THE
AMARANTHINE LAW

Praise for Gun Brooke

Ice Queen

"I'm a sucker for a story about a single mother, and in this case, it really adds depth to Susanna's character. The conflict that threatens Susanna and Aislin's future isn't a convoluted series of events. It's the insecurities they each bring into the relationship that they're forced to acknowledge and deal with. To me this felt authentic. The book is a quick read with plenty of spice."—*Lesbian Review*

Treason

"The adventure was edge-of-your-seat levels of gripping and exciting...I really enjoyed this final addition to the Exodus series and particularly liked the ending. As always it was a very well written book."—*Melina Bickard, Librarian, Waterloo Library (UK)*

Insult to Injury

"This novel tugged at my heart all the way, much the same way as *Coffee Sonata*. It's a story of new beginnings, of rediscovering oneself, of trusting again (both others and oneself)."—*Jude in the Stars*

"If you love a good, slow-burn romantic novel, then grab this book."—*Rainbow Reflections*

"[A] light romance that left me with just the right amount of "aw shucks" at the end."—*C-Spot Reviews*

Wayworn Lovers

"*Wayworn Lovers* is a super dramatic, angsty read, very much in line with Brooke's other contemporary romances...I'm definitely in the 'love them' camp."—*The Lesbian Review*

Thorns of the Past

"What I really liked from the offset is that Brooke steered clear of the typical butch PI with femme damsel in distress trope. Both main characters are what I would call ordinary women—they both wear suits for work, they both dress down in sweatpants and sweatshirts in the evening. As a result, I instantly found it a lot easier to relate, and connect with both. Each of their pasts hold dreadful memories and pain, and the passages where they opened up to each other about those events were very moving."—*Rainbow Reviews*

"I loved the romance between Darcy and Sabrina and the story really carried it well, with each of them learning that they have a safe haven with the other."—*The Lesbian Review*

Soul Unique

"This is the first book that Gun Brooke has written in a first person perspective, and that was 100% the correct choice. She avoids the pitfalls of trying to tell a story about living with an autism spectrum disorder that she's never experienced, instead making it the story of someone who falls in love with a person living with Asperger's... *Soul Unique* is her best. It was an ambitious project that turned out beautifully. I highly recommend it."—*The Lesbian Review*

"Yet another success from Gun Brooke. The premise is interesting, the leads are likeable and the supporting characters are well-developed. The first person narrative works well, and I really enjoyed reading about a character with Asperger's."—*Melina Bickard, Librarian, Waterloo Library (London)*

The Blush Factor

"Gun Brooke captures very well the two different 'worlds' the two main characters live in and folds this setting neatly into the story. So, if you are looking for a well-edited, multi-layered romance with engaging characters this is a great read and maybe a re-read for those days when comfort food is a must."—*Lesbians on the Loose*

September Canvas

"In this character-driven story, trust is earned and secrets are uncovered. Deanna and Faythe are fully fleshed out and prove to the reader each has much depth, talent, wit and problem-solving abilities. *September Canvas* is a good read with a thoroughly satisfying conclusion."—*Just About Write*

Fierce Overture

"Gun Brooke creates memorable characters, and Noelle and Helena are no exception. Each woman is 'more than meets the eye' as each exhibits depth, fears, and longings. And the sexual tension between them is real, hot, and raw."—*Just About Write*

Lambda Literary Award Finalist *Sheridan's Fate*

"Sheridan's fire and Lark's warm embers are enough to make this book sizzle. Brooke, however, has gone beyond the wonderful emotional explorations of these characters to tell the story of those who, for various reasons, become differently-abled. Whether it is a bullet, an illness, or a problem at birth, many women and men find themselves in Sheridan's situation. Her courage and Lark's gentleness and determination send this romance into a 'must read.'"—*Just About Write*

Escape: Exodus Book Three

"I've been a keen follower of the Exodus series for a while now and I was looking forward to the latest installment. It didn't disappoint. The action was edge-of-your-seat thrilling, especially towards the end, with several threats facing the Exodus mission. Some very intriguing subplots were introduced, and I look forward to reading more about these in the next book."—*Melina Bickard, Librarian, Waterloo Library, London (UK)*

Pathfinder: Exodus Book Two

"I love Gun Brooke. She has successfully merged two of my reading loves: lesfic and sci-fi."—*Inked Rainbow Reads*

Advance: Exodus Book One

"*Advance* is an exciting space adventure, hopeful even through times of darkness. The romance and action are balanced perfectly, interesting the audience as much in the fleet's mission as in Dael and Spinner's romance. I'm looking forward to the next book in the series!"—*All Our Worlds: Diverse Fantastic Fiction*

The Supreme Constellations Series

"*Protector of the Realm* has it all; sabotage, corruption, erotic love and exhilarating space fights. Gun Brooke's second novel is forceful with a winning combination of solid characters and a brilliant plot. The book exemplifies her growth as inventive storyteller and is sure to garner multiple awards in the coming year."—*Just About Write*

Protector of the Realm "is first and foremost a romance, and whilst it has action and adventure, it is the romance that drives it. The book moves along at a cracking pace, and there is much happening throughout to make it a good page-turner. The action sequences are very well done, and make for an adrenaline rush."—*The Lesbian Review*

"Brooke is an amazing author. Never have I read a book where I started at the top of the page and don't know what will happen two paragraphs later. She keeps the excitement going, and the pages turning."—*Family and Friends Magazine*

By the Author

Romances

Course of Action

Coffee Sonata

Sheridan's Fate

September Canvas

Fierce Overture

Speed Demons

The Blush Factor

Soul Unique

A Reluctant Enterprise

Piece of Cake

Thorns of the Past

Wayworn Lovers

Insult to Injury

Science Fiction

Supreme Constellations series

Protector of the Realm

Rebel's Quest

Warrior's Valor

Pirate's Fortune

Exodus series

Advance

Pathfinder

Escape

Arrival

Treason

The Dennamore Scrolls

Yearning

Velocity

Homeworld

Lunar Eclipse

Renegade's War

The Amaranthine Law

Novella Anthology

Change Horizons

Visit us at www.boldstrokesbooks.com

THE
AMARANTHINE LAW

by

Gun Brooke

2022

Credits
Editor: Shelley Thrasher
Production Design: Stacia Seaman
Cover Photos by www.pexels.com
Cover Design by Gun Brooke

Acknowledgments

Me, writing a paranormal love story? If anyone would have suggested such a thing a few years ago, I would have balked at the idea. I love such stories as a reader—and same goes for crime novels—but writing them…whoa! But in January 2021, I got this idea for a story (and it was meant to remain a fanfic story at first) after watching art restoration videos on YouTube. When my mind goes "What if…?" I know it'll bug me until I write. So, firstly, I want to acknowledge the YT channel *Baumgartner Restoration* for the information and inspiration.

Thank you to my editor, Dr. Shelley Thrasher, for helping me sort this manuscript out. You are such a pearl and I adore you.

Thank you also to Len Barot, Sandy Lowe, Ruth Sternglantz, Toni Whitaker, Cindy Cresap, and Stacia Seaman, plus everyone else at BSB who create such a lovely, inspiring home for us authors. You are all amazing.

Regarding this book, I want to give extra thanks to my first reader, Annika in Germany. You were such a tremendous help and the perfect mix of blunt and encouraging. You rock!

My readers, whether you buy my books or read my fanfic, or both, I owe you so much. Kind words, pointers, suggestions, and general appreciation goes such a long way. I feel truly blessed.

Malin, Henrik, Pentti, Ove, Monica, the grandkids—I could never do without you. Birgitta, Rose-Marie, Soli, Kamilla, Georgi, Joanne, Sam, girls from the acrylic paint group, you all know how much you mean to me. I know this'll sound sappy, but without my dogs, everything would be harder, so, my darling pooches, keep up the good work.

Writing used to be known as quite a solitary endeavor, but as you can tell from the list above, it isn't always. I'm very grateful for every single person above.

For Elon

For the BLAs

PROLOGUE

1769
Aboard a sailing ship on the Atlantic Ocean

"Here, Sarah. Drink this."

Sarah looks up at her mother. The light behind her creates a halo. Maybe Mother is now an angel. Then Sarah feels Mother's cool hand against the back of her neck as she helps Sarah drink from the cup. The liquid is hot and bitter, and Sarah tries to pull away, but Mother insists.

"Are you sure this will help her?" Father asks from somewhere in the shadows. "After all, we don't know that woman."

"You know as well as I do, if she doesn't get any better, if she can't keep water down, she won't make it." Mother's voice is harsh, but Sarah can hear the anguish. When she holds the cup back to Sarah's lips, she drinks more of the strong liquid, wanting to please Mother. Reassure her.

Father's face appears next to Mother's. He too looks pale. "Come on, little sparrow. You have to fight. Mother is going to give you some water soon to rinse down that brew." His big, callused hand cups her cheek.

Sarah groans. The water aboard the ship is vile, barely better than what Mother is forcing on her.

"I have some I boiled earlier today over there." Mother points to the corner where they keep a jug.

"You are clever to do so, dear." Father runs a finger down Sarah's nose, but she doesn't have enough strength to offer him her usual smile at his caress. "Dear God, she's so thin."

"So were the two Halliwell girls across from us, but look at them now. No matter what that woman put into this tea, those girls are alive because of it. The parents of Sarah's little friends, Rosalee and Iris, are giving it to their little girls as well. Even those two wretchedly wicked little sisters in the aft are doing better. Whatever this plague is, it has hit all the youngest girls the hardest."

Father sighs. "I know you're right, dear. It's just that I observed the woman as she made her brew. I'm not comfortable with the way she chanted. There's something strange about her."

Sarah flinches when Mother snaps her head around to glare at Father. "I honestly don't care if she was summoning the devil himself," she whispers intensely. "Our little girl won't see the next sunrise if we don't do this. I would never be able to live with myself if I didn't try everything available."

Father puts his arm around Mother's shoulders. Normally Mother would shake his arm off with a huff, because that's her way. Mother is not sweet and cuddly like Iris's mother. But this time, Mother must be truly upset that Sarah is ill. She puts her head on Father's shoulder and hides her face against his neck, sobbing quietly.

Sarah closes her eyes, imagining she can feel the hot, bitter tea slosh around in her belly much like the waves carry their ship toward the Americas. That is, of course, unless Mother's fears come true, and Sarah goes to heaven before the sunrise.

CHAPTER ONE

Present Day

The young woman before her should normally be unremarkable by Tristan's standards. Average height, long dark-brown hair, beautiful amber eyes, and full lips that easily stretch into a captivating smile all add up to a pretty creature. Still, the sum of her parts is nothing Tristan hasn't seen a million times before. Yet—the fidgety young woman holds...*something*. Despite her ordinariness—emphasized by jeans, a gray T-shirt, and a black leather jacket, this girl possesses a quality that creates, if not cracks, then indentations in the armor Tristan, out of necessity, constructed around herself a long time ago. How peculiar. And how inconvenient.

"Olivia Bryce. What makes you think you're a good fit for my company and able to do this job at the required level?" Tristan asks, easing up on the corner of her large oak desk. She lets her boot-clad foot dangle slightly, noticing how Olivia gazes at the motion for a few moments before returning her focus to Tristan.

"I've attended art school and have a degree in chemistry. I would consider an internship with your fine-art-conservation company a fantastic opportunity." Olivia shifts from one foot to the other. Does she realize that she tends to pull at her fingers when nervous, Tristan wonders.

"Of course you would. But how would employing you benefit Amaranthine Inc.?" Pursing her lips, Tristan takes pity on Olivia and motions at the antique leather visitors' chair. After returning to her own office chair, an impressive piece that is even older and made from skillfully carved oak, Tristan sits down. She folds her hands on the desk, studying Olivia.

"I've dreamed of working for you ever since I discovered art restoration when I was fifteen. My first passion was drawing, then painting, and I *lived* for going to art museums whenever possible. The old masters mesmerize me, and I will find a way to work on preserving their art, no matter what, but doing it here would be perfect." Olivia stops talking and blushes. "Sorry. When it comes to this subject, I get very excited very fast."

"Well, being interested in the job is considered the baseline when seeking employment, don't you think? What sets you above the other applicants—some, if not all, with more experience than you?" Tristan tilts her head and deliberately raises her perfectly groomed eyebrows, knowing full well what impact she can have on people.

"Interested? That doesn't even come close to how I feel. I *burn* for this. I live and breathe art and conservation. The others may have more experience, but as they've worked and trained in other places, they might also have picked up habits you would find undesirable. Are you their first choice, their *dream*, like you are for me?" Olivia sits at the edge of the chair, gesturing emphatically.

Tristan can't help but be impressed. The girl is nervous, yes, but she's fearless, and she's not above fighting a bit dirty. Suggesting her competition might have learned methods that Tristan would have to make them unlearn is a valid point, but rather audacious to bring up when you're just—Tristan glances at Olivia's application form—twenty-four.

Recalling the other eight individuals she has interviewed over the last two weeks, a task so tedious and unimpressive that Tristan is ready to push needles into her eyes, she can't remember any of them catching her attention like Olivia has.

"All right," Tristan says slowly, leaning forward. "Three months' paid internship. My assistant will deal with the details and show you around. You start tomorrow."

"Tomorrow? I'm…You're hiring me?" Olivia stands up, exuding energy as if she's ready to burst.

"Don't make me regret it. I'm not a patient woman, and I hate repeating myself."

"Whoops. Sorry. Okay. Tomorrow. What time?" Olivia smiles broadly, and Tristan thinks she may even have tears in her eyes.

"Pay attention. Talk to my assistant." Rolling her own eyes, Tristan stands up slowly. "We're done."

For a horrifying moment, Olivia looks like she's about to start crying or, God forbid, hug Tristan, but then she merely nods, whispers a barely audible "thank you," and is out the door.

Sitting back down, Tristan shakes her head. Has she just made a mistake or perhaps the best decision in a long time? Olivia's education and the work samples she sent ahead digitally were fine, but only time would tell if she had what it took to work at Amaranthine Inc. Looking around her office, taking in the brick walls, the oak shelving and beautiful antiques she has lovingly collected for many years, Tristan seems to see it all with new eyes. Meticulously maintained, these props have provided a backdrop for her, added to her reputation for being the best at what she does. Now, Tristan thinks of how Olivia seemed when she entered the office, her obvious exuberance as she looked at one antique after another.

Until Olivia.

❖

"I'm Dana Parker, and I oversee everything to do with administration for Tristan," the thin, strawberry-blond woman behind a less impressive desk than Tristan Kelly's—though definitely an antique—says with a faint Scottish accent. Dressed in a charcoal skirt suit and a white blouse, she wears her hair in an austere twist and seems to be about Liv's age. Liv's thoughts stray to her first impression of Tristan—a woman in her forties with short, white-blond hair, blue laser-focus eyes, a long, aristocratic nose, and a deceptively soft-looking pink mouth that appeared ready to spout scathing remarks. Where Dana dresses as a conservative, young professional, Tristan wears all black—chinos, shirt, boots, giving the impression that she needs only a helmet and a leather jacket to mount her motorbike.

A recluse of sorts when it comes to social media, Tristan Kelly barely has any digital footprints online. Amaranthine Inc. has a classy, understated website where visitors can read about the long list of art pieces that the company under Tristan's reign has saved for posterity.

"This way, then." Dana motions for Liv to follow her through the foyer and through a massive wooden door. Behind it, a corridor leads to locker rooms, a break room, and—and this is where Liv loses her breath. Her reaction compares to when Tristan challenged her reason for applying for the internship. Now Liv stares at the large hall where five people—three women and two men of varying ages—are working on different canvases. Her gaze falls upon two empty tables, sitting at the far end of the room. The one to the left looks unused. The one to the right is empty, but bottles, brushes, and other tools are clearly in use.

"The left one will be your workstation, but I recommend that you don't touch a thing before one of your supervisors tells you it's okay." Dana motions for Liv to walk with her to meet a thin, bald man. "Olivia. This is Graham Berry. He is in charge when Tristan's not here. Graham. This is Olivia Bryce, our new intern." Dana's manner of speaking makes it obvious how much she doubts this fact.

"Welcome, Olivia." Graham holds up his gloved hands, palms toward them. Unlike Dana, he has a warm, welcoming smile as he wiggles his fingers. "We'll shake some other time."

"Please, call me Liv. Most people do. I'm so excited for this opportunity." Liv peers at Graham's workstation, where he has smeared a dissolvent on part of the painting that is so dark and yellow, it's hard to even see the motif. Squinting, Liv can make out just enough details. "A portrait. And in pretty bad shape."

"Yes. Restorers have maltreated this work over the years. Varnished with conflicting media, which makes removing it difficult. I may end up making it worse. Well, if it gets too hairy, I'll ask Tristan. She's the genius around here." Graham smiles warmly. "I look forward to working together, Liv."

"Thanks. Likewise." Liv thinks she sees Dana grimacing, but since she'll actually be learning from Tristan and Graham, what Dana thinks of her doesn't matter.

After receiving an access card, Liv says good-bye to Dana and exits the building. Standing on the sidewalk, she looks back at the brownstone. Four stories high, it originates from the seventeenth century, or so the website states. Amaranthine Inc. occupies the two first floors, but the website doesn't specify the function of the other floors. The building is well maintained, and Liv can almost feel its vast history. For Tristan to own such prime real estate on the Upper East Side is just one proof that her company is thriving.

Turning her collar up against the January wind, Liv begins walking toward the closest subway station. She wants to make sure she has everything prepared, even if she has spent weeks getting ready for this interview and is also itching to sit down with her sketchbook and do some basic drawings. The tiny studio apartment she rents doesn't allow for her big easel, which she's stored at her parents' house in Boston. Until she can afford a larger place, she must settle for a table easel and her sketchbooks.

The thought of her parents in the ranch-style house Liv grew up in makes her rigid. Her mother isn't happy with Liv's choice to make a life for herself in New York, but at least Chloe Bryce isn't as bigoted and overbearing as her husband, Brian, Liv's stepfather. Having grown up with him since the age of four, she remembers him as her only father figure, as her biological father died before Liv was born. Brian's strict and judgmental attitudes toward anything outside what he considers the norm nearly destroyed Liv when she realized she was a lesbian at age fourteen. She came out to her friends at fifteen but delayed telling her parents until she headed for college. This revelation created a chasm between her and Brian, and it made her stop calling him her dad. Liv talks to her mother every couple of weeks, but their conversation is stilted, as if they are running out of topics. Liv's mother has most likely succumbed more and more to Brian's world views since Liv is no longer around to balance things out.

Liv pulls the zipper of her leather jacket higher and, before she rounds the corner at the end of the block, takes another look at the brownstone. It is getting dark, and the light from the first floors sparkles and moves in the uneven glass of the windowpanes. Lifting her gaze, she notices that lights are on at the top floors as well, but these are more muted. Does perhaps Tristan live up there? Not that it is any of her business, but the woman has captured her imagination. Not to mention that Tristan is so damn beautiful, she should come with a warning label.

Snorting at herself, and to change the course of her thoughts, as well as the topic of her mom and Brian, she hums a melody and lengthens her stride when she sees the subway station ahead. She has one last shift at the hole-in-the-wall deli to take care of and a paycheck to collect. Tomorrow her new life will begin.

CHAPTER TWO

Tristan steps into the old elevator and pulls the gate closed behind her. The only button glows an understated gold against the copper panel. She is used to the slow ascent up to her private two-floor dwelling, where she has lived on and off since she came to New York. In her apartment, the familiar scent of potpourri mixed with the scented candles she always lights as soon as she steps off the elevator wraps around her. Sandalwood, orange, and dark vanilla soothe her senses and calm her mind. She learned a long time ago that scents are part of the solution when she is desperate for stillness. And after meeting Olivia Bryce, she is taken aback at how much she must reel herself in.

Was it a mistake to hire Olivia as the new intern? From a professional standpoint, she has a feeling, and she is rarely wrong, that she has found a diamond in the rough. Olivia's portfolio, education, and obvious passion for art and restoration set her apart from the other applicants. Two of the others had worked in the business for a decade, which they stated with such pride and even with a hint of condescension. Tristan had nearly scoffed in their faces. A decade? Try a lifetime.

Undoing her shirt, she hangs it over a chair and toes off her boots, placing them underneath, before heading to the kitchen. She opens the fridge and pulls out a Carlsberg, drinking directly from the bottle as she walks back to the living room. She is tired but not ready for bed. Knowing full well what a night's tossing and turning do to her, she instead settles into a familiar routine. Turning on the TV, she browses through the news channels, eventually giving up on the repetitive content and moving on to the cooking shows that often relax her. Tristan watches a Japanese cook at a food cart in Kyoto slice and dice with great precision. Each quick move with the knife makes a percussive sound that aligns her heartbeat.

When she was a little girl, the sound of the ax as her father chopped wood, or the use of knives when her mother and older sister prepared food, had the same effect. Tristan would sit by the fire in the cabin, watch the flames dance, and listen to the thudding sound from outdoors, and the sharper, rhythmic drumming from the kitchen area. Mother kept their home meticulously clean, especially the cooking area. Father would step in from the cold, his arms full of firewood, and Tristan would hurry to help him stack it neatly. He then winked at her and whispered about how important it was to not anger Mother. Tristan would giggle at his irreverent words. They both knew Mother's scathing tongue was all talk. Beneath the stern exterior beat a warm, loving heart when it came to family matters. As for people outside of their family circle, Father always said that annoying neighbors needed to watch out since Mother harbored no love for them.

After an hour of watching the skilled chefs, Tristan gets up, stretching her back until two vertebrae pop. She knows she looks good, but on days like today, she feels every single one of her years. She goes through her evening routine, removing makeup and quickly rinsing in the shower, and then tumbles into bed. Curling up around a pillow, a nearly forgotten childhood habit that manifests itself when she is tired or stressed, Tristan hugs it close. Amber eyes appear before her inner eyes, plump, soft-looking lips smile broadly, and hands flicker in the periphery.

"Goddamn it," Tristan snarls and rolls over onto her right side. She forces herself to think of her next project in the workshop. She plans to restore an eighteenth-century portrait of an Italian contessa. Its male owner claims to be a descendant of the woman in the portrait and is paying a lot of money for Tristan to do the job herself. It strikes her that it might be a great project to use as an introduction for Olivia to observe.

Groaning, Tristan plunges a fist into one of her pillows. She has come full circle, and her thoughts have returned to Olivia again. What the hell is it about this young woman that tugs at her this way? Tristan has met people of great wealth and beauty during her years, but this is a first. Attraction at first sight is one thing, but being unable to stop thinking of a girl she knows *nothing* about...? Ridiculous. It is also dangerous. Having kept her guard up for so long, Tristan can't afford to lower it now. The few times it has inadvertently happened, nothing good has come from it. The word *disastrous* comes to mind, and it's not an exaggeration.

Tristan hums as she pulls several pillows closer. Suddenly the one behind her is her sister, a vivid memory from when they shared the narrow bed in the corner of their humble cabin. Corinne would align her voluptuous body with Tristan's and keep her little sister warm during the cold winter nights after the fire died in the fireplace. Outside, the wind would whistle and howl, wild animals would pass by and some even scratch at the walls, which would frighten Tristan more than anything. Corinne would hum, much like Tristan does now, and whisper, "You're safe, little sparrow," in Tristan's ear, and eventually, they'd both fall asleep.

Fortunately, on some nights, like tonight, the humming works its magic even all these years later.

CHAPTER THREE

L iv admits she's nervous when she puts on her apron and then waits by her workstation while Tristan talks to one of her other employees, a stunningly beautiful woman. Not sure what to do with her hands, she pushes them into the large pocket in the front of the apron, but then she thinks it looks silly, like a kangaroo with cold paws, and pulls them out, opting to lace her fingers instead.

After a few minutes, Tristan approaches and waves Liv over to her table. "Marlena is going to take over my ongoing project so you and I can start from scratch. Some of what I do is rather universal, but some things might be new to you." Tristan doesn't wait for Liv to respond but walks over to the wall to where several wrapped packages stand. Liv doesn't wait around to be asked but hurries to help Tristan lift the large painting onto the table. Tristan merely nods and begins opening the wrapping carefully.

Marlena comes up to them and eyes the new project in all its layers of wrapping. "I looked up information about this painting when I saw it on the roster. That's quite the undertaking, Tristan." She turns to Liv and smiles warmly. "I'm Marlena. I was in the zone when you walked the premises yesterday. I promise I wasn't being deliberately rude."

"I'm well acquainted with the zone," Liv says and returns the smile. After trailing Dana, whose cool demeanor didn't exactly give her the warm-and-fuzzies, yesterday, she's relieved that Graham and Marlena are more welcoming. When it comes to Tristan, she's impossible to read. Not unwelcoming, but not exactly warm in her greeting either.

"I'll just grab this painting and get it out of your way, all right?" Marlena, whose accent suggests she may be from Eastern Europe, slides her hands under the smaller painting next to the package. Liv assists her, and when she returns, Tristan has uncovered all but the last layer of protective packaging.

"Can you tell me about this painting?" Liv flexes her fingers as she ends up perpendicular to Tristan.

"It's a portrait, painted in the late 1700s, by Serafina Natale. It's of a woman, known only as Signorina Santo. The owner claims to be related to Santo."

"I haven't heard of Serafina Natale," Liv says.

"Doesn't surprise me. She's not well-known these days." Tristan pulls off the last layer and taps her lower lip at the state of the painting. "If she was as famous now as she was back then, they wouldn't have let this masterpiece come to this." Shaking her head, Tristan pulls out a magnifying glass and studies a few spots, pointing things out to Liv, who has put on her own magnifier, which attaches to her head.

"That's some thick varnish," Liv mutters.

"Exactly. And to develop my answer about Natale, she was a renaissance woman if there ever was one. She was a painter, author, feminist, and farm supervisor—among other things."

Intrigued, Liv decides to google the painter the first chance she gets.

Tristan goes over the canvas with her gloved hands, feeling gently along long cracks. "Here's penetrating damage. You'll learn a lot from this piece, Olivia."

The way Tristan says her name, with the tiniest of emphasis on the first *i*, sends shivers along Liv's bare arms. Forcing herself not to fidget, she watches Tristan go through the familiar procedure of turning the painting over on top of acid-free paper and then removing it from the stretcher by pulling the old tacks out. She saves them in a glass bowl, and Liv guesses she'll reuse the ones that are intact. After all the tacks are removed, Liv sends Tristan a questioning glance, and Tristan nods. Carefully, Liv lifts the stretcher and sets it to the side, leaning it against the wall. Turning back, she joins Tristan in examining the back of the painting.

"What do you see?" Tristan asks.

"Some strange residues, probably from a previous restoration." Liv leans closer and manages to accidentally nudge Tristan's shoulder as her boss does the same. "Oh, I'm sorry."

"No matter." Tristan doesn't turn from the canvas, but Liv thinks she can see how she rolls her shoulder as if the touch hurt her, or something. "Some binder, but we won't know until we attack it. I think scraping is our best bet. You've performed that technique, according to your credentials?"

"Yes. At one point, someone had glued the canvas to a piece of plywood. Once we detached it, we had to scrape off the glue."

"Was it a large painting?" Tristan looks up, clearly interested.

"No. It was fifteen by twenty inches. This is thirty by forty, right?"

"It is." Tristan examines the edges of the painting. "We'll have to flatten the canvas first before we can do anything about the back. How would you do this?"

"I'd cut off a piece of silicone release paper and use it between the back of the canvas and a small tacking iron to flatten the edges." Liv holds her breath as she waits for Tristan's response, even though she knows her answer is correct.

"Exactly. Go get what you need." Tristan lifts the stretcher off the floor. "I'll give this to Paul. He's our wood guy and works in another room with frames, stretchers, and such."

"Should I wait for you before I start?"

"No. I'll be right back. Just mind the heat setting." Tristan walks off with the stretcher, and Liv hurries over to the part of the room where supplies are stored. She finds what she needs and is cutting off the silicone release paper when someone says her name. She turns around, and a smiling Graham is standing behind her, holding large scissors.

"Great minds think alike," Graham says and motions with his head toward the paper.

"Oh, you can have this," Liv says and hands him her rectangle she has just cut.

"Thank you." Graham stays beside her as she cuts another rectangle. "I see you're getting your hands dirty right away."

"Um. Yes?" Questioningly, Liv turns around after finishing.

"Makes me wonder what skills you have that no other newbies here did on their first day. Marlena had to watch only, for several days. The others even longer. And here you are getting material and fetching tools."

"Tristan wanted me to start the flattening process." Confused, Liv blinks. "I did ask."

"Hm. She's not big on questions, our boss. So, let's see. You get to start working on an important piece, and she didn't bite your head off for asking questions…" He smirks, but his gaze is still kind.

Walking back to the table, Liv plugs in the tacking iron. "How am I supposed to learn if I can't ask questions? That doesn't make sense."

"Exactly. Do share, Graham, how that can possibly be the case?" Tristan shows up behind Graham, making him startle.

He chuckles and shakes his head. "Please. I've been here long enough to know where all the skeletons are buried, Tristan. You never let your interns work on a painting on the first day. I'm just curious what talents Liv has that the rest of us didn't." His eyes sparkle as he regards Tristan.

Instead of getting annoyed, which Liv feared she might, Tristan rolls her eyes and flicks her fingers at Graham. "You ridiculous man. What skeletons?"

"There has to be at least one. Remember that intern that figured it was a good idea to use sandpaper from the woodshop on a painting? We never saw or heard from him again," Graham says and rubs his chin. "Exhibit A."

"He was fired. And I made sure he never worked in fine-art restoration again." Tristan speaks mildly, as if reminiscing about inviting the unfortunate intern for tea.

"Right. Sure." Graham laughs. "I'll get out of your hair. See you at lunch, Liv?"

"Yes, absolutely. Thank you." Liv nods and then checks the tacking iron. "It's the right heat. Still want me to continue?" She isn't sure after what Graham has just said, joking or not.

"You heard Graham. Enough with questions that force me to repeat myself." Tristan watches intently as Liv begins flattening the canvas.

Liv works with her usual complete focus, moving the tools along the edge of the canvas, careful to apply only the exact pressure needed. She has almost finished when someone speaks Tristan's name in a curt British accent, startling Liv just as she's lowering the iron again. Afraid of dropping it on the back of the canvas, she fumbles to get a better grip and feels it singe her skin on the outside of her left index finger. Whimpering, she puts the iron down where it can't hurt anything or anyone and is lifting her hand to examine the burn when someone yanks her by the arm, dragging her over to a sink.

Tristan lets the faucet run and then shoves Liv's hand under the cool water. "How bad?" she asks, her voice not cool at all anymore. Still on the lower register, it is a definite growl.

"I'm so sorry," Liv gushes, blinking to get the tears off her lashes. "I wasn't prepared. That's never happened to me before, I swear." So certain she has screwed up enough for Tristan to do what she did to the guy with the sandpaper, she feels her stomach tremble.

"Dana should know better." Tristan whips her head around and stares at her assistant. "What could possibly be so important that you couldn't be more careful?"

"You…you have a call from the Louvre. In Paris." Dana stares at Tristan and then Liv's hand. "I apologize."

"I will call them back." Tristan is still holding Liv's wrist, forcing her to keep her fingers under the running water.

"I can manage, Tristan," Liv says, knowing full well everyone is looking at them.

"I will call—them—back." Tristan's voice is barely audible, and Dana scurries away.

"This is why we don't have cell phones in the workshop. We can't have any flinching or dropping things…or injuries." Tristan bends to examine Liv's fingers but doesn't remove them from the water. "We caught it in time, I think. A little while longer under the faucet and then cool-spray."

Eventually, Tristan lets go and tears off some paper towel, handing it to her. "Now let me see." She is intent on Liv's injury, and what can she do but hold up her finger to let Tristan examine it. It stings a little bit, but not at all as it did initially.

"Here. First-aid box." Marlena shows up with a large plastic container and then returns to her table, but only after gently patting Liv's shoulder.

Tristan applies the cool-spray and then bandages it. "It's pink, but no blisters as far as I could tell. The lidocaine and aloe vera in the spray will help."

"Thank you." Liv leans against the counter. "That got way more dramatic than was called for. I'm normally not clumsy around my work. May I finish?"

Tristan blinks. "But your hand—"

"Is much better, thanks to your quick reaction." Liv would have done the same for her hand, but to be honest, it would have taken her longer. "I'd like to finish it before we move on to the next step."

"Very well. Just be very careful." Tristan seems pensive as they return to the table.

"Not that it's any of my business," Liv says, as she remembers the reason for Dana showing up in the first place. "Don't you need to go call the Louvre?" She checks her time. "I mean, it's already four p.m. there."

Tristan stops immediately. "Perhaps too much drama even for me," she mutters and leaves the workshop.

"As I said," Graham calls out from his table. "What sorcery do you possess, Liv Bryce?"

CHAPTER FOUR

Tristan opens her laptop and starts logging on to Zoom. Vanessa Mercier from the Louvre is connected already, but not at her desk yet, so Tristan has an unobstructed view of the window behind Madame Mercier's desk. It's dark as it's evening in Europe, and the lights make Paris sparkle like a diamond. She hears steps against a hard floor and the rustling of clothes before Mercier sits down in her leather chair. A woman in her early middle age, thin, bordering on emaciated, perfect makeup and long, light-brown hair, Mercier smiles politely into her webcam.

"Ms. Kelly, I'm so glad to finally meet you face-to-face…" Mercier's voice falters, and she blinks a few times. A faint frown on her no-doubt Botoxed forehead comes and goes before she continues. "Your work and your excellent reputation precede you, of course."

Tristan doesn't reveal her shock. This woman is no stranger. In her mind, she exchanges the long, Veronica Lake–styled hair for a short, blond sixties bob with bangs, and the chic and professional-looking suit jacket and blouse for a Mod Mondrian sixties dress with matching long earrings. The face was fuller then, but it's her. The name's new too, of course.

Vanessa Mercier keeps talking about the painting in poor condition that the Louvre just acquired, which she wants Tristan to work on. She smiles too broadly when she describes it as a true find that could draw the masses of art and history aficionados from around the world. Except for her rapid blinking every now and then, Tristan wouldn't have guessed that anything was amiss. Her mind spinning, she decides that if Mercier doesn't intend to acknowledge any mutual recognition, it's probably best to play along.

They talk about the painting and the potential peril of transporting it to New York and Tristan's busy schedule. Tristan hopes she can remember the details of the conversation after they disconnect. In twenty minutes, they agree to talk again once Mercier has sent digital images to Tristan and make final arrangements.

After disconnecting the Zoom platform, Tristan leans back in her office chair. She can hardly breathe. The call has yanked the proverbial rug from under her feet. How hasn't she known that Mercier, whom Tristan originally knew as Rosalee, works at the Louvre?

Tristan is aware that she's well-known among her peers, but an unknown to everyone else, which could explain why Rosalee had no idea who she was. She remembers the skinny little girl from her childhood, even if it was so long ago, and how they had clung to their respective mothers as the ship they were on crashed into each wave. Rosalee had already been ill then, and Tristan's mother had kept her and Corinne away from the girl and her siblings during their journey. Later, they had become friends, but that seemed like another lifetime. Being in contact on and off over the years, they gradually grew apart, and the fact that they both had to be careful about their past made them part ways. The last time Tristan ran into Rosalee, she went by yet another name, just like Tristan did, and was working as an assistant to a politician in London.

Running her hand over her face, trying to stroke away memories as if they were cobwebs, Tristan stands and walks over to the door and locks it. She opens her safe, hidden behind a desk, that is connected to the wall on hinges and pulls out the thick ledger with a leather and gold cover. After returning to her desk, Tristan opens the ledger and runs her index finger along the beveled gold letters. *The Amaranthine Law.* She slowly turns the pages, some of them quite brittle, until she reaches the spread that says *The Carmichael Family.* She steels herself and locates Rosalee's name. Under it is a list of four other names in Rosalee's column. Tristan uses a fountain pen and enters *Vanessa Mercier.* In the column next to the name, she writes down Rosalee's/Vanessa's location, workplace, and the date. Tristan glances at the other columns, which hold the names of Rosalee's three sisters. They are all dead, which she knows, of course. Flashbacks of gaunt little girls huddling in a corner of a cot make her shudder. Tristan groans and rubs her cheeks more vigorously, trying to yank herself out of the past. If Rosalee recognized Tristan, it was in their best interest to not address their acquaintance—ever.

Tristan puts the ledger securely into the safe again and pushes the desk back against the wall. Unlocking the door, she walks out into the foyer and finds Dana sitting rigid and typing fiercely on her laptop.

"Dana." Tristan stops by her desk. "I took care of the call to the Louvre. And Olivia is all right."

Only a barely noticeable flutter of Dana's mascara-coated eyelashes reveals her relief. Tristan knows her assistant well and now understands that it will take more coaxing from her to soothe Dana's easily frayed nerves. Very few people understand this austere Scottish girl the way she does.

"Why don't we ask how many will join us in an impromptu visit to Marlena's parents' bar after work? They serve food nowadays, so I'm told." Tristan digs deep not to wince at her own suggestion. Going to a bar is fine. Sitting alone at the counter and staring into a bourbon is all right. She's done this many times. Going as a group, getting a table, socializing, and eating typical bar food—not her thing. Still, for the sake of her business, and for Dana, and to integrate Olivia quicker, it might be the smart thing.

Dana blushes and relaxes marginally. "I'll ask everyone at lunch and take care of it. It's very popular, but Marlena's father has promised that her friends will always get a table, no matter what."

"Give Marlena's father my credit card information. My treat." Tristan walks into the workshop and over to Olivia, who has swept loose debris off the back of the painting and now is scraping off the dried glue using a scalpel. She's sticking to a corner and edge, probably not wanting to assume she's allowed to do too much. Wearing gloves, she doesn't seem to be in pain. Tristan breathes a little easier. She isn't used to feeling this protective of very many people, and she truly doesn't know Olivia. Tristan does understand that she's not ready to analyze her own reaction.

Tristan inspects Olivia's work so far, pleased with what she sees. "Acceptable. Keep going. I'll start on the other side." Willing her normally so steady hands to cooperate, Tristan pulls up a stool, puts on gloves, and attaches a new blade to a scalpel handle. As it turns out, sitting across from Olivia, working in silence, and tuning out the voices from the others behind her, finally settles her. Tristan scrapes with the scalpel, and from the corner of her eyes, she sees Olivia's hands slowly approach hers.

Finally, Tristan can breathe.

❖

Liv is taken aback at how different Tristan seems when she returns to the workshop. Her movements are jerky and her eyes opaque. She pulls on the gloves and fixes a blade to her scalpel with unsteady hands, which makes Liv worry about her boss cutting herself. Then, when Tristan begins to scrape at the back of the canvas, it is as if she snaps out of whatever funk she's in. Liv keeps working, and soon the actual canvas appears between them.

The minutes tick by, and the work is as hypnotic as it is repetitive. Liv tells herself she can't become distracted by the woman across from her. Imperfections might show up after being hidden under the glue, and she can end up damaging the painting further if she scrapes right into them.

"Dana is planning to ask everyone if they'd like to go to an, well, I suppose, after-work thing, at a bar close to the workshop. I hope you can join us, as it would be an excellent way to speed up getting to know your colleagues," Tristan says quietly.

Liv is surprised, and not quite sure why. Perhaps it's the fact that Tristan said "us." But who is she kidding? Of course she wants to go. "I have no plans tonight. I'd be happy to. Actually, last night was my last shift at the deli." Wanting to slap her hand over her mouth, she's certain Tristan hates small talk.

"A person has to make a living. I haven't always done this, you know," Tristan says absentmindedly, her gaze on the canvas.

Relieved to an absurd degree, Liv smiles. "I'm all for honest employment that teaches a person a great work ethic."

Tristan nods. "Yes."

The second silence stretches, but it is not uncomfortable. Liv's thoughts make a beeline for what she should be wearing but then remembers that Tristan said they were going to a bar. Her jeans and white button-down shirt will do fine. She glances furtively up at Tristan, even if she knows full well what her boss has on. All black—again—and with an ornate, of course antique, gold necklace. No hoops in her ears today, but instead gold studs in the shape of a bird in flight. The gold looks amazing against her pale skin— Liv bites down so hard on the tip of her tongue she almost gives a little yelp.

Focus. That was the plan. Focus.

CHAPTER FIVE

L iv knows she's begging for trouble when she takes the opportunity to sit next to Tristan at the round table. Marlena's father, who insists they all call him Rajmund, has placed their beverage of choice in front of them, and as Liv sips her beer, she sees Graham across from her, winking. Raising her eyebrows and trying to look innocent, Liv knows he knows she knows. She decides to not let that get to her. Socializing with Tristan in a casual setting is golden in more ways than one. Professionally, for sure, but more than that, for getting to know this intense, enigmatic woman. Aware that it is smarter to let the others keep the conversation going, to begin with, sort of listen and learn, Liv leans back in her chair while nursing her beer.

"That painting you and Liv are working on," Graham says lightly, "looks like it's going to be quite the task. Whoever decided to glue it to something?"

"Probably two restorations ago. Though I wouldn't call it a restoration. I think someone glued it to a board, and then someone after that tore it from said board and used a stretcher. This treatment didn't do the canvas any favors," Tristan says, drinking her beer from a bottle. "It's a damn crime."

"Good thing you have one more person working on it," Marlena, who sits close to Dana, says. "All that scraping is a surefire road to insanity, if you ask me."

Liv forgets about her decision to watch and learn about the group's dynamic before speaking. "It can be," she says and places her glass on the coaster. "Then some days you just get into the zone, and time doesn't matter."

Tristan clears her throat. "That's true."

Liv nods. "When I was in college, the students were given a canvas to work on, free of charge for the client, and it turned out that the cracked layer on top of the painting wasn't varnish…it was polyurethane. I had to scrape it off, in small pieces, and after talking to the client and explaining that it was impossible to not lose some of the paint underneath, they still wanted us to continue. I spent a lot of hours on it, and that's when I truly learned about the zone." Suddenly a little embarrassed that she's given a whole speech about her newbie foray into the profession that the others around the table, barring Dana, have worked in for years, Liv grabs her glass again and takes a large gulp. She doesn't embarrass herself by choking, but it's close.

"Polyurethane!" Marlena makes a face. "I've had to deal with that a few times, and it sucks. Ask Dana what I think of it. She's seen my reaction the last two times."

"I will not utter such words," Dana says primly and sips her white wine. "It's unbecoming, though understandable."

For some reason, everyone chuckles, making Dana raise her chin.

"I know, Dana. I use a bit of undesirable language when I'm frustrated." Marlena leans in and kisses Dana's cheek, making her blush.

Graham snorts but doesn't elaborate as Rajmund brings in the preordered food. He hovers a bit and then beams as they all dig in, humming around the Polish dishes. Liv cautiously eyes Tristan, and when their eyes meet, a sensation as if someone has snapped a rubber band against her makes her wonder if her boss is as aware of the strange sort of chemistry forming between them as she is.

Liv carefully moves her injured finger, which stings, but not too badly. She can still feel Tristan's firm grip on her wrist when holding the finger in place under the faucet. Not only that, their proximity, standing so close together, Tristan's hip pressed to hers, hadn't made it easier. And what the hell happened that had Tristan looking rattled when she came back from her call? She'd been pale, but with dark red spots burning at the top of her cheekbones. Her eyes hadn't given a single thing away, yet it was obvious to Liv that Tristan was concerned. No, more than that, alarmed. It seems to have passed now, though. Tristan chats amicably with Paul—the "wood guy" who takes care of stretchers and frames in the wood workshop—who sits on her other side.

Liv keeps light conversation going with the others, and even Dana grants her a faint smile, which Liv suspects is no small feat. It's obvious to her now that Marlena and Dana are a couple, and as different as they are, they send off good vibes.

"So, how was your first day, Liv?" Graham asks. "And Tristan, you must be thrilled to have Liv on board, as you gave her an actual job to do today."

Liv knows she must appear totally put on the spot, and a quick glance at Tristan proves she too has a look of concern.

"Um. Actually, I loved it. I know this is what I want to work with—it's truly my passion," Liv manages to say without sounding too gushing or revealing how out of breath she is. She turns to Tristan, expecting her to respond to her part of Graham's questions.

"I have no idea what you're talking about," Tristan says coolly. "Of course, Olivia's here to work. The hands-on approach is the best way, wouldn't you agree, Graham?"

Graham chokes on the fork of vegetables he's just put in his mouth and reaches for his beer. Making a big production of swallowing, he then shakes his head and holds up his hands, palms forward, in mock defeat. "I yield. We won't mention how the rest of us could only look at what you were teaching for days on end before you let us touch anything. Some of us almost a full week."

"That'd be me," Paul says, raising his glass to Graham. "I had to wait for six workdays before I was allowed to unbox a painting by myself."

Tristan glares at the two men, but then she smiles, which turns into a chuckle. "You're both horrible people. Olivia must think I'm a real dragon." She shifts her gaze to Liv, who can only stare at the now warm and sparkling blue eyes. Gone is the flat expression from earlier in the day, and instead, Liv sees something that pulls her farther in. She's not quite sure what it is, but images of candlelight, a soft bed, gentle voices are mixed with passionate caresses, gasps of pleasure, and, oh God, moans and whimpers.

Is this what being struck by lightning feels like? Liv sits straight up, staring at Tristan, not sure what else she's trying to deduce from those beautiful eyes and the unexpected softness of her features.

"Perhaps you better put your fork down. You look like you're contemplating stabbing someone," Tristan says, her voice a low purr now. She's clearly teasing, but why? It's as if she's suddenly flirting.

Liv wills her hand to relax her grip of the fork, her injured finger stinging again. "I promise, I'm not dangerous in any way, Tristan," she says, trying to answer in jest.

Tristan tilts her head in a way that's becoming familiar—and lethal to Liv's peace of mind. "Oh, I wouldn't say that, Olivia. I wouldn't say that at all."

CHAPTER SIX

Two weeks after the night out at Rajmund's bar, Tristan realizes she's found a gem in Olivia. Interested, eager, and always quick to research their works of art, Olivia is making herself irreplaceable. Tristan enjoys teaching her—and admits to herself that she likes it too much. Something is so alluring in those keen, golden-brown eyes, which look at Tristan as if she possesses the answers to all mysteries. Thank God, Olivia isn't the puppy-love kind. Tristan has had her fair share of experiences with young interns who've idolized her and indulged in some sticky, uncomfortable hero worship. This isn't what Olivia exudes. Instead, she challenges Tristan when it comes to a more unconventional method of work. Tristan knows that some of her techniques are not the most modern, but they work for her, she's comfortable with them and she's used them forever. When Olivia argues for the latest finds in fine-art restoration, it turns out to be invigorating to spar with her.

Now, she meets Olivia in the foyer as the young woman comes in from the cold, carrying a tray of hot beverages. The scent of coffee makes Tristan's mouth water.

"My turn to do the coffee run today." Olivia smiles. "I couldn't find you before I left and wanted to beat the lunch crowd, but I took a chance and brought you your usual super-strong latte."

"Very thoughtful. Why don't you hand those over to Graham and come join me in the office? I'd like to sum up how you've experienced the first two weeks here." Tristan takes her latte and is turning to leave when she catches Olivia's panicked expression.

"Already? Two weeks?" Olivia grips the tray hard.

"Calm down. It's just a talk. You're fine." Tristan expects her usual exasperation at emotional displays to appear, but instead, she wants to kick herself for startling Olivia unnecessarily. Oh, this is not good. She can't go soft and mushy over this girl.

"Okay. I'll be right there." Olivia nods and scurries over to the door leading into the workshop.

Tristan enters her office and leaves the door ajar. Her desk is cluttered, as she's been using it to clean and polish an antique sextant. She merely pushes the tray aside and sits down while pulling a pen and legal pad closer.

Olivia stops in the doorway and hesitates briefly. She's holding on to her coffee, and after a few moments, she steps inside. "Should I…?" She motions behind her with her thumb.

"Yes. Close the door, please." Tristan makes sure her voice is noncommittal and cool, which is her preferred approach. "First of all, how's the unboxing of the Russian icon coming along?"

Brightening, and relaxing, Olivia sips her drink before answering. "I'm peeling off the last cloth layer. The client was afraid the paint would come off with the old fabric, but so far, I see no trace of that happening. I'm so excited to see what condition it'll be in once we remove that covering."

"And the final touches of the Natale painting?" Tristan taps the back of her pen against her lower lip. This motion seems to distract Olivia, who doesn't answer right away.

"Um. I still think we should airbrush a second layer of varnish and buff the surface if you think it's too glossy." Placing her coffee on a coaster on the desk, Olivia gestures for emphasis. "It would hold up better, and since buffing isn't permanent, there's really no risk."

Tristan nods slowly. "Very well. I'm not a fan of the airbrush equipment. I was trained using classic techniques. Perhaps it's time to join the twenty-first century."

"A combination of the old and new technique is the best of both worlds." Olivia takes her mug again but doesn't drink from it.

At Olivia's words, Tristan feels a twitch in her chest, painful enough to contract her muscles. She is about to say something when her office phone rings, making her flinch. Rattled at her own reaction, Tristan picks up the receiver. "Tristan Kelly."

"Sarah. It's Rosalee," a female voice says. It's familiar, and cold dread runs down Tristan's spine like beads of ice. Rosalee. She sounds out of breath. Even agitated.

"I'm Tristan Kelly." Tristan isn't about to acknowledge anything just yet. She stands up but forces herself to remain calm. "Who is this?"

"I know you recognized me. You had to. I knew it was you, Sarah. It took me only a few moments. Oh, dear God." Rosalee gives a strange, choppy kind of laugh. "The name of your firm made a lot more sense, suddenly. Now that we're in contact, there are matters—"

Suddenly remembering Olivia, Tristan turns to dismiss her, but the concern in Olivia's eyes makes her falter. Olivia indicates Tristan's free hand, which is trembling. Tristan clenches it but can't bring herself to tell Olivia to leave. Olivia's presence seems to help ground her. Later, she will examine this peculiarity, but right now she has to handle Rosalee.

"What do you want?" Tristan asks, hearing the menace in her own voice.

"This…finding each other by happenstance, is a godsend. We should meet."

"Godsend." Tristan huffed. "Hardly the right word, given the circumstances."

"Point taken." Rosalee takes a trembling breath. "How many do you have on your list that are still with us?"

Stunned at Rosalee's words, Tristan is transported back to when they lived in the same small town in Maine. Rosalee was still married, and Tristan was a widow. Was it then they had begun their lists? They had looked up the ones from the ship they could find and traveled up and down the coast until they located all but two, who were dead, both from horrible accidents.

Tristan had saved and bought the ledger as a young woman, and she took it with her everywhere she went. She had worked as a teacher back then, and the pay wasn't great, but the ledger had been with her ever since, the list of names changing. Rosalee had used a similar system, and now, should Tristan play nice and simply go along?

Slowly sitting down, Tristan suddenly feels Olivia's hand on her shoulder, and she covers it with her cold, trembling one. "All right, Rosalee, what do you want?"

"There have been new developments for some of us during the

last decade, and as you always were the reclusive one, you may not be aware. Come to Paris and work on the painting. As it's a remarkable piece, nobody will think it strange for you to do so."

Tristan looks up at Olivia. "I'm not making any promises. It would take a few days to arrange the trip."

"I understand."

"If this is some trap..." Tristan clenches her teeth around the words.

"Absolutely not. I would never do that." Rosalee sounds sincere.

"I'll be in touch." Tristan hangs up, not bidding Rosalee farewell. She sits as if frozen until she feels Olivia gently squeeze her shoulder.

"Tristan? What can I do?" Olivia crouches next to her.

"Excuse me?" Blinking, Tristan isn't sure how much time has passed after she hung up. Unbidden thoughts and memories keep whirling in her mind. Already knowing she has to go, that she has to see Rosalee, she chuckles mirthlessly. "Oh, Jesus. Do you have a passport?"

"Yes?" Olivia's eyebrows go up, but she doesn't take her eyes off Tristan.

"Then I suppose you're coming with me to Paris to work on a painting at the Louvre."

Chapter Seven

Liv has never flown first class before. She has her own little alcove in the center row, as Tristan prefers the window seat, and she's taken aback by the amount of space. As soon as she sits down, a flight attendant offers champagne, or any other beverage Liv might prefer instead. She's not about to choose champagne, which, the few times she's tasted it, has gone straight to her head and tends to give her a headache. She can't arrive with a hangover.

The plane levels out after taking off, and Liv takes a deep breath of relief. She doesn't like flying. A lover of trains, she has crossed the US several times in both directions. As the only other means of traveling to Paris is by cruise ship, she is realistic enough to accept air travel as the only reasonable choice. And she understands the chance of her traveling in first class ever again is infinitesimal. Might as well enjoy it.

"I overheard you tell Marlena this is your first transatlantic flight." Tristan puts away her tablet. "Once they serve the meal, I suggest you try to get some sleep. When it comes to jet lag, I always find traveling to Europe much harder than flying in the opposite direction. We need to stay sharp, for many reasons." Her eyes darken, and she adjusts the cuffs of her powder-blue cashmere sweater, which she wears with black slacks.

"Can you tell me about the curator we'll be working with? I'm not even sure if her name is Rosalee or Vanessa," Liv asks cautiously.

Tristan doesn't answer at first but squints at Liv before shifting farther toward the window. "Well, don't just sit there. I'm not going to yell across the aisle for everyone to hear." Tristan displays her regular annoyed-but-not-really expression.

When Liv finally catches on, she unbuckles and sits next to Tristan. Even if the seat is comfortably wide, it's not really meant for two. Liv feels Tristan's hip against hers, which makes her shudder. She's not sure she manages to hide her reaction.

"Both names are correct," Tristan says. "And I've known Rosalee for many years. Longer than I care to remember."

"If you don't like her, why are we heading to Paris?" Liv knows she's pushing it, but she's enthralled with Tristan and the fact that she's starting to share personal details.

"Actually, I was fond of Rosalee when we were children. Our parents started out as friends when we met during a…trip. Rosalee was fun, full of mischief, and as my sister was a great deal older than me, we found each other, Rosalee and I."

"Did you outgrow each other?" Liv shifts again, sitting more turned toward Tristan while trying not to push against her with her knee.

Tristan gives another one of her mirthless chuckles. "I suppose. It took a while. All through childhood, once Rosalee's father decided to remain in the same area near us, we played and dreamed about the future. I suppose, all these years later, so much has changed, and the two of us as well, that nothing is recognizable. I do have to admit, though, I heard something in Rosalee's tone that reminded me of the young girl she used to be. I'm not sure, except for the art piece we're restoring, what she might want. I may have to rely on you to work independently more than usual. We'll be collaborating with some of the Louvre's staff. You won't be tossed to the wolves alone."

Liv winces. "My French isn't what it was in high school. I focused on Spanish and Italian in college."

"You'll be fine. They speak English, and there are enough similarities between the languages for you to understand and make yourself understood." Tristan rubs her neck. "I hate sleeping on planes."

"Need a neck rub?" Liv hears herself ask before she can harness her tongue. Maybe it's because Tristan has finished talking about Rosalee and her childhood, and to be honest, her reminiscing has only managed to stir more questions in Liv, but Tristan cocks her head and seems to take Liv's offer seriously. "I'm sorry," Liv hurries to say. "I'm overstepping."

"I think you're being quite caring." Tristan shocks Liv by removing her sweater right there and then turning her back to her, wearing only a sports bra under a tank top. "If you injure me, we'll have words."

Liv looks at Tristan's pale, perfect skin, her mouth going instantly dry. "I don't have any oil." Her meek words make her want to groan out loud.

"Wait." Tristan opens her messenger bag and pulls out some hand cream. "Will this do?"

"Sch-sure." Liv squirts some into her palm and warms it between her hands. The moment she lays them on Tristan's beautiful shoulders, she knows it's a mistake that's going to cost her. Not now, perhaps not even in Paris, but afterward, when they get home—being allowed to touch this woman, just once, is going to cost her.

CHAPTER EIGHT

Instantly, Tristan knows it is a huge mistake to allow Olivia to touch her. Colossal. She's been able to rationalize—somewhat—her feelings when she's around this woman, but to accept a neck rub, in public, even if they are well out of sight of anyone but the occasionally passing flight attendant, is a miscalculation. Olivia's hands are warm as they rest against Tristan's knotted muscles on either side of her neck. She just keeps them there, which makes Tristan tremble. She hopes Olivia doesn't notice, but maybe she does, since she starts moving, applying enough pressure to do something about the knots, but not hurting her. Or at least not too badly.

"This good?" Olivia murmurs into Tristan's ear. "Harder? Or too hard?"

"Hm. It's okay." Tristan has to clear her voice. "Like that."

"Okay." Olivia shifts, and now both hands are resting on the left side of her neck. One hand holds Tristan in place with the palm just above her clavicle, the other gently kneading the sore trapezius muscle. She keeps the movements going until Tristan wants to tip her head back and let out the moan hovering in the back of her throat.

Olivia moves her hands to the right. She also shifts behind Tristan, sliding closer. Now not only does Olivia's perfume wrap around Tristan, but firm, round breasts press softly against her back. What is Olivia thinking? Doesn't she realize how that makes Tristan feel? Like being raked over embers.

Perhaps she does. Olivia gasps and moves back enough for the contact to disappear, and now Tristan acutely misses it and wants more.

"I apologize." Olivia whispers the words, and they are caught in Tristan's hair, sending tingles along her scalp. "This good still?"

"Mm-hmm." No way can Tristan talk without giving herself away. Her belly is on fire, and the heat that follows every single vein in her body is such a new feeling, Tristan doubts she's ever responded like this—to anyone. If she has, it must have been so long ago, she's forgotten it. She doubts she'll ever forget this experience.

Eventually, Olivia stops the therapeutic kneading, and Tristan thinks she's done. She begins to turn, but Olivia's hand on her shoulders makes her stop.

"Hey. I need to make sure you're all taken care of," Olivia says. Her choice of words sends Tristan's left hand up to cover her mouth. She clamps down hard, to keep the moan from escaping this time. "Like this." Olivia palpates the muscles gently, sliding her fingers along them. "I can't find any knots. How does it feel when I do this?"

Like I could come if you keep touching me. "I think you managed to get them all." Tristan's voice is strained. "Thank you."

"No problem. I'll go back to my seat now. I think dinner's about to be served." Olivia stands, but before she has a chance to leave, Tristan turns and takes hold of her wrist. Blinking in clear surprise, Olivia remains on her feet, looking down at her.

"Yes?"

Tristan studies her carefully. Olivia's eyes are darker than usual. Her cheeks are flushed, and, having studied this face more than what is appropriate since the day she first interviewed her, Tristan can tell that Olivia's lips are swollen and damp. Oh, thank God. It may not be convenient or advisable, but it is such a relief to realize that Tristan isn't the only one that the massage has affected.

"Tristan?" Olivia looks concerned now.

"Nothing. Go eat and then get some sleep. We hit the ground running when we get to Paris." Tristan lets go of Olivia, again missing the connection so much it pains her.

The way Olivia cradles her wrist and holds it against her chest suggests she may be feeling the same.

CHAPTER NINE

Rosalee looks the same in some ways and vastly different in others, compared to when Tristan last saw her in person. So many years have passed. Tall, gangly, plus appearing utterly elegant, à la Paris, Rosalee, nowadays going by Vanessa Mercier, strides along the corridor toward them.

"Tristan." She air-kisses Tristan's cheeks and then extends a hand to Olivia. "I'm Vanessa. Welcome to Paris. How was your flight?"

So, small talk first. Tristan applies a polite smile. "Uneventful. We're eager to get started, as our time here is limited. Originally, the Louvre was supposed to send the painting to New York. All these last-minute changes have reduced the number of hours we're able to spend on this project. If I hadn't brought my intern, I don't think it could have been done at all."

Rosalee pales. "I had hoped we could talk first."

"Why don't we make it a working dinner tonight?" Tristan is entirely content with putting off whatever Rosalee wants to talk about.

"I don't mean to be rude, Tristan, but I meant just between us." Looking awkward now, Rosalee tugs at her long Chanel necklace. "I hope you understand, Olivia?"

"I do, completely," Olivia says calmly. "I thought I'd take the time to go shopping a bit anyway, if it's all right with you, Tristan?" She smiles broadly. "Not every day you have a chance to make a find in Paris."

Tristan isn't pleased but figures she might as well bite the bullet. Before she and Olivia fly back to New York, Rosalee is going to have her meeting no matter what, and perhaps doing it the first day will reduce stress during the rest of her time at the Louvre.

Rosalee guides them to the workshop where other restorers are working on their respective paintings. At the far end, a large workstation is set up, and the painting is sitting on an easel, covered with a cloth.

"Here it is. I'll let you get sorted." Rosalee checks her time. "It's two p.m. When will you be done for the day, do you think?"

"Seven." Tristan steps closer to the painting and removes the cloth. She has seen digital photos of it and its wear and tear, and damages.

"I'll send a car for you. You can drop off Olivia where she wants to go." Rosalee remains by their side, looking uncertain, but eventually bids them a good day and walks off on her lethal heels.

Tristan casts a glance at Olivia, who appears puzzled as she studies Rosalee's departure. "Olivia?"

"Yes?" Swiveling, Olivia joins Tristan by the easel. "Holy crap. It looks worse up close. Perforations, at least four. The varnish looks thick. The frame needs a lot of woodwork. Is that on us?" She looks dismayed.

"No, not the frame. The Louvre has a wood workshop almost up to my standard. They'll deal with it. This, however," Tristan says and motions toward the painting, "this is going to be a baptism by fire for you. I hope your performance is as consistent as it has been back home. If you're ever unsure of what to do, ask me. All right?"

"Absolutely. I realize it's a privilege to be here. You could have picked any one of the others with much more experience." Olivia nods.

No, she couldn't have. Tristan's abdominal muscles clench. She needs to spend time with Olivia, alone, to figure out what's going on between them. The whole neck-rub scenario only emphasized things, but it did little to explain why. And Tristan knows herself well enough to admit she always needs to know exactly why.

They start on the painting as they have worked on other projects, and once they remove the frame and stretcher, they're relieved to find no strange substances on the back. While Olivia starts gently brushing away the debris with a special sponge, Tristan prepares the tools they need to strengthen the frail edges.

They work in silence, and only after two hours, when Tristan stretches and feels a vertebra in her neck pop, does she acknowledge how pleasant the silence between them is. They have exchanged only a few words and briefly greeted their French colleagues, who have come up to introduce themselves. The rest of the time, they have anticipated each other's moves and worked seamlessly together. "We need coffee, Olivia."

"I'll go get some—no?" Olivia stops midstep when Tristan shakes her head.

"No. *We'll* go get some. We need to stretch our backs. Or at least I do. Comes with age." Tristan chuckles to herself.

"How can you move with more elegance and grace than I ever could, no matter how tired you are?" Olivia shakes her head. Then she blushes and covers her forehead. "That sounded creepy. I mean, I'm not stalking you, even if it sounds like it, by noticing how you move. Damn. I'll just shut up." Now she looks up to the ceiling and groans.

Tristan's chuckle turns into full laughter. "I take that as a compliment, even if it isn't true. You move like a young panther." Olivia's candor is clearly contagious. Tristan notices how Olivia's eyes grow wide and lengthens her stride. She stops by one of their colleagues and asks for the break room and if they can get coffee there. The man makes a typical French shrug and answers, "Yes, madam, of course," sounding offended that she would even think to ask such a thing. "Any type of coffee imaginable."

When they reach the break room, they find it empty. A somewhat intimidating espresso machine sits in the corner, but as they near it, Tristan is relieved to see it has options for preselected varieties. She presses a sensor that immediately makes a double espresso latte for her. Olivia chooses the same, and they sit down in the corner on a three-seater couch.

"Ah, padding." Olivia sighs and sips her coffee. Her eyes widen again. "Oh, my God. This coffee...it's...it's insane."

Tristan drinks from her mug and agrees. It's incredibly good coffee. "Yes. Insane."

Olivia drinks some more of her latte and then places the mug on the coffee table. Turning toward Tristan, she tilts her head and studies her for a few unnerving moments. "Can you tell me more about Rosalee? About what's wrong? And why she changed her name?"

Tristan wants to. Only the horrific memories from her youth, when she trusted in someone enough to share the truth, keep her from doing so now. Granted, times have changed, but not *that* much. Not nearly enough. "Rosalee and I grew up under simple circumstances. I think we both wanted to shed that skin when we became adults and began making our respective plans. Now, Rosalee isn't aware that you know her original name. It might…startle her to learn that you do, so may I ask you not to reveal this fact?"

Olivia's eyes narrow, but then she nods. "Of course. I won't tell a soul. We all carry baggage, no matter how old we are."

"Do you as well, Olivia?" Tristan doesn't like the pained expression that ghosts across Olivia's face.

"Yes, but I'm working on carving out my future by doing this." She motions in the direction of the workshop. "And by being here," Olivia adds, making a smaller circle between them.

"I hope it will live up to your expectations," Tristan says, clinging to her mug. She hopes Olivia takes that remark as if she's talking about the internship, but a small, insistent voice keeps drowning out Tristan's voice of reason, hoping that Olivia will find spending time together like this appealing.

"It already has. More than you realize." It's time for Olivia to grab her mug and drink from it. She licks an errant drop from her lower lip, and Tristan wants to throw herself across the empty cushion between them and capture those lips with hers.

"Tristan?" Olivia whispers.

"We—we should go back." Tristan stands up, drinks from her mug, and tosses the rest of the coffee into the sink. "We need to get a lot more done—oh!"

Olivia's hand is on her arm, effortlessly making Tristan pivot. Sparkling amber eyes lock on to Tristan's as Olivia slides her hand down her arm. There, she gently squeezes Tristan's hand before letting go. "I'm not trying to embarrass you. I didn't intend to on the plane, or now. You have nothing to worry about when it comes to me. I promise." Her expression is so honest, so guileless. Olivia evidently believes every word she's saying.

Tristan, however, knows better. She has everything to worry about when it comes to Olivia Bryce.

CHAPTER TEN

If, only a few days ago, anyone had told Liv she'd be strolling along the Seine and, later, along the Champs-Élysées, she would have called them batshit crazy. Yet here she is, in the early evening, after a lovely dinner by herself, shopping. Well, mostly window shopping, as the stores on the famous street are beyond her price range. She loves looking at the clothes from an artistic point of view and isn't at all upset that she could never afford a pair of Louboutin pumps. The height of the four-inch heels alone would be enough to deter her if the price hadn't already.

The street vendors are more her thing, and she finds some beautiful custom jewelry that could have belonged to a woman a couple of centuries ago. The stones are made of glass, some even crystal, and the colors are amazing.

After strolling through the famous area, content to look at the people and the beautiful lights, taking in the feeling of being in Paris, Liv begins to lose momentum. Her thoughts go to Tristan. How is the dinner with Rosalee working out? She checks her cell phone and sees it's time to return to the hotel. Flagging down a taxi, she gives the driver the name of the luxurious establishment where she and Tristan stay in a two-bedroom suite. Liv hadn't expected this, and Tristan's assumption that she's all right with the arrangement should perhaps feel like arrogance, but it doesn't.

Spotting three missed text messages, Liv clicks on them, and her heart jumps when she sees they're from Tristan. Shit. What's wrong now?

8:40 pm
Have you found a decent place to eat?
8:56 pm
Olivia. Have you eaten? Are you all right?
9:09 pm
Why aren't you answering? If you haven't texted me back in 15 minutes, I will call you.
Damn it. Liv taps her screen furiously.
9:22 pm
Sorry, Tristan. I'm fine. On my way back to the hotel in a taxi. All is well.

She sends it off, with one minute to go. It takes ten seconds before a ping lets her know Tristan has texted her back.
9:22 pm
Fine.

Slumping against the backrest, Liv isn't sure whether to roll her eyes at Tristan being so huffy, yet clearly worried, or strangely flattered that Tristan worries at all. She settles for the latter, even if the "Fine" sounded damn huffy.

She crosses the hotel lobby and heads for the elevators, her legs like lead now, jet lag simmering behind her eyelids. It's possible she might doze off in the elevator. Better not lean against the wall. After reaching her floor, she walks down the corridor, her steps inaudible against the carpet. She fumbles for her keycard when she gets to the suite but can't see it in her wallet. She goes through her pockets, and her bag, but finds no sign of the card. Groaning, she thuds her head against the door. She can of course take the elevator back down again and have the desk clerk make her a new one, but the elevator is so far away—oddly it feels much farther than it was just moments ago.

Liv sits down on the floor, her back against the door. She'll find the phone number to the hotel and ask them to come up with a key. Yes, that's a great idea. She's not in anyone's way here by the door, as the suite is at the far end and just around the corner of the main corridor. The only ones who have any reason to walk here are Tristan and her.

Resting her head against the door, she taps on her phone, trying to figure out which number is for the desk. Or maybe call housekeeping? No. That's not right. Has to be the desk. They can send a bellhop.

Liv's thoughts return to Tristan and the enigmatic Rosalee. Two women, both from similar circumstances, but so different. Tristan—strong, stern, and aloof. Rosalee, on the other hand, seeming jittery, bordering on nervous, as if something is very, very wrong. Will Tristan share anything with her? Of course, none of this is any of Liv's business. Totally true. Yet she and Tristan move around each other in elliptical orbits, sometimes close enough to touch, sometimes, like now, at a distance.

Was Tristan worried or merely annoyed? Why was that so important? You could argue that Liv's in Paris with Tristan only to assist her, but that would be untrue. At least on Liv's part. What if Tristan has brought her for other reasons as well? Liv's thoughts whirl, and soon she slumps sideways, barely propping herself up against the door frame.

The next thing she knows, someone is holding her shoulder in a firm grip, shaking her.

"Liv! Why on earth are you sitting on the floor? Are you all right?"

Liv blinks and looks up into blue eyes regarding her through narrow slits, and it takes her a second to realize it's Tristan crouching next to her. Her lips are pressed into a thin line as she shakes Liv again.

So, yeah. Annoyed *and* worried.

CHAPTER ELEVEN

Tristan walks into the restaurant, of course the most hyped in all of France, according to her Google search. Rosalee always dreamed of flair and extravagance, even when they were young girls back in the countryside, not far from Plymouth. The very modern restaurant features bold colors, and Tristan suspects the menu will offer everything from classic French cuisine to almost avant-garde cooking.

Rosalee gets up from the booth she's booked when the maître d' shows Tristan to her table. Tall, thin, and with tension written all over her, the fire-engine-red lips greet Tristan with more air-kisses.

"Welcome, my dear," Rosalee murmurs and motions toward the booth. "Please, have a seat. I took the liberty of ordering drinks for us. I seem to remember you are fond of bourbon?" Fidgeting in a way that reminds Tristan of Olivia, Rosalee plays with the napkin-wrapped utensils.

"I am. Thank you." Tristan sips the bourbon and approves. "All right. I'm in Paris despite it throwing my entire schedule out the window. What can possibly be so important?"

"It's beyond important," Rosalee says quietly. "It's a matter of, well, life and death. As of twelve days ago, only you and I are left." She shudders. "It frightens me as much as it is a relief."

Tristan grows rigid. "What do you mean?" She has an inkling, and the idea of it all is indeed intimidating. "Iris?" she asks, her voice strained.

"Iris." Rosalee takes a large sip of her colorful, pink cocktail. "She's used the name Anneliese for the last twenty years."

"How?" Tristan clings to her glass of bourbon.

"This time it does look like a genuine accident. A pileup in the Swiss Alps. It was in the papers. I found out only because I have software that alerts me when anything remarkable happens to you or her. As it turns out, it never was reliable when it came to you. I thought your new alias was Pamela Newton, for some reason."

"I see." Tristan recognizes one of her smokescreen names. Inside, she begins to tremble. She is appalled and sad about Iris's fate, in so many ways. Clearly Iris's death was accidental, not from natural causes. This meant Tristan, and Rosalee, still had very little hope to have a normal, humane ending to their lives one day. "And as tragic as that loss is, why am I here? What's really going on?"

Paling, Rosalee clears her throat. "Some people know."

Tristan flinches. "Excuse me?"

"That's my theory at least. I'm not sure who among us has broken the Amaranthine Law." Rosalee shakes her head. "I only know it wasn't me—and I think I know you well enough to assume it wasn't you."

"It most certainly wasn't." Tristan speaks through clenched teeth, her heart hammering as she tries to estimate the fallout if what Rosalee thinks is true. "Perhaps Iris, before she passed."

"I doubt that. Iris was so private and quite the recluse, most of the time." Rosalee frowns. "Did you bring your ledger? We need to compare notes."

"I did, but it's in the safe in my hotel room." Tristan sighs. "If we're the last ones left, who can know? And, more importantly, who can prove anything?"

"Don't be naive, Tristan." Rosalee snaps the words out impatiently, but then closes her eyes hard for a moment. When she looks over at Tristan, she has an expression of defeat, her complexion more gray than white. "Aren't you just so very tired of it all sometimes?" Rosalee whispers.

"Sometimes." But not lately, Tristan realizes. "You're not going to do anything stupid, are you?" She deliberately nails Rosalee with her best glare.

"I would be lying if I told you I haven't thought of it during the years. I bet you have too. But now, I'm not going to break the law.

Those who did…the wounds will never heal for us. It's bad enough to deal with the ones who passed accidentally. But to break the law. Never." Rosalee regains some of her color, and her voice is stronger. "So, who can know?"

"Wait…" Tristan thinks back to when she browsed her book of *The Amaranthine Law.* "You say we're the only ones left, but that's what we *think.* You're here in Europe, I reside in the US. It would be easy for any of the others who moved to South America, or Africa, to fake their passing a little too well, don't you think?" Tristan pauses as the waiter approaches to take their orders, and they rattle them off. Rosalee flicks her fingers dismissively when they're done. "Tell me why you think someone outside our group knows anything."

"I received a letter. Then an email a few weeks before Iris passed. The former was posted in Melbourne, Australia. That means nothing, of course."

"And what did the letter and email say?"

"I didn't bring the letter, but here's the email." Rosalee hands over her cell phone. "It's short."

Tristan takes the phone. Putting on her reading glasses, she scrolls through the short message.

Rosalee,

 After several lifetimes, you do not have the right to walk this earth unchallenged. Your past speaks for itself, and so do your actions…or inactions. Your punishment will be carried out swiftly, and the same goes for Sarah, who also swore to abide by the Amaranthine Law.

 The moral right is on our side.

 We are coming for you.

The email was unsigned, and the sender had used a common email server.

"I guess the regular letter you received was also anonymous?" Tristan hands the phone back to Rosalee.

"It was. The message was worded a bit differently, but the meaning was the same." Rosalee shudders. "When I realized who you were, I knew that fate had stepped in, yet again…that you could help me."

"How am I supposed to do that? I have no hidden computer skills that allow me to track this email." Tristan frowns.

Placing her hand on Tristan's, Rosalee leans across the table. "Listen to me. You used to have connections within the police force."

Appalled, Tristan pulls her hand free. "Are you insane? That was too long ago, and even if I still did, I would never expose us like that—and thus break the Amaranthine Law. We all swore to uphold it. You half coerced me into flying here. It wasn't my first choice, and you know it. We always risk exposure, but more so when we cross borders. IDs are getting harder and harder to forge."

"I know. And I'm sorry that I couldn't see any other way out. I need you here. We were close once. We were the best of friends."

"A lot has happened since then. We're not the same people." Tristan winces as the waiter interrupts again, placing the starter dish before her. Once he leaves, and Tristan imagines he's happy to escape waiting on them as the tension is ominously thick, she catches Rosalee's gaze. "Do you understand what I'm saying?"

"I do, but I don't accept it. We need to deal with this situation. We have to find out what exactly happened to Iris. I'm afraid. Who knows what the people behind the email and letter can do?" Rosalee grips her utensils hard. "I insist we deal with this once and for all."

"Insist?" Tristan merely glowers.

"Yes. With the best of intentions for both of us." Rosalee speaks in a gentler tone. "Please, Sarah—" Rosalee sighs. "Tristan. Please."

"All right. We'll get together again tomorrow—and in private." Tristan is curt. "Bring your data and we'll compare. I agree that the email is worrisome, but I refuse to commit to something that sounds like a mere hunch on your part. Too much has gone on in my life for me to see ghosts where none exist."

"Yet," Rosalee says, slumping against the backrest.

Tristan keeps eating, even though she has lost her appetite during their conversation. She needs the sustenance, as it seems she might have double duty on this trip. Her thoughts whirl, but eventually she manages to push them to the back of her mind. Only one thought remains and moves to the front of the rest. Olivia. How is Olivia doing in the center of an enormous city that is entirely unknown to her?

Tristan pulls her cell from her messenger bag and sends off a text.

When she has no reply, she texts again. And then again, this time with caution. Just as she's hovering with her finger over the call button, Olivia texts her back, seeming completely oblivious to how she's worried Tristan. Wonderful.

❖

After leaving Rosalee and hailing a taxi, Tristan is exhausted. Jet lag is creeping up, and it's relentless. She tumbles out of the taxi at the hotel and forces herself to lengthen her stride as she walks toward the elevators. She pulls out her keycard and holds it tight, wanting nothing more than a quick scalding shower and then sleep.

The corridor is ridiculously long, and she feels foggy when she rounds the corner—and sees Olivia sitting with her back against the door to the suite. Her senses on high alert again, she runs the last steps over to Olivia, throwing herself to her knees next to her. Olivia is pale and doesn't even move. Tristan grabs her shoulder and shakes her. "Olivia! What on earth are you doing sitting on the floor? Are you all right?" Her heart is pounding.

Olivia wakes up, her arms flailing as if she's lost her balance. Staring at Tristan, she seems embarrassed and afraid. "Tristan. Okay. I'm okay. I just lost my keycard."

Lost her keycard. That's all? "Well, get up. Fortunately, I have mine." Tristan realizes she's biting Olivia's head off, but she can't dial down her worry just yet. She draws a deep breath and attempts a less curt tone. After all, anyone can lose something. "You look as exhausted as I feel," she says. She gets up and then holds out a hand to pull Olivia to her feet.

"I am." Olivia grimaces painfully when she's fully vertical. "Ow. My joints won't be thanking me for that resting place."

Olivia opens the door after Tristan pulls out her card. "After you."

Entering the hallway, Tristan does her best to dampen her internal reactions that her escalating emotions have been fueling since they stepped onto the plane. The massage Olivia gave her that had them both breathless. Worry because of the emails and letter sent to Rosalee. More worries for Olivia not texting her back in a timely fashion, and concern—no, *fear*—when she found Olivia slumped against the hotel-room door just now. Tristan drops her bag onto the floor and then turns to Olivia, who is half out of her coat. Gripping her upper arms, she notices how slender Olivia is, but also how she has wiry muscles under the sweater sleeves. She pushes Olivia against the wall next to the mirror and growls. "Don't say a thing. Not a thing."

CHAPTER TWELVE

Liv has eyes only for Tristan as she stands there, motionless, her back against the wall. Tristan is well within Liv's personal space, scanning every inch of her face. What is she looking for?

"You frightened me this evening. Twice," Tristan says through clenched teeth. "You took your sweet time answering my texts, and then I find you in a...a...*pile* on the floor. I can't tell you the thoughts that went through my mind."

Liv waits, knowing it will be a mistake to speak too soon. Tristan doesn't look as if she's done. And she isn't.

"I have sat listening to Rosalee telling me things that might turn my life to shreds, and despite that, all I could wonder was if you were all right. Alone in a city unfamiliar to you, where you don't speak the language."

Thrown off by Tristan's words, Liv fumbles in her mind before she finds her own voice. "Turn your life to shreds? How?" What could Rosalee possibly say to yank the rug from out under Tristan like this? And was that why she reacted in such a frantic way to a few delayed texts?

Tristan gives Liv's arms a small push and then lets go, only to place her palms against the wall on either side of Liv's head. This position brings Tristan even closer. Her perfume fills Liv's senses and floods her entire system. It's tinged with a barely-there scent of bourbon, but Tristan isn't intoxicated. Liv has no idea what that would look like but knows this isn't it.

Not sure what her next response ought to be, Liv slowly raises her hand and runs her fingers along Tristan's jaw. This gesture halts time.

Tristan even stops breathing. Her lips part, and her stormy-blue eyes probe Liv's.

"I'm sorry I worried you," Liv says quietly. "I'm even more sorry that Rosalee upset you."

If Liv thought her apology would reduce the tension between them, she was mistaken. Tristan places a hand over Liv's before she has a chance to remove it and keeps it there. "You're sorry." She takes a couple of deep breaths. "Apology accepted. Don't do it again." She still doesn't let go.

Liv has lost her own breath, not to mention what she was thinking just before this happened. Wait. Yes. Rosalee. But it seems less important now. What matters is how Tristan keeps them connected. The warmth of her hand on the back of Liv's. The incredible feeling of Tristan's impossibly velvet skin against Liv's palm.

"I can't promise," Liv says, gently moving her fingers to caress Tristan's cheek. "But I'll do my best. I can promise that." The sensation of touching Tristan travels up her arm and into her chest, where Liv's heart picks up speed in a way that makes every single beat almost painful. She wants to reverse their positions, place Tristan against the wall and cover her with her body, shield her. Hold her. And, oh God, claim her.

"You better." Tristan steps back, lowering her hand. Liv feels the loss of the touch acutely and doesn't know what to do with hers. She pulls off her coat and hangs it and, turning to Tristan, sees that she's still just standing there, looking lost in thought.

"Here." Knowing her action can backfire, Liv still helps Tristan out of her coat and hangs it next to her own. Something about their respective wraps hanging next to each other with no space in between is remarkably touching. "I need mineral water. Can I get you anything?" Liv asks while she kicks off her boots.

"Pellegrino." Tristan answers absentmindedly. She bends to unbuckle her boots and toe them off before placing them on the shoe rack.

Liv explores the tray of beverages and then the complimentary refrigerator content. "No Pellegrino, I'm afraid. Perrier? Evian? Badoit?"

"Badoit." Tristan disappears into her bedroom, and Liv hears the door to her ensuite bathroom close. She pours two glasses of Badoit, adds a few ice cubes, and makes a quick trip to her own bathroom. Catching her reflection in the mirror, she sees how pale she is. The dark circles under her eyes are impressive. She decides on a lightning-quick shower before returning to the living room area.

Tristan sits on the couch, her legs pulled up, holding a thick, old, locking book, perhaps a photo album, on her lap. She drinks from her water and has already finished half of it. If Liv's dark circles are bad, then Tristan's look like semicircular bruises. She has removed her makeup, so perhaps that's why they're more noticeable than only moments ago.

Liv takes a seat in the armchair to Tristan's right, mimicking her pose. Pulling up her phone, she pretends to check texts while stealthily studying Tristan, who at first glance seems relaxed, but who really is gripping the book. When she suddenly puts the glass down on the side table between them, the sharp noise makes Liv jump.

Tristan is clasping the book to her chest, her eyes ablaze, but her body language radiates anxiety. Unable to witness such torment in this formidable woman and not do something about it—*anything*—Liv also puts her glass down and moves to sit next to Tristan.

"Please. Let me help you if I can. I know it's none of my business, I really do, but I can't bear to see you like this."

Tristan slowly turns her head, and when she meets Liv's gaze, her eyes are flat, the fury gone. "You mean well, but there's nothing, absolutely nothing, you can do. I've always known this day would come. In fact, it's taken far too long. It has lulled me into a false sense of security." Tristan tips her head back and draws a trembling breath. "I should put you on a plane back to New York and have Graham take over the mentorship."

"No!" Liv closes the last few inches between them. Rounding Tristan, she places her hand gently on her closest shoulder. "Don't send me back. You can't deal with the painting for the Louvre and whatever's going on with Rosalee at the same time. You...you need me here."

At first it doesn't look like Tristan has heard her. She seems to look straight through Liv, and Liv wonders what she's really seeing. Not anything good, that's a safe bet. Wanting to break through Tristan's haunted reverie, Liv does the only thing she can think of. Moving her hand over to the other shoulder, she tugs Tristan into her arms, book and all.

CHAPTER THIRTEEN

Olivia holds her so close the hard leather cover of her ledger digs into her. Tristan doesn't move, despite the discomfort. It has been so long—too long—since someone held her like they truly cared.

"Wait. Better put this aside," Olivia says, her voice choked as she pushes at the ledger until it ends up on the floor beside them. Tristan flinches and moves to pick it up, but Olivia's arms are back around her, and now she's pulled into a much closer embrace. Groaning, she closes her eyes, not sure what to think or how to respond. What is this? Pity? Or Olivia simply being her compassionate self? Or, worse, is this a sign that this girl genuinely cares? If that's the case, Tristan needs to pull back.

But, oh, how can she? Olivia smells so good, and she's all softness, curves, and... Tristan feels her arms move, and she can swear it's not initially of her own volition. Then she does commandeer her arms and wraps them around Olivia's neck and buries her face in her long hair. It's intoxicating. She hasn't had this in such a long time, she might have just dreamed that it ever happened. "I'm sorry," Tristan murmurs. Of course, Olivia has no way of knowing why Tristan apologizes.

"You haven't done anything wrong. I'm sure of that. And please, just let me hold you. It's all I want," Olivia says.

Tristan knows a lie when she hears one. Or, not a lie exactly, but more of a self-deluding statement. Olivia's goodness tells her this is a platonic, comforting hug, and Tristan knows that's how it started—but it's not just that anymore. Olivia trembles against her, her breath catches every now and then, and when Tristan tests the waters by pushing her fingers into Olivia's hair at the back of her head, the young woman whimpers.

"It's not all you want," Tristan says with a practiced calm and pulls back far enough to read Olivia's expression.

Olivia's eyes are nearly black. Gone is the brilliant amber, the sparkling, brandy-colored irises, and instead, there's…well, the most alluring coffee-colored black. "No, that's not true, I—" Olivia's hands move restlessly against Tristan's back. "Of course. You're right. It's not *all* I want. I suppose I want a lot when it comes to you."

"So, you're saying that you can't remain supportive? Can't be 'there for me' without trembling or losing your breath?" Tristan tilts her head, and she can see Olivia's eyes mist over and hates herself for sounding matter-of-fact.

"I can." Olivia speaks firmly, but the barely visible tremors belie her words. "Not saying it'll be easy, but I can. If that's all you want—or need—from me, but I don't think it is."

"Don't you realize that friendly support is all I could ever allow myself to want from you?" Does Tristan sound as desperate as she feels? "I have many reasons for not crossing that boundary."

"I can think of several," Olivia says, giving a short, choppy kind of laugh that isn't based in any sort of happiness. "I'm not your type. Or you're not gay, or bi. You don't like me. You have workplace rules. I realize all this."

"And still…" Is Olivia aware they're still holding each other?

"And still, something in me has felt more from the start. I'm really careful with my feelings. I've had to be for years, but even so, they are what they are." Olivia wipes quickly at her eyelashes before returning her hand to Tristan's waist. "So, are you going to tell me, or will I have to keep guessing?"

"What…oh. Actually, none of the above. I don't have a type. I have been with both men and women. I do like you. Yes, I have workplace rules, but I make them, after all." Tristan smiles at Olivia's slowly parting lips.

"You—you like me?" Of course, Olivia latches on to those words.

"I do. And I think you can feel it. I let you get away with more than anyone else in an exceptionally long time. In fact, I talk to you like I haven't done in ages." Tristan sags sideways with her arms still around

Olivia. "I should tell you to go to bed, Olivia. We're both exhausted, and we have a long day ahead of us tomorrow."

"Yet you're holding on to me like you don't want me to let go," Olivia says slowly. "Despite your effort to verbally push me away, you haven't let go once."

Ah. Perceptive of Olivia. "I know." Tristan allows the words to slip through her teeth.

"We should sleep, but you're here on the couch, and it makes me think whatever Rosalee said left you all worked up—and it might have something to do with that old book. Or am I reading too much into things?" Olivia glances down at the ledger.

"No, not really. Rosalee has, for the longest time, had the ability to corner me, and this time, though I can't really blame her entirely, is no different. She brought me news, and I wasn't prepared for it. I just want to work on the painting and then for us to return to New York." Tristan rested her head on the top of the backrest. "I'm so jet-lagged I can't think straight."

Olivia smooths back Tristan's hair and runs her thumb along her cheekbone. "So, let's get some sleep. I don't want to keep you up by adding to the emotional turmoil. You obviously have enough on your plate." Olivia shocks Tristan by pressing her lips to her temple. "Just don't sit up here fretting over that family Bible or whatever it is."

Tristan has to smile. She supposes it can be looked upon as a family Bible of sorts, though it has nothing to do with faith or religion. "I need to make a few notes, but I won't sit up all night. I'm already half asleep."

"All right." Before Tristan has a chance to react, Olivia bends and picks up her ledger, brushing along the beveled gold letters. *The Amaranthine Law.* That's an interesting title. And it looks like an antique." She hands it to Tristan, who barely stops herself from snatching it from her. Instead, she calmly takes it and leaves it sitting on her lap. "It is. A family heirloom, you could say."

"I see." Olivia clearly doesn't but only smiles. "Well, call me overprotective, but I'll be poking my head out to make sure you're not still here, once I've brushed my teeth and texted a friend."

Tristan nods. "Very well."

Olivia stands, and Tristan is suddenly bereft. The warmth of the embrace is gone, and she wishes she could pull Olivia back onto the couch again. She wants to curl up against her, feel the affection in the way Olivia's hands move along her back and up and down her arms. Instead, she watches Olivia walk to her bedroom and disappear out of sight.

Opening the pages where she's put the ribbon that marks them, Tristan plucks her fountain pen from the coffee table and writes down the gist of what Rosalee told her earlier. When she sees the information, as sketchy as it is, in writing, it emphasizes how uncertain her situation is. More so now than usual.

Tristan closes the ledger and places it on the coffee table. She plans to put it back in the safe in a moment, once she persuades her body to move. She's all set for bed, having taken care of her evening routine already, but it is as if those few steps over to the bedroom and the already turned-down bed are too many. Groaning, she lets her head fall back against the backrest again.

She has no idea how long she's dozed when gentle hands nudge her. "Tristan?"

"Hm." Tristan recognizes the voice, and she wants only to roll over and make room.

The hands shift, and something, hair, perhaps, caresses Tristan's cheek. "Let me help you. The couch is great but too short. You'll thank me in the morning."

"Or now," Tristan murmurs, feeling drunk. She tries to open her eyes, and on the third attempt, or maybe fourth, she manages to look up at the beautiful creature before her. At first, she thinks Olivia might be naked, but then she sees the tank top and sleep shorts, both of them quite skimpy, and she moans, cursing the fate that tests her this way. "You should stay away from me." She slurs her words. "To be honest." Standing on wobbly legs, Tristan pushes Olivia's hands away. "Take my word for it."

"I do—except when I don't." Olivia's voice is like honey, reverberating enough to echo deep within Tristan. "I'm just going to make sure you end up in your bed to get some decent sleep, all right?"

Oh, God. Tristan tries and manages to walk into her bedroom. Only when she's in her bed, covers up to her chin, does she realize she has forgotten the ledger on the table. By then it's too late, as a deep sleep claims her.

CHAPTER FOURTEEN

L iv is dressed and busy getting some coffee going. Black for herself, as she seriously needs it, and a strong latte for Tristan. Yawning, she stretches and glances out the window and finds that it's still quite dark. It's seven a.m., and they're going back to the Louvre to continue working.

Tristan strides into the sitting area, snatching her large book off the coffee table. "How long have you been up? Did you look at this?" she says, her voice like a whip.

"What? Your Bible? No. I'd never—"

"Are you saying you're not in the least bit curious—not tempted at all?" Glaring, Tristan walks to the closet, and Liv hears her open the safe. When Tristan returns, Liv gives her the latte in a tall mug.

"This is what I've been doing after I got ready. For us." Not pleased with the sudden third degree and how Tristan's glare is piercing her, Liv calmly sits down in an armchair and pulls out her phone.

Tristan stands motionless with her coffee mug for a moment, both hands clutching it. Then she sighs and sits down in the same spot on the couch as the night before. "Did you manage to get some sleep?" Her voice is quieter, but the edgy nerves are still present.

"Yes. Thank you." Not about to stir the dragon, Liv keeps her eyes on the phone, pretending to read the news.

"God damn it. I apologize." Tristan presses her lips together. "You didn't deserve that."

Liv puts her phone down and moves to sit next to Tristan. All the feelings from last night flood her, make her go molten inside. "What just happened? Why would you think I'd snoop around your personal belongings?"

"Because I'm not a very trusting person. Normally. And, when I remembered I didn't put my ledger away, I…I panicked." Tristan probes Liv's gaze, making Liv wonder what she's looking for. Signs that Liv is not being truthful? She hopes not.

"Whatever you wish to share with me, no matter how I'm dying to know everything about you, is worth something only if you do just that…share it. Voluntarily." Liv places a hand on Tristan's knee. "If we have no trust or little patience, then it's meaningless."

Whether her words or her touch relaxes Tristan is hard to tell, but her shoulders go down, and she drinks her latte for the first time.

Liv removes her hand reluctantly and adds some more distance between them. Reaching for her phone again, she spots a white square on the floor. Curious, she changes direction and picks it up. After she turns it over, she sees it's a photo of a woman in vintage clothing. Judging from the cut of the garments and the hairdo, Liv guesses the 1920s. She's about to hand it over to Tristan, who appears lost in thought, when she catches a closer glimpse of the face. Pulling it near again, Liv squints. It's uncanny how much the woman in the photo looks like Tristan.

"This must have fallen out of your journal. It was half under the couch," Liv says and holds out the photo to Tristan.

Tristan flinches and puts down her mug with one hand, yanking the photo out of Liv's hand. "Yes. It's mine."

"All right. And before we go through the drama from earlier, part two, yes, I did look at this one. She resembles you. She's stunning. Your grandmother, or even great-grandmother?"

Tristan holds the photo to her chest, all color drained from her face. "No. Please don't ask me. I don't want to keep lying. Just…can we postpone talking about the book and the photo until tonight? We have to leave for the Louvre in minutes." For the first time since Liv has known Tristan, her voice holds a pleading tone. This doesn't sit well with Liv. She'd never want Tristan to have to beg for anything. Ever.

"Absolutely. Remember, you don't have to tell me a single thing if you don't want to. That doesn't mean I'm not interested, because I am. Everything about you matters to me." Is she giving away too much now, to reassure Tristan? Probably. Could it come back to bite her? Oh, for sure. That's practically a given.

Tristan tucks the photo into her messenger bag and stands. When they both pause just inside the door, putting on boots and coats, Tristan stops Liv as she's about to turn the door handle. "Wait." She cups Liv's cheek and slides her thumb along her eyebrow. "Thank you. I don't deserve your understanding, but I appreciate it."

Liv understands even less than before. Why is Tristan so hell-bent on keeping her distance and assuming Liv will eventually conclude that she's a horrible person? Liv can't stop herself. She covers Tristan's hand with her own and pulls it down to her mouth. Gently, she presses her lips to Tristan's palm, at the same time inhaling more of her scent. Their eyes meet, and Tristan shakes her head sorrowfully.

"You're going to make this so much harder than it has to be, aren't you?" Tristan's voice is as soft as the words are accusing. She pulls her hand away from Liv's mouth, and, after only a fraction of a moment's hesitation, she instead cups the back of Liv's neck. So slowly, as if to give Liv ample time to object, Tristan pulls her close and kisses her.

Liv runs her hands up Tristan's arms and circles her shoulders. She returns the kiss, moving her head to find the best angle. Trembling, she can't believe how such a chaste kiss can send her into such turmoil. The world spins around her, and she moves her lips gently against Tristan's, and when Tristan reciprocates, Liv can barely breathe.

Tristan pulls back, though still holding on to her, and Liv tries to find her bearings by blinking repeatedly. "Oh."

"Yes. Oh." Perhaps Tristan is trying to be facetious, but the tremor in her voice reveals she's just as affected. "We have to go." The last four words convey some of her usual tone, but Liv needs a few more seconds to process the kiss that, no doubt, will haunt her for the rest of the day.

"Is this part of what we need to table until tonight?" Liv says and reluctantly lets go of Tristan to put on her scarf.

"I only now realized that it is." Tristan straightens Liv's bangs. "Tonight, Olivia."

As they ride the elevator down to the lobby, Liv finds herself hoping Tristan won't assign her any of the tasks that involve a scalpel. She might just accidentally create havoc with it as she thinks about "tonight."

CHAPTER FIFTEEN

The painting lies between Tristan and Olivia like some sort of neutral zone that serves to keep them from getting stuck in each other's gaze, or, Tristan thinks, as a safeguard keeping her from repeating the kiss from earlier in the day. She tries to push the memory away, but how can she? The taste of Olivia, the scent of her, and the way she made Tristan feel are all branded into her soul and swirl through her veins in a never-ending spiral.

The talk they're going to have tonight…Tristan swallows hard at the thought of it. It's not going to be what Olivia thinks, of that Tristan's certain. The hope in Olivia's eyes this morning, and the way she's given Tristan warm, not to mention heated looks whenever their eyes do meet, suggests Olivia hopes for more intimacy.

Wound so tight inside that Tristan fears her heart might rupture, she turns to her go-to emotions when she's cornered. Anger. Annoyance. Coldness. She bends over the painting, working on removing varnish from the lower left corner. Cursing under her breath, she realizes that her solution of chemicals isn't strong enough. After she snatches up the small jar, she walks over to the sink area where the bottles and cans of chemicals are stored. She pulls her notebook from her pocket and browses through the formulas that she's invented herself, realizing that the mix is correct, but the ratios are wrong.

"Can I help?" Olivia comes up to her.

"I need to remix this. Follow along in my notes, and you'll learn faster." Tristan knows she sounds abrupt and standoffish. She doesn't dare look at Olivia, or she'll crumble. Why has she allowed the situation between her and Olivia to progress this way? Only heartache can come from it—for both of them.

Olivia merely takes the notebook and helps Tristan double-check the proportions, not commenting further. As they turn to go back to the table, Tristan's cell rings. Pulling off a glove, she picks it up. It's an unknown number. After hesitating briefly, she hits reply. "Tristan."

"Sarah, it's Rosalee." Rosalee's voice is strained, and the fact that she calls her "Sarah" is worrisome.

"What's wrong?" Tristan walks back to the desk in the corner of the room, still within earshot of Olivia, but not any of the others in the workshop.

"I received another letter. It came to the office." Rosalee draws a trembling breath. "This is bad."

"What did this one say?" Tristan straightens up so fast, her lower back smarts.

"Similar to the email I showed you, only this one had printed pictures of me and you. And of your intern."

Tristan has to support herself against the desk and hits one of the jars of chemicals. She barely registers how Olivia rescues it at the last moment. Photos? Candid photos of her and Rosalee is one thing. But Olivia is here just by association and completely innocent.

"Where are you?" Tristan clenches her hand into a fist. "At the Louvre?"

"Yes. I'm going to pack up some things in the office, and then I'll go to a good friend's country estate and work from there. This is more than I can take. Why now, after all these years? We've all been so careful. Or most of us have." Rosalee gives a muted sob.

"Can anyone trace you to your friend's estate?" Tristan is used to thinking at least ten steps ahead, and now her brain is almost on overload.

"No. Nothing is even in my friend's name. It belongs to a distant relative of theirs. It probably makes me a bad friend and a calculating bitch, but it's one reason I befriended this person in the first place."

"Whatever it takes. Listen. Don't use your car leaving here. When you're done in the office, choose the least conspicuous exit. Have a taxi waiting, and then take a bus or a train. You must act fast. You know that, right?"

"I do. But what about you—and your friend?" Rosalee sounds calmer.

"We'll pack up the painting, and you'll have to sanction with your boss that we can take it with us and work on it at another location if they want my company to do it. If not, then we have to leave it for another conservator to continue the work." Tristan's heart picks up speed as well. What the hell's going on? Living with the possibility of being discovered has always been a risk, but this, Rosalee receiving letters and emails, where Tristan is mentioned by her original first name, and then the recent death of Iris...

"I won't have time to find my boss and go into a lengthy discussion. Perhaps if we get all this sorted somehow, you can return to finish the work, but...it's just a painting." Rosalee now sounds eerily calm, as if she's reached a conclusion and her course of action is set.

"Very well. This number, is it a new cell?" Tristan squeezes her cell between her shoulder and ear and pulls off her other glove. She nods at Olivia to do the same and sees that she's already begun.

"It's an unregistered mobile." Rosalee snorts mirthlessly. "Like in some damn spy movie."

"I'll start up one of mine as well. The number will end with 4434 when I call you. All right?"

"Understood." Rosalee pauses, and Tristan can hear the rustling of paper in the background. "Be safe. And take care of the girl. Collateral damage...can't happen."

Oh, God, no. "I hear you. I'll text you from my other phone once it's charged. Take care." Tristan disconnects the call. Taking a thin instrument from the counter, she opens the small compartment on her cell phone and pulls out the memory card and the SIM card. The latter she cuts in two, and the memory card goes into her wallet.

"Tristan? Are we really packing up?" Olivia is wide-eyed, and who can blame her?

"I'm sorry, but yes, we are. A new, unforeseen development has shortened our stay in Paris. We'll have to pack up here and go back to the hotel to get our things." Tristan's mouth is dry. "Can I ask you to just trust me on this, for now? I promise to explain as much as I can later."

Her brow furrowed, Olivia watches her closely but then nods.

"Okay. I don't know your friend at all, but I trust you. Just tell me what you need."

The relief that she isn't going to have to waste time convincing Olivia of anything right this minute makes Tristan stagger. She had tensed up completely during her phone call with Rosalee. She rights herself and holds up her hand when it looks like Olivia's going to try to help. "Go get some acid-free packing material. I'll make sure the woodwork people know they can still work on the frame, but then store it along with the painting."

They hurry through their tasks, and Tristan's planning like she always does. She has a go-bag, a habit since she was young. The one she has back at her condo is larger, but the small one she uses for traveling fits in the safe in the hotel room. The bag can never be left for anyone, like a curious maid, to browse through, which means keeping it the right size for safe storing. The concern now is that, of course, Olivia doesn't have anything like that. She's just with her boss on a business trip meant to last a week, perhaps ten days.

They casually wave to the other conservators and hurry through the corridor. Tristan wonders if Rosalee is still in her office, but it will take too long to check. Tristan has called an Uber, and it's waiting at a side exit. They get into the backseat, and the driver pulls into traffic.

Olivia startles Tristan by taking her hand. "Breathe," she whispers, and Tristan realizes she must have been practically holding her breath for quite some time. She exhales and gasps for air. Tipping her head back, she feels Olivia slide closer on the seat. "That's better." Olivia presses her lips to Tristan's jaw, just beneath her ear.

The kiss is reassuring rather than romantic, but Tristan still wants to forget where she is, hell, *who* she is, and kiss Olivia senseless. Drown in this girl and let all that pent-up desire free, finally. At one time she wouldn't have hesitated. She would have taken the chance to erase the thoughts that pained her and not considered the lover she was using. Not with Olivia. Never. Tristan understands in this moment that she'd rather put an end to the gauntlet she's run forever rather than allow Olivia to be—what was it Rosalee said earlier—collateral damage.

CHAPTER SIXTEEN

"Pack your things. Quickly." Tristan barks the order and then disappears into the closet. Liv remains just inside the door, blinking at the sharpness in Tristan's tone. "Now, Olivia. Please." The last word comes out softer and makes Liv move.

Liv travels light, which in this case is a double blessing. She also tends to be neat with her belongings, which makes it even easier to just push everything into her carry-on, which is all she brought. After fetching her toiletries, she puts them into their designated compartment, double-checks that she has taken everything, then goes back to the living room area and finds Tristan waiting, carrying only her messenger bag and a small black backpack.

"But...your things?" Liv knows she probably sounds stupid, but how can they be in such a hurry that Tristan leaves her clothes behind?

"No time." Tristan looks up from her cell phone, which isn't the same one as before. This one is smaller. "I've bought tickets for us on the train to London. You'll fly back to New York from there." She opens the door after tucking the phone away in her inner pocket. "Come on. Another Uber is waiting."

Liv walks into the corridor and lengthens her stride to keep up with Tristan as she rushes toward the elevator. "What do you mean, *I* will fly back? What about you?"

"I'll explain more on the train." Tristan presses the button to summon the elevator.

"No. Now." Enough is enough. Liv has agreed to crazy shit for long enough now, and she's not going anywhere until Tristan levels with her. She takes a step back, for emphasis.

"Olivia. You have to trust me."

"Why? You have me jumping through hoops without trusting me with any information. You know I care about you, and you're using that affection to get me to just trot along. No more. You have to tell me *something*." Liv leans back against the wall, folding her arms.

Tristan glowers, but then she sighs and pinches the bridge of her nose. "I apologize. I've never had to worry about another person when I've had to depart quickly."

"Depart quickly? You're joking. You 'depart quickly' if you're late for the damn movies. This is like you're trying to run from the cops."

Tristan gapes for a moment and then snorts. "You have a point." She walks over to Liv and clasps her shoulders. "All right. Someone, and don't ask me who, because I don't know, has been writing threatening emails and letters to Rosalee. This person has now sent her candid photos of you and me as well. I can't risk anything happening to you, so we're leaving. So is Rosalee." Tristan presses her lips to Liv's in a brief, hard kiss. "And I promise to tell you more when we're able to sit down without being overheard. Please, Liv. Trust me."

Not sure if it is because of the kiss, or the word *please*, or the unfathomable fact that someone out there might pose a threat, Liv complies and steps into the elevator when the door opens. Tristan joins her and seems a little less stressed.

"You destroyed your SIM card." Liv sucked her lower lip in for a moment. "Should I do the same?"

"I want you to be able to call for help if you need to. Why don't you just remove it before we get into the Uber and tuck it away?" Tristan stops Liv from walking out of the elevator and exits first. "I hate not knowing whom to look for," she mutters as she heads for the south entrance of the lobby.

Liv gives the handle of her carry-on bag to Tristan and then removes the SIM card. Placing it behind her driver's license, she puts her wallet and the phone back into her small cross-body bag.

The Uber is there, this time a large SUV, and the driver looks baffled that they have hardly any luggage. "But your luggage, *mesdames?*" he says, looking behind them as if they've hidden it from him.

"No luggage. Gare du Nord, please. We're pressed for time," Tristan says.

The driver merely nods and pushes open the sliding back door for them. Tristan hoists Liv's bag in after her and climbs inside. "There."

As the Uber driver zigzags through the busy Paris lunch-hour traffic, Tristan takes Liv's hand, squeezing it. "You're being more than patient, all things considered. I'll do my best to explain later, but it'll be difficult for you to understand."

"Difficult?" Liv knows Tristan doesn't think she's slow on the uptake, which suggests she means "difficult," as in hard to grasp. "No matter what, I'm not sure sending me back to New York and you staying behind alone to deal with things alone is the best choice."

Tristan sits in silence for a while, still holding on to Liv, and then the softest smile grazes her lips. "You say that now, and I know you mean it. Only yesterday, and even this morning, everything was still manageable. Now, it's not." She raises their joined hands and kisses the back of Liv's hand. "The truth is, I would never forgive myself if something happened to you because of me."

Liv doesn't care if the Uber driver can see them in his back mirror. She pulls her hand free and grabs hold of the lapel of Tristan's coat, tugging her close. She hears Tristan gasp as she hugs her tight.

"Liv!" Tristan clings to her, and though it's only for a few moments, she pulls at Liv with such fervor, it's as if she's trying to merge them.

"No matter what, I'm here now." Liv tips Tristan's head back and kisses her, and there's nothing remotely chaste about this kiss. Their tongues meet, caressing and tasting, and Liv whimpers...or it might be Tristan.

After they end the kiss, they sit back, not even looking at each other, but still holding hands.

CHAPTER SEVENTEEN

Tristan's shoulders are so rigid, she's afraid her trapezius muscles might just rupture. She and Olivia sit in a part of the train to London where they're alone, and it has just started to pick up speed. The closest passengers are well out of earshot. This is why she's so tense. Olivia expects to be informed about what's going on, and as they're virtually alone, Tristan is running out of excuses.

To Tristan's surprise, Olivia doesn't jump at the first opportunity. She merely gets comfortable and settles into her seat after stowing her carry-on bag on the overhead shelf. Their trip will take about four hours, which means they will reach London around five p.m.

The silence draws out between them, and Tristan caves first. She's not sure if this has been Olivia's plan all along, although she doubts Olivia is that calculating.

"You have questions," Tristan says, finally.

"I do." Olivia shifts, almost sitting with her back to the outer wall. "This situation seems to have very little to do with me, but I'm clearly involved somehow, judging from the photo you talked about."

"I've already told you I've known Rosalee since we were children." Tristan lowers her voice further. "We had a friend the same age, maybe a year or two older, called Iris. She died not long ago. Rosalee suspects that someone else among the ones we knew back then might be out to cause us harm. In what way, I don't know, but if this is the case, they're trying to intimidate Rosalee, and clearly, someone has followed you and me in Paris." Tristan was hoping it was only in Paris. The idea of someone stalking her, or them, in New York, her home, turns her stomach.

"And this person, were they an adult when you and Rosalee were kids?"

"No. They will have had to be a child too. One of the girls we knew. At least it must have started with that." Having her thoughts still on the horror of having to deal with this situation even in New York makes Tristan speak before she edits her words.

"A child who still holds a grudge?" Olivia frowns. "That doesn't sound plausible."

A lot about this doesn't sound plausible at all. Tristan pushes her fingers through her hair. "I know." She isn't sure what to say and definitely not *how* to say it. "Some events in my past defy logic, Olivia. I never share any of this because the only time I did…let's just say, it didn't end well. I know I can't ask you for such a leap of faith, and it's seriously ironic that not being able to tell you requires just that from you, another leap of faith."

"Okay." But it's not okay for Olivia, Tristan can tell. She's still frowning and holds her arms tight to herself, her fingers laced hard. "So, what can you tell me? I mean, you did say you were going to explain."

Tristan's mind whirls. "This phone is a burner phone. You've realized that. I've also destroyed my old passport and am traveling under another name. If someone refers to me as Tristan Kane, just go with it."

Olivia blinks but doesn't speak. Oddly, her clasped fingers have relaxed some.

"This is because I've had to disappear before, change identities, and so on. I always travel with three passports and three burner phones. It's necessary. I must be prepared at any given moment. Not exactly ideal, but after all these years, I'm used to it."

"How long have you had to do this? Disappear?" Olivia places a hand on Tristan's knee. The touch is warm, and Tristan relaxes against the backrest. Her shoulders still hurt, but she can breathe better.

"For most of my adulthood, you could say. A long time."

"Which means you've had to give up friends and family several times." Olivia's eyes well up. "That must be so horrible."

"Yes. Several times." Tristan fights back a burst of humorless laughter that wants to erupt. "Several times" is an understatement. "That's why I normally don't allow myself to go beyond casual friendship these days. Though I admit, my company and my employees are all more than that."

Slipping her arm behind Tristan's shoulders, Olivia tugs her closer. "And casual friendship, is that what we share?" Her voice trembles, but she's not taking her eyes off Tristan.

Tristan leans in, fast and hungry now, and kisses Olivia. She runs her tongue along those plump lips, wanting in but still controlling herself enough to ask. "Olivia?" she whispers against her mouth.

Olivia parts her lips and pushes the fingers of her free hand into Tristan's hair, holding her in place. She takes over the initiative, and Tristan finds herself completely devoured. She surrenders, what else can she do, and for these precious moments, she allows the pretend world of "anything is possible" to exist in her mind. She wants to sit like this with Olivia—kissing, caressing—and not think about anything else. Not work. Not the faceless individual who stalks them, and not the fact that even if this were the case, she cannot be with Olivia, or anyone else.

They slow the kisses, passion turns to tenderness, and with that change, reality sets in. "Darling," Tristan says, only realizing after the fact how she began the sentence, "this is unwise. You're irresistible, but I can't allow you to—"

"As your explanations are so damn cryptic, and being on a train isn't ideal, I insist you try to clarify what you've told me." Olivia smiles softly. "If you think I'm going to let you fend for yourself, even if you have throughout your life so far, you're mistaken. You don't know this, but I used to compete in tae kwon do. I still keep it up on my own at the dojo. Or I did, until I started my new job with you. I can be useful."

Tristan is at a complete loss for words. Martial arts? She is surprised, but giving it more thought, she shouldn't be. It does rhyme well with the Olivia she's glimpsed now and then—the one who isn't intimidated by Tristan, or anyone, she wagers, and who obviously is stubborn as hell. "You don't understand." It isn't just about being able to physically defend themselves. There's so much more.

"Then you have to make me understand. Because until you do, I'm not going anywhere." Olivia's assertiveness appears to grow exponentially, along with her determination.

"But I can't explain things. You have to take my word for that." Tristan is angry and frustrated now, but mostly because being here with Olivia has sparked the terrible, heart-crushing sensation of hope in her heart. Can she explain in a way that won't turn Olivia's look of affection and warmth into one of scorn or loathing? She doubts it. She's played out that scenario and doesn't care to repeat it—especially not with Olivia.

"Do you trust me, Tristan? I mean, do you have faith in my willingness to keep an open mind?" Olivia gives her a quick kiss.

Tristan's breath catches. "I believe in your good intentions. This goes beyond that."

"It doesn't matter. You have carried this burden alone for far too long, whatever it is. This can be the turning point. Please, Tristan. Let's go somewhere safe and really talk this time."

There is honey in those soft, cognac eyes. Has Olivia ever looked at another woman this way? It's not a nice thought, but she hopes not. As much as she's tried to convince Olivia to stay away, Tristan yearns to be the only one on the receiving end of Olivia's molten gaze. "You will end up regretting this," Tristan whispers, "and I will too. I planned for the possibility that you might be this stubborn. I was going to slip away in the London crowd and leave you behind with the ticket to New York."

"I guessed that." Olivia's lips tremble. "I tried to think of plans to stop that possibility. Cuffing myself to your wrist came to mind."

Tristan smiles against her will. "We'll go and continue the talk. I happen to have a small condo in London that's in another name." She clears her throat. "Promise me that when you decide to leave, and sooner or later you will reach that conclusion, you'll go to Heathrow and board a flight."

Olivia shakes her head. "I'll go so far as to say '*if* I decide to leave,' I'll promise to do what you ask. *If.*"

Tristan pulls Olivia closer, and they settle into more comfortable positions. Fully relaxed now, as Olivia has promised, Tristan knows there is no *if*—only *when*.

CHAPTER EIGHTEEN

Liv looks around the impressive Victorian railway station, St Pancras, as she and Tristan make their way toward one of the exits. Tristan's expression goes from soft and, well, loving, to stony as soon as the Eurostar train pulls into the station. She slips on her messenger bag and the small backpack and merely stands there waiting for the train to stop and the doors to open, like a statue, not even holding on.

"Are we getting another Uber?" Liv easily follows Tristan's stride, but it's tricky to maneuver the carry-on bag among the throngs of people rushing to and from platforms.

"No. A London taxi will do." Tristan pulls up her phone and taps at the screen. She doesn't slow down, and the people in Tristan's way move aside as if she's royalty. Perhaps they sense her determination and are not prepared to play chicken with this woman. Probably smart.

The long row of taxis makes it easy to find a ride, and they climb into one of them. Tristan gives the address, and soon they're in rush-hour London traffic. Liv, who is used to New York's version of this congestion, is jarred by the fact that the taxi is driving on the "wrong" side. When they reach a large roundabout, she gasps when the driver takes a left, even if she realizes that's how it works here.

Tristan chuckles. "First time in London, I assume?"

"Uh-huh. And this driving on the left feels weird. Yikes." Liv slides closer to Tristan. "Have you been here often?"

"Many times. I lived here once. I was born here." Tristan bites her lips and looks away from Liv. "It was a different city then. A lot different."

"You're from here? Huh." Liv thinks back to the bio of Tristan she read in *Apollo* magazine before she applied for the internship. "I read that you're from Philadelphia."

"I know. That's the official story. I was born in London, and my family and I emigrated to the US when I was eight years old."

Why is that a secret? Liv knows the back of a taxi is not the place to ask these questions but makes a mental note to inquire when they're settled in Tristan's condo. Which is another secret.

The taxi pulls over, and Tristan pays the driver. Stepping out, Liv looks up at the office building, confused. "Here?" she asks, turning to Tristan.

"No. Two blocks from here." Tristan looks around and then starts walking. Liv grabs the handle of her bag and catches up with her. The streets in this area aren't as busy as the part of London they've just driven through—a few people on the sidewalks and no gridlock at the intersections.

Then Tristan turns and abruptly walks over to a window displaying women's clothing. She seems to be perusing skirts, which is odd, since Liv hasn't seen her wear anything but slacks, jeans, or chinos. Now her gaze darts all over the display in the window.

"Tristan?" Liv murmurs. "What's going on?"

"Shh. Give me a moment." Tristan focused on the items in the window, but not on one in particular. Instead, she shifts her angle and squints, as if she's trying to read the price tags. "Listen to me," she says, her voice low and stark. "There's a man thirty feet behind us on the other side of the street. I recognize him from the station. Now he's stopped when we stopped, pretending to tie his shoe. Can you believe it? We're going to have to lose him."

Lose him? All this secret-agent vocabulary makes everything surreal. "You sure?" Liv tries to find the man in the window's reflection, only now realizing what Tristan is doing.

"Quite sure. We can't lead him to my condo. Around the corner, a block from here, is a small square, or used to be. I believe it's a parking lot now. We need to get there, as it's another good place to hail a taxi. We have to run, which means ditching your bag. Do you have anything you can't live without in it?"

Liv trembles now. Tristan sounds so collected and matter-of-fact that Liv doesn't even consider questioning what's going on. "Clothes and toiletries. Nothing I can't buy again. I have everything important in my bag." She pats her cross-body bag.

"Good. Follow me." Tristan hooks her arm under Liv's, startling her, and starts walking down the street. When they reach the next building, she nods to the right. "There's a place you can get rid of the bag. The cars block us from view here."

Liv nods and slips the carry-on up a few steps and out of sight into a doorway. Once she's done that, Tristan lets go and starts running. Liv wants to look behind them but knows she has to keep up with Tristan. She can't lose sight of her.

They sprint past several shops, and then Tristan makes a sudden right turn, and Liv follows. They're in a narrow alley between two buildings, and to Liv, it seems the walls are closing in. Old cobblestones make it hard to run without slipping or twisting an ankle, but Tristan doesn't slow down. Liv's ankle boots aren't ideal for running either.

The alley leads to a courtyard. Has Tristan made a mistake? Are they trapped in here? Liv is filled with questions but is too winded to speak. It's not because she's not in shape. She runs in Central Park twice a week, and training at the dojo as often as possible keeps her strong, but this reaction is more a question of nerves.

"Don't slow down." Tristan dashes along the wall, and after they've crossed the courtyard, she turns right again, and they're in another alley. Before they turn, Liv risks a glance across the courtyard and sees not just one man, but two, rush in.

"Two of them!" Liv gasps as she and Tristan sprint down the new alley.

"Fuck!" Tristan lengthens her stride. "We have to get to the square, and there better be a taxi."

Liv's legs are burning, mainly from struggling to keep her feet level on the cobblestones. The alley seems longer and narrower with each step, but eventually, they burst out on to the next sidewalk. Twenty yards to their left is what could be described as a square, albeit it is filled with vehicles. Along the far side, a row of taxis is waiting for passengers.

Tristan waves, and a taxi begins moving toward them. They meet it halfway. Tristan stops as it pulls up next to them and yanks the door open. Liv throws herself into it, and Tristan slams the door behind them. "Drive. Just drive. I'll give you a hundred percent tip if you get us to this address in less than five minutes." She rattles off a completely different address than before.

"Will do," the driver, a young girl, says and floors it.

Liv holds on to the handle next to the seat as the woman turns a corner, and she pictures the wheels on the left side of the car losing touch with the ground. Tristan is half-turned on the seat, peering out the back window.

"You ladies being followed or something?" the driver asks as she tosses the taxi to the left in another intersection.

"My husband hired someone to spy on me," Tristan says easily. "I'm grateful if you can keep well ahead of whoever among your colleagues they're about to use."

"Ah, those tossers in line after me? No problemo." The girl circles another building, throwing Tristan into Liv, who catches her just in time to keep her from slamming her head into a window.

"You have to hold on," the girl in the front yells. "We're almost there."

"Pull up to number four." Tristan pulls a credit card through the machine on the acrylic glass between them and the driver.

"Here we are then." The stunt-driver-wannabe slams the brakes and moves into an impossibly small spot between two cars. "Nobody's behind us yet, so hurry inside." She grins at them through the rearview mirror.

Tristan exits and moves to the heavy wooden door in the industrial-looking building. Liv manages to remember to thank the driver when she steps out of the taxi.

"Be safe. I'm off now so they don't spot me. They'll think I'm still driving you, maybe." The girl races off so fast, the tires squeal.

Tristan is holding open the door. After entering the building, Liv leans against the wall as the door closes behind them with a loud thud. Through the dark windows, she sees another taxi rush down the street, passing them without hesitation.

"Damn…" Liv whispers, and then she's in Tristan's arms.

"I'm so sorry, darling." Tristan kisses Liv's neck. "Let's go up."

"Yeah. I hope you have something stronger than Earl Grey, because I need a drink."

Tristan chuckles against Liv's skin. "I do. I have everything we need, for now."

They enter the elevator, and its size suggests this used to be an industrial building back in the day. Tristan presses the button for the fourth floor, and they ascend to a place where they will finally feel safe.

For now.

CHAPTER NINETEEN

Tristan's small condo is as she left it when she had business in London a year ago. A firm maintains it and always keeps it stocked with food in the freezer and pantry, stuff that lasts a long time and is rotated out as soon as it expires.

"A drink, you said. You'll find a fully stocked bar in the living room. Help yourself." Tristan reluctantly lets go of Olivia and turns to the alarm console on the wall just inside the door. She switches it back on. When she turns around, Olivia is still there, standing motionless in the small hallway. "Are you all right?" Tristan closes her hands around Olivia's upper arms.

"I'm fine. Just trying to wrap my brain around what the hell you've gotten yourself into that makes people literally chase you through the streets." The words seem accusatory, but Olivia's voice is soft, almost pensive.

"It's not something I did. It's what happened to me, and who I am," Tristan says starkly. "I don't know about you, but I need something to eat and, yes, a drink. Something strong."

"I'll make you something. I tended bar during my college years. That, together with training kids in the art of tae kwon do, kept my loans to a minimum. I was pretty good at both those jobs." Olivia pulls off her coat and hangs it next to Tristan's. "Any request?"

"A Bloody Mary, please. You should find tomato juice in the pantry. Spices too."

"On it."

Tristan washes her hands under the kitchen faucet and then explores the freezer. She's quite used to frozen dinners, and as Olivia opens the pantry door behind her, she pulls out a few different boxes. "Anything in particular you like?" She motions to the counter.

"Anything with chicken. Nothing with potatoes." Olivia disappears toward the living room, carrying the items she's found in the pantry.

Tristan places one box after the other in the micro and then plates the contents on real china. They may be on the run, or in hiding, but they're not going to eat directly on cardboard. Tristan sets a tray and enters the living room, which contains a small, round table with three chairs. She's just finished emptying the tray when Olivia brings their drinks.

"Bloody Mary for you and a gin and tonic for me." Olivia sits down and takes a proper gulp of her drink. She coughs and clears her throat. "Now we're talking."

Tristan takes a sip and winces at how strong it is. "This...oh, dear...the lining in my stomach might never recover." Despite this statement, she drinks some more.

They eat in silence, both hungry, and Tristan is grateful for the reprieve. After they finish, they move to the couch, and now it's entirely natural for Olivia to curl up next to Tristan with her hand on her thigh. Tristan feels the warmth of the touch permeate her skin through the fabric of her black denim pants.

"You ready to tell me some more?" Olivia places her drink on a coaster on the small glass-and-metal coffee table.

"Yes." Not really, but Tristan reaches for her go-bag. She opens the zipper to the largest compartment and pulls out her ledger and her wallet. Her heart has begun to drum faster against her ribs, which lends a foreboding sensation. "Open mind, remember?"

"Absolutely." Olivia hasn't moved and looks at Tristan rather than the large book.

"May I ask a favor?" Tristan feels ridiculous, and Olivia probably thinks she's stalling. Perhaps she is. No. No, she isn't.

"Sure."

"Kiss me?" Tristan leans in, stopping just one breath short of Olivia's lips.

Olivia doesn't answer but wraps her arms around Tristan and pulls her close. She begins with small kisses just below Tristan's left ear. Then she creates a trail that burns gently as she kisses along Tristan's jaw, over to her chin. There, she slowly nibbles her way up to Tristan's lips, and after a few, ghastly long seconds, she claims Tristan's mouth with hers. "Part your lips, Tristan," she murmurs. "Let me in."

Olivia must know that she doesn't have to ask, yet Tristan understands why she does. The request is hot and sexy, it makes Tristan want to give in fully, and Tristan complies eagerly. The kiss lingers, the intensity going from fiery to tender and back again. Finally, Olivia pulls back, but the emotional heat just conveyed by her lips now lives in her eyes.

Tristan draws a trembling breath, drinks from her Bloody Mary, and then pulls the ledger onto her lap. "I think it might be less confusing, if that's at all possible, if you read through this with me."

Olivia shifts until they're sitting hip to hip. "Okay."

Tristan opens the large book, and the first page shows an ink drawing of a small cabin among tall pine trees. Tristan runs her finger over the door to the cabin. "I drew this when I went home to attend my father's funeral. All the shadows you see in the windows are the mourners. My mother and sister are in there."

"But not you?" Liv leans closer, as she can hear Tristan's forlorn tone.

"Only for a little while. I left the next day." Tristan turns the page. "Here are the names I've used over the years." She points to the list of names, each followed by a set of numbers.

"Sarah, Mary, Elizabeth, Anna, Virginia, Tyra, Paula…Tristan…" Liv reads just as many different surnames in another column, which ends with Kelly. "What are those numbers?" she asks.

"We'll return to that. Now let me show you Rosalee's page." Tristan flips a few pages, and there it is. Rosalee Carmichael. In her case there are seven names, and the latest one is Vanessa Mercier. Tristan turns over one page, and there is the name Iris Schmidt. Another set of seven names, the last one being Anneliese Manz.

Liv tries to fathom what this information means, what the names and the numbers suggest, but she draws a blank. She glances at Tristan, who is so pale now, her skin looks transparent. Liv takes her hand, which is ice cold. "Tristan? Why have the three of you changed names so often? This isn't making sense."

"Three? Oh, right. Actually, there were nine of us, initially. All girls." Tristan takes a deep breath and squeezes Liv's hand so hard that it hurts. "You asked about the numbers. Well, after I show you how to interpret them, they'll make a weird sort of sense."

Liv waits, but it is as if Tristan's eyes have become stuck on Iris's list of names. "Please."

Tristan flips back to the page with her names. "Here." She points to the first set of digits. "This is how long I waited until I changed names the first time. When Sarah became Mary."

Liv leans in farther to read. "That number? Fifty-two? What? Weeks? Months?" Liv tries to calculate in her head, thinking out loud. "You're forty-six according to Wikipedia…" Liv feels a blush creep up her cheeks. Surely Tristan must have realized she would have googled a potential employer, but it was still an awkward statement.

"No, Olivia." Tristan raises her chin. "I was born in London on June 11, 1761."

CHAPTER TWENTY

Tristan watches Olivia's expressions shift like water. Stunned surprise. Disbelief. Shock. Confusion. Concern. But what she doesn't see is more important. No scorn, mirth, or mocking. And even more important, Olivia stays by her side. Though her eyes are grapefruit-size at Tristan's words, they radiate the same warmth as before.

"1761." Olivia's voice is without inflection.

"Yes." Tristan's not about to get into the "I know it sounds crazy and unbelievable, but I swear I'm not insane..." litany. If Olivia is about to take a leap of faith, she will have to do it without Tristan begging her. It's the only way, and Tristan knows the chances are infinitesimal for this to happen.

"Are you saying that this list of names, they're not just some witness-protection-program, having-tons-of-passports thing? You've been living the lives of all these people?" Still not raising her voice, Olivia looks down at the ledger and back up again. "Tristan?"

"In a nutshell, yes." Tristan is cold now. She's shivering and just wants to close the ledger and be done with it. The risk of Olivia walking out the door and leaving her obviously delusional boss in the dust is great. Why not get it over with?

"Tell me more. Just...tell me more." Olivia strokes an unsteady hand across her forehead, messing up her bangs. Tristan absentmindedly lifts her hand and combs them down with her cold fingers.

"You're freezing." Olivia reaches behind her and tugs at a blanket. "Here." She wraps it around them both, effectively creating a cocoon of them and the ledger.

Grateful, Tristan tugs at it and closes her eyes for a moment.

When she opens them, she has steeled herself against the onslaught of fear. "My family—my mother, father, sister, and I—were among a large group of people who left Liverpool for Plymouth in 1769. It was a horrible journey, during which old people and children died in the middle of the Atlantic. I, to this day, don't know what illness spread among the most fragile on the ship, but the adults called it a plague. In retrospect, I think they named it that because of how fast it burned through both crew and passengers, and how quickly some people died." Tristan reaches for her drink, making sure she takes enough to burn her throat. She needs the sting to focus as her own words take her back in time. "Our small corner below deck was right next to that of the Carmichaels, Rosalee's family. She was the first to get sick among them, and she turned into a shell of herself, wraith-like. I begged to go sit with her, but Mother didn't allow it. It didn't matter. I got ill as well. My sister, Corinne, was sixteen, almost an adult. She and my parents didn't catch the disease."

Pausing, Tristan quickly wipes at her damp eyelashes, feeling as if her pent-up emotions are right there, ready to burst through her skin and make her bleed. Olivia hasn't said a word, but she also hasn't cringed, winced, or made any sort of disdainful face at Tristan's words. Now, she slips her arm around Tristan's back, holding her. How incredibly strange this is. How unexpected.

"Among all the children that became ill, nine came through it, and they were all little girls, ten and younger. The affected boys, older children, and some adults were not so lucky." Tristan snorts unhappily. "Lucky. Well, I suppose that's one word for it." She tips her head back against the couch. "By the way, what's with us and couches, Olivia? We seem to have a propensity for advancing our, eh, relationship on couches."

"Where else should we sit? The floor?" Olivia gives a tremulous smile.

"You have a point." Grateful for the reprieve, Tristan turns her face into Olivia's neck, amazed that she hasn't rejected her yet. *Yet.* She shudders.

"Just take your time. I can tell how hard this is for you." Olivia kisses the top of Tristan's head. "When you're ready, I'm listening."

Which, of course, isn't the same as believing, but that would be too much to expect of anyone.

❖

Liv watches how Tristan straightens and turns a few pages in the ledger before she continues her incredible tale.

"We arrived in Plymouth, and my parents were relieved and excited to have reached our first destination. So was Corinne, but I was distraught over leaving Rosalee and the other little friends I'd made. It was as if we shared a bond after having lived through that plague. Little did we know what it'd mean for us.

"The upcoming years were hard. My father had a little capital he'd saved for the purpose of starting over in this new land. We settled on the outskirts of a village in Maine. After a few years, others we knew from the ship joined us, including the Carmichaels. Mrs. Carmichael had passed by then, and Rosalee's father was alone with the children. My mother helped take care of them, as they lived close to us."

The details of Tristan's story are minute, and the emotions in her voice, restrained and yet so raw, grate on Liv's nerves. She hardly dares breathe to not miss a word.

"To make this story short, the years went by, and our lives unfolded the way lives back then often did. My sister got married at eighteen. So did I, ten years later. We worked hard. Five years into my marriage I noticed how Rosalee, who was also married by then, and I seemed to live parallel lives. No children. If we were injured, we healed fast and never succumbed to infections. We were never sick. When the smallpox epidemic hit, we nursed one sick family member after another, and we were fine. We also looked a lot younger than our peers. Our husbands were frustrated with us for not having children, preferably sons, and Rosalee's husband abused her daily. Having a body that absorbs your bruises in less than a day was a blessing and a curse. Eventually, she ran away from him. I was forty years old, already a widow, and looked eighteen. Words like 'witchcraft' began to circle, and that's when my mother urged me to follow in Rosalee's footsteps and leave our settlement in Maine. She and my father had saved enough for me to start over. So, I did, a first of many start-overs. I almost tried marriage one more time, but never again after that."

Liv looks down at the ledger, where someone, in small, ornate handwriting, has entered dates, names, locations. She turns the page. More dates and notes. Her gaze falls upon a longer entry.

New York, December 22nd, 1809—I miss my family the most at Christmas. I envision my mother and Corinne, in their respective homes, preparing the food and helping at church. Mother provides for the less fortunate whenever she can. I try to follow her example, and God knows the need here in New York is great. Owning a restaurant makes saving scraps of food easy enough, and it can mean the difference between life and death for a child trying to survive on the street.

Liv's eyes fill with tears. She uses the blanket to dab them away and turns more pages. Originally Sarah wrote these entries, but the new names show up as the years pass. Liv notices a pattern of about thirty or forty years between the changes.

Trying to think critically, Liv regards the pages from an art restorer's point of view. The pages are fragile, and the large book is clearly old. Leather bound, it shows cracks where the leather has gone dry or become damaged. The ink changes throughout the pages, and so does the handwriting, to a degree. The word choice changes as well, going from very formal to more casual. If Tristan has forged this document, she's done it in an ingenious way. Of course, as an expert art restorer, she would have the knowledge. But why? What motive could a person possibly have to create such a ruse—then keep it a closely guarded secret? That part simply doesn't make sense.

"I can practically see your thoughts spinning," Tristan says quietly. She looks drained as she clutches her half-finished Bloody Mary. "You can probably guess why I never share this with anyone...at least not anymore. It's an unfathomable recollection of my past."

It was. But Liv homes in on the "at least not anymore" part. "Who did you tell?"

Tristan flinches and returns the glass to the coffee table. "The man who was supposed to be my second husband. He adored me and was ahead of his time when it came to his outlook on life. Just not *that* ahead. I told him my true age—I was seventy-eight—and about being barren, and he laughed it off. Called me his eccentric angel, of all things. I refused to marry him until enough time had passed, to prove I wasn't lying. As time went by and he aged, and I did not, he was not amused. When people started to point out our age difference, he ended up doing what my parents had done—paid me off to go away." The pain is evident in Tristan's voice. "I left with my ledger," she says and strokes the pages of the large book, "and enough money to take me to Philadelphia."

It is of course an impossible tale. And yet…Liv groans and grips Tristan's hands between hers. Tristan's are still ice cold. "Are you saying you're immortal?"

"The title of my ledger would suggest that, wouldn't it?" Tristan's smile is more of a grimace. "Amaranthine. It means, among other things, undying, a flower that never fades, and a red, burgundy color." She shakes her head. "The Amaranthine Law is something I, Rosalee, Iris, and a few of the other six girls set up in 1855. We all agreed to a set of rules to keep each other safe."

"So…not immortal?" Liv persists, needing to hear Tristan say it, no matter how unfathomable such a statement would be.

"No. I have aged. I no longer look to be in my early twenties, do I? I look the age I try to be. I can pass for anything between forty to sixty. That's the best span for me right now, that and modern times allowing for nips and tucks that make seventy-year-olds look decades younger."

"What does the Amaranthine Law state?" Liv watches Tristan pale.

"We have broken several of the statutes, anyway, starting by my meeting with Rosalee. We've become exposed. People have died. The Amaranthine Law that was supposed to protect us is crumbling at our feet." Tristan yanks her hands free and stands up, rigid arms and fists at her side. Her blue eyes are nearly colorless, and they scorch Liv like white flames. "I think this is the endgame and—oh, God, Olivia—you're caught in the middle of it all."

CHAPTER TWENTY-ONE

Tristan is pacing. She's told Olivia, well, not everything, but more than she's told anyone in almost two centuries. She can't imagine what's going through Olivia's mind. Perhaps anything from "let me get away from this insane woman right this second" to "let's call an ambulance," or better yet, "let's call the police."

"What are you thinking?" Tristan swivels, placing her hands on her hips, as she has no idea what else to do with them. "Don't just sit there. Say something."

"Hey. Give a girl a break." Olivia frowns and stands up. "You just dropped a mother lode of, let's just say, unusual information on me, and I need a moment to process. Or a drink. Preferably both." Olivia takes her gin and tonic and empties it in two gulps. Coughing, she walks over to Tristan and grasps her shoulders firmly. "You have to stop pacing. You're driving me nuts. I can't think."

"Okay. Let's sit down."

"No." Running her hands up and down Tristan's upper arms, Olivia seems to look straight through her. "I...I can't sit down either. Perhaps pacing is a good idea." She doesn't move, though, but pulls Tristan close. "If this is confusing as all hell to me, how strange must it feel to you, to be forced to share something like this? I'm so sorry I did that. That I nagged you."

"You deserve to know." Tristan can barely enunciate the words, as raw emotions overwhelm her. How can this woman think of her, a virtual freak of nature, more than herself? "You are involved, and my main priority now is to get you back to New York, or anywhere in the States, safely."

"Now, this is where we'll have words." Olivia pushes her fingers into Tristan's hair and gently tugs her head back a little. "We are going to see this through—together. You've told me as much as you can for now, I'm sure, but I think there's tons more. I mean, why, for instance, is someone after you and Rosalee? And why now? I realize I'm just involved by happenstance, but who says that whoever is after you won't think I know too much and keep chasing me once you've managed to ditch me in New York?"

Tristan grows cold. She has assumed that if she can get Olivia away from her, distance herself, then Olivia will be fine, and Tristan can deal with what's going on or disappear—again. "Goddamn it." She groans. "You're right. Of course you are."

"On occasion, yes." Olivia smiles sorrowfully. "But look at it this way. Two minds instead of one. We're smart people, both of us. We'll figure it out. And remember, I wasn't kidding about the tae kwon do. I'm good to have in a fight."

Tristan believes Olivia but still shakes her head. "No way can we ever let them get that close. Trust me." She feels maneuvered by the faceless person or persons behind the chase through the London streets. This response makes her angry, but the fact that she's wrapped up in Olivia's embrace makes it impossible to start pacing again. Yet for some reason, pushing Olivia away is equally impossible. They're standing so close together, chest to chest, and Tristan buries her face in Olivia's hair.

"We need to rest. Once we've done that, we have to plan." Olivia seems oddly comfortable with taking the initiative.

Tristan holds her breath for a moment before she asks the question that burns beneath her skin. "Do you believe me at all?"

Olivia shifts her hands and cups Tristan's cheeks. "I have two choices. Either I believe you, or I believe that *you* believe this to be true. Then there's the fact that we were indeed chased. Also, your childhood friend—no matter when she was your childhood friend, exactly, is really beside the point—she's being stalked as well. That part, the stalking, is what's important now."

"In a way you're right, but looking at it from another perspective, you're only half right." Tristan takes Olivia by the hand and returns to the couch. "Let me show you something a few pages into my ledger."

"Tristan…you're exhausted." Olivia tries to resist. Is she mindful of them being tired, or has she had enough of the ledger?

"I am." Tristan rubs her neck after they sit down. "But it won't take long, all right? Just humor me for a few more minutes."

"Okay."

Tristan takes her bag and pulls out the photo that fell out… goodness, was it yesterday? She places it next to the ledger and opens the large book on a page farther into it. She pushes it closer to Olivia. "Here's a picture of me from 1851. It's faded, of course, but it's the original." She looks down at the familiar photo of herself at the photographer's studio in Boston. "It was my ninetieth birthday. I told everyone it was my twenty-fifth, and they still thought of me as a hopeless spinster. Most of the women my age that I knew were married."

Olivia bends over the ledger, squinting at the photo. "God."

"Pretty sure God has nothing to do with any aspect of my life. Our neighbors in Maine were all certain that Rosalee's and my eternal youth was the work of the devil." Tristan turns a page. "This is from the boardinghouse I owned in Baltimore. My staff and I. 1869. I left the boardinghouse to the staff when I 'died.' They were kind to me."

"Oh." Olivia sniffles. "Is there more?"

"There is." Tristan shoots Olivia a worried glance and sees how she wipes at silent tears. Another page shows Tristan sitting between two other women. "1883. I let myself inherit enough money under a new name, Virginia Knox, that I could move to London. Here I started a fashion house that became quite popular. I let the other two women be the face of the business."

"Did…did they inherit the business as well? Later?"

"Yes. Or in one case, her daughter did." Tristan closes the ledger. "So, either you think I'm a completely delusional woman who carries around a make-believe ledger of old photos to fool herself…or you are willing to give me the benefit of the doubt?" Her head pounds, and she rubs her temples.

"I was already giving you the benefit of the doubt." Olivia stands abruptly and extends her hand. "And we're not going to talk about this anymore tonight. I can tell you're fading, and to be honest, so am I. I want a hot shower and to go to bed."

Tristan slowly takes the proffered hand. "This is a one-bedroom apartment with a king-size bed. Are you willing to share my bed, Olivia?"

"Yes." Olivia colors faintly but pulls Tristan to her feet.

Tristan makes the bed while Olivia showers. Taking sleepwear with her, she then checks the door and the alarm system. When she finds the bathroom empty, she steps in under the hot spray of water, letting it hammer her aching shoulders. Her ankles hurt as well. Running on cobblestone streets is insane. After drying her hair, she finds Olivia sitting on the foot of the bed, dressed in a T-shirt and panties.

"I assumed it was all right to borrow some clothes." Olivia tugs at the T-shirt. "This was the largest one I could find."

"Of course." Tristan is wearing a long sleep shirt. "Let's go to bed."

They crawl in, and Tristan turns off the light. A faint night-light in the hallway keeps it from going pitch-black.

"Are you afraid, Tristan?" Olivia asks in a whisper.

"Only for your sake." Tristan turns onto her side, facing Olivia. "Are you?"

"Yes, but not because of anyone catching up with us. Not yet anyway."

Tristan places a hand on Olivia's shoulder. "Then why?" She doesn't understand.

"I'm afraid of waking up and finding you gone. That you'll decide that you need to protect me by disappearing after all. That I'll…lose you."

Tristan stops breathing for a moment. "I can promise you that I won't leave you voluntarily. I will certainly not sneak out in the night in some misguided attempt to keep you safe. You're right about what you said—we need to figure this out together."

"Okay. Good. But what then? Once we have figured things out?"

A cold fist squeezes Tristan's heart until it can't refill with blood. Ironically, not even this sensation will come close to ending her life. Olivia still doesn't know, or doesn't understand so much, and one of those things is—they have no future. A woman like Tristan can never have one.

CHAPTER TWENTY-TWO

L iv sits up in bed, disoriented in the unfamiliar room. She pushes long tresses of hair off her neck, feeling nearly suffocated. She must have tossed and turned. A soft whimper startles her, and she glances to her right. Tristan is curled up on her side, facing away from Liv. Leaning in, Liv places a gentle hand on Tristan's shoulder. Tristan's trembling so much now, Liv can hear her teeth clatter.

"Tristan. Please. You're dreaming." Liv rocks her carefully. "Just a dream, okay?"

Tristan goes rigid, and it is as if she has tied her body into a knot. Fearful now, Liv moves closer and aligns herself with Tristan's, hoping that some shared warmth will permeate the woman next to her. Effectively spooning Tristan and tucking the covers tightly around them, Liv pulls her knees in behind hers and worms her left arm under Tristan's neck, wrapping her right arm around her upper body.

Tristan slowly stops shivering. Her breathing begins to calm but is still shallow. She moves her arms restlessly until they hook around the one Liv has wrapped around her.

"Are you awake?" Liv asks quietly. "You had a nightmare."

"C-cold." Tristan's voice is stark and raspy, not at all her usual silky way of speaking.

"I'll have you warm in no time. Just try to relax." Liv presses her lips behind Tristan's ear.

"I was back on the ship to the colonies. So many faces around me below deck. Not the real faces of the passengers, but yours, Graham's, Marlena's, Dana's…and yes, Rosalee's, but not as a child, but the way she looks now. You were all ill with the plague. I was the only one not affected by it—and you all blamed me. Called me a w-witch. An abomination that needed to be burned at the stake or thrown overboard."

Her heart aching at the raw pain behind Tristan's words, Liv shifts and rolls Tristan toward her. She adds a blanket from the foot of the bed, on top of the duvet, before taking Tristan in her arms again. "It sounds awful. Try to let it go. It was a dream."

Tristan doesn't reply but doesn't pull away either. She rests her head on Liv's shoulder, and now her breathing is even and deeper. Liv wills herself to relax, only now realizing how Tristan startled her. She hates that Tristan is in such pain.

"What time is it?" Tristan asks huskily. She rolls onto her back and groans. "Damn, I did a number on my back."

Liv's gut reaction is to offer another back and neck rub, but she also knows that Tristan is proud and definitely not one to take kindly to being fussed over. "No idea. Wait." Liv pushes up on her elbow and glances over to the rather old-fashioned clock radio on the nightstand on Tristan's side of the bed. "Two thirty. Middle of the night."

"If I didn't know I'll need all the rest I can get, I'd get up and make coffee," Tristan mutters. "It's what I do in New York when I… can't sleep."

Ah. Tristan regularly has nightmares and disturbed sleep patterns. "I put on a podcast and let whoever's talking lull me back to sleep," Liv says lightly. "My mind just doesn't know when to shut up sometimes."

"Really? A podcast? I can sometimes go back to sleep on the couch in front of the TV, watching cooking shows. It's almost the only time I watch the damn things. If all else fails, I go down to my workshop and work on a project."

"I've been known to paint or draw in the middle of the night."

Tristan shifts and looks up at Liv, her eyes reflecting the night light from the hallway. "What has you so unsettled that you can't sleep, Olivia?"

The way Tristan speaks her name…does she know how much of a caress it is? Olivia…like something exotic and beautiful. "I lost a lot when I moved to New York. My parents gave me a year to 'get my act together' and then use my scholarship to Harvard. They're both proud pro-bono lawyers with quite the entourage in Boston, and they have always expected me to join the firm. I do admire them. They're working with the people who can't afford legal representation, and they do deserve all the accolades. No doubt about that."

"But?" Tristan kisses Liv's neck softly.

"But it was never my path. For me, art and art restoration come in at shared first place. If I can't paint, or help rescue and restore paintings, I...I don't know. I have no plan B, really."

"And your parents?"

Liv sighs and hides her face against the top of Tristan's head. "They were already looking for an apartment for me, and setting up an internship at the firm, when I called to say I was still not returning to Boston."

"And you hate disappointing them." Tristan speaks in a noncommittal tone.

"I do, but it's not the first time. This is about my career, which is bad enough, I suppose, but when I came out and my father, or, stepfather, rather, set the tone, as he is as bigoted as they come...and my mother allowed his hate speech to continue, it really screwed with my mind. I suppose not wanting to be a lawyer was just another nail in the coffin."

"I'm sorry you had to go through this. Was it long ago?" Tristan smooths back Liv's hair.

"I came out to my parents when I was fourteen, and then I went back into the closet as far as they were concerned. I found my stride in college and refused to hide my true self after that. I kind of knew it wouldn't go well but hoped I was wrong. That it was just nerves. That Mom and Brian would come around."

"Instead, they let you down."

"Yes."

Liv is amazed at how easy it is to talk to Tristan. Perhaps because Tristan's told her such a fantastical tale about her past, practically nothing's off the table.

Tristan nudges Liv over onto her back. "I don't know when I realized I could find my own gender attractive. It was perhaps during the Civil War. It's been so long, I can't remember...what?" Tristan stares down at Liv.

"C-civil War." Liv tries to stop the slightly hysterical laughter from erupting. "I th-thought I was late in finally making a stand when it came to myself...but you were...a hundred?" She hiccupped. "I'm sorry. I'm not laughing at you. Honestly." Snorting, Liv buries her face in the pillow, trying to calm down, but the irrepressible laughter keeps coming in wave after wave.

"I'm absolutely thrilled that you find this so amusing," Tristan says haughtily, but Liv can hear the smile in her voice. "Not to mention how wonderful it is to be the source of such delight on your part."

Liv flings her arms around Tristan and pulls her close. It's as if the laughter has pushed them both past their respective ghosts…at least for now.

Tristan then shoves anxiety even farther away by kissing her. This doesn't allow for any other thoughts than how hard Liv is falling for Tristan, and how much she wants her. Slipping her hands under Tristan's sleep shirt that has ridden up over her hips, Liv finds smooth, warm skin. She spreads her fingers wide, wanting to cover as much of Tristan as possible, and returns the kiss by parting her lips and letting Tristan deepen it. Tristan nibbles and caresses with her lips and tongue, and Liv reciprocates by exploring Tristan's mouth.

"You taste like some exotic fruit," Tristan murmurs against Liv's lips. "You also make me forget about anything but you, and all I want is to drown in you. I want you to know that."

Hearing traces of regret, Liv wants to hold Tristan closer to keep her from withdrawing, but she can feel it's already happening. Tristan is too selfless to just take what she wants in this moment, and Liv understands but also hates this noble trait.

Tristan ends the heated embrace with sweeter kisses that calm rather than ignite.

"I'd make love with you in a heartbeat if you'd let me," Liv whispers as they settle down among the pillows, duvets, and blankets.

"Oh, don't tempt me, Olivia." Tristan takes a deep breath. "You think too highly of my self-restraint."

"No, I don't. You're a woman of principle, though part of me wishes you weren't." Liv kisses Tristan's shoulder where the neckline has slipped and reveals the velvety skin. "And I'll do my best to be good."

Tristan doesn't answer but moves in behind Liv and places a hand on Liv's thigh. Certain neither of them can go back to sleep, Liv settles for just enjoying being this close to Tristan and reliving the kisses in her mind, and that's what she does until she falls asleep, two minutes later.

CHAPTER TWENTY-THREE

If the previous night was intimate and tender, the breakfast in the small nook in the kitchen is quiet and pensive. Preoccupied, Tristan lets her mind run different scenarios of what might be the reason for the stalker—or stalkers. She has no idea if one person or several is behind it all.

"I received a text from Rosalee last night," Tristan says, finally looking up at Olivia, who appears as lost in thought as Tristan felt a moment ago.

Olivia blinks, and then her attention is back. "She okay?"

"She's arrived at her destination. That's all she wrote, but I would assume if she'd run into trouble, she'd allude to it." Tristan drinks the last of her coffee and pours half a mug more. "More coffee?"

"No, thank you. I'm fine." Olivia taps her lower lip. "Did you tell her about the people who were after us yesterday?"

"No. Or at least not yet. Why?"

"Because she may have had something happen and reasoned like you do—keeping the information close to the vest." Olivia stands and rinses her mug. "She might not trust you, or us, completely. Or at all. Or she may be the one behind it." She turns around, resting her hip against the counter. "Isn't that one of the potential scenarios you were busy sifting through earlier?" The way Olivia tilts her head makes her hair fall like a mocha waterfall over her right shoulder.

"You have got to stop reading my mind," Tristan says dryly. But she's shocked at how accurately Olivia manages to reason as she does. "And you're right. Yes, I did worry that Rosalee somehow, if not maliciously, but by being careless, helped put us in this situation."

"You don't know her anymore, I suppose. I mean, tons of time has passed. She may have used us to throw the scent off herself. It's not nice, but it's human. I mean, self-preservation." Olivia moves to stand behind Tristan, placing her hands on her shoulders. She doesn't start a massage but caresses her gently.

"Yes. I thought about that too. Or perhaps Iris's death wasn't an accident—but manslaughter or murder. One of the emails delivered to Rosalee held a very obvious threat, and the reason was the Amaranthine Law, which the sender saw as an abomination."

"This law…can you tell me about it?" Olivia sits down but remains on the same side of the table.

Tristan isn't sure about pulling Olivia further into this mess by sharing the details of the "law" she and the other girls who survived the plague on the ship once wrote when they were in their nineties and fully aware they might not die for a very long time. "If you're certain."

"The more I know, the more I can help you." Olivia runs her thumb along Tristan's cheekbone. "Please."

"Very well." Tristan pulls the ledger that sits at the other end of the rectangular kitchen table from her. Opening one of the first pages, she looks down at the ornate, rather pretentious handwriting. "The Amaranthine Law. Paragraph one. It is forbidden to discuss our longevity with anyone outside our group of nine. The people we live among will not understand, and such discussion will endanger us all. Their intolerance for the true nature of our fate might very well mean certain death. Addendum. We are all likely barren, which is in this case a blessing, but this addendum insists that no children can ever be born to any of us, as the repercussions would be heartbreaking and cruel to both mother and child." Tristan hasn't read through the law in many years because she knows it by heart. Now, when she does, the feelings of dread, of truly being an abomination in the eyes of the world, and mostly, in her own opinion as well, resurface.

"Want me to read? You're shaking." Olivia places a hand on top of Tristan's.

"I'm all right." Tristan can feel Olivia flinch and realizes she just used her most lethally soft tone. "Truly." She clears her throat. "Paragraph two. We must obtain new identities when a certain amount of time has passed and well before our longevity causes speculation among those who know us. We can allow no socializing or relationship with anyone from our former existence except for correspondence via mail if an emergency should arise. See Paragraph five.

"Addendum one. At least seventy years must pass before we may return to a place where we've lived before.

"Addendum two. Stay well within the law at all costs, and thus do not attract unwanted attention from the authorities.

"Paragraph three. Potential property and wealth should be donated to deserving individuals. If enough funds exist to not raise suspicion, the option to leave them to be inherited by our next persona can be invoked.

"Paragraph four. With our longevity comes great responsibility for dealing with people of normal life expectancy. We cannot live a completely solitary life, but this paragraph still maintains that we do not cause those of normal stature any undue bodily or emotional harm by constantly deceiving them. Addendum. Do not share the true nature of our longevity with a person outside our group. Do not readily display your rapid healing abilities. Always be prepared to change into a new persona.

"Paragraph five. We will immediately share any information about what made us age at this remarkably slow pace among us." Tristan stops reading and leans back, away from the ledger. "Nobody has ever come close to finding out about the plague on the ship, or what makes our genetic makeup different. Even during later years, one can't just submit a DNA sample with such a risky outcome. A strange reading is bound to provoke scientists and the authorities alike. I have used many contacts over the years, fending off questions as to why I want human tissues and blood analyzed. Nothing even remotely conclusive ever came of them." Sighing, Tristan visibly shudders.

Olivia wraps her arms around Tristan, who finds herself in a tight embrace. "I know some people are living under a similar threat in this world. To exist like this for…for centuries, though…and for a reason that is no fault of your own, is not fair. It shouldn't still have to be like this for you."

"Someone is out there making sure that Rosalee and I know they know. No matter their agenda, it's ominous. Threatening. And I can't risk you getting hurt. No matter what happens to Rosalee or me, we have lived long, rewarding lives during all the insanity, but you…are twenty-four years old, Olivia. You have your entire life ahead of you."

Tristan clutches at Olivia, her actions belying her words, but she means every single one of them, even if they shred her heart.

Olivia is quiet but holds on just as tight. Her embrace is both a bliss and a curse. Tristan has endured a lot of pain throughout her long life, but nothing has prepared her for the searing agony of pulling back from Olivia. When she puts enough inches between them to be able to think rationally, she suddenly knows what they must do. She lets her usual mask of control slip back into place, and she can tell the second Olivia notices it, as her face grows still and pale.

"The day to finally part hasn't come yet," Tristan says stoically. "How do you feel about going to Switzerland?"

CHAPTER TWENTY-FOUR

Liv still can't comprehend how fast they managed to leave Tristan's London condo, catch a taxi a few streets away, and now be at Luton Airport, where Tristan has arranged for a private jet. Torn between trying to act casual about this extravagant way of traveling and wanting to ask where the hell Tristan has stowed away this vast amount of money, Liv stays in the background for now.

"We're in luck. Not only do they have a jet ready to embark to Geneva in two hours, but we're also able to share it with some representatives of an IT company that apparently likes to split the cost. That way our names aren't at the top of the contract." Tristan looks pleased as she adjusts her scarf. "You're looking a little pale. Hungry?"

Liv shakes her head and wishes she hadn't. She is quite dizzy, but not from a sugar low. "Things are moving fast." And she is also trembling inside in a highly unpleasant way—has been ever since they read through the damn Amaranthine Law.

"Well, we have two hours to kill. Let's go to the VIP lounge and find a quiet corner. I'm traveling under the name Tory Kline, and that woman is quite well off."

"I guessed as much," Liv mutters as she follows Tristan through the part of security where nobody has to wait in line, and they're whisked through in minutes. The VIP lounge is nice, the sitting areas arranged to create privacy for work and rest. Dividers provide protection from prying eyes, and Liv sits down on a plush couch after pulling off her coat.

A host shows up, and Tristan orders some snacks and hot tea. When he returns with a tray, she tips him and asks for privacy. The tip must've been good because the young man looks like he's ready to post armed guards to accommodate Tristan.

Tristan sits down next to Liv and takes her hand. "You're cold. Come here." Wrapping an arm around Liv, Tristan takes their discarded coats and covers them both. "London can be damp and raw this time of year."

Liv knows this is only part of the explanation. She's probably shivering because of everything that's going on. She suspects Tristan is aware of this fact, but if she doesn't want to speak about this possibility up front, then Liv's not going to bring it up. "Yes. Damp and raw." Liv can hear the hollowness in her voice and, obviously, Tristan too, as she hugs Liv closer.

"Why don't you have some tea? The cucumber sandwiches look all right. And there are scones with jam and clotted cream. Very British." Tristan tips Liv's head back by placing a curled finger under her chin. "Please." She kisses Liv lightly.

Yeah. Perhaps something to eat will help steady her. It's ridiculous to be this taken aback, but this revision of her entire view of the world, and, God knows, her lifetime expectancies in general, has thrown her off her game. Secretly pinching her thigh through her jeans, Liv winces at the pain but manages to sit up and peruse the tray. She pours them tea, pleased to see that she's not shaking on the outside, at least.

It's amazing how food can, at least temporarily, settle a person. Nutrition, being warmed from within by the tea, and Tristan, who doesn't remove her arm from around Liv's shoulders, all help make her feel more like herself. And so the questions begin popping out.

"Tory Kline? Is that to keep the same initials?" Liv whispers the words after swallowing the last half of a scone and licks her lips to catch errant traces of clotted cream.

"Exactly that." Tristan finishes off her mug of tea. "Keeps having personalized luggage and other items possible." She keeps her voice barely audible. "After a while, you learn these things."

Anything to make life easier, if there was such a thing when it came to Tristan's. "Why Geneva?" Liv realizes how shaken she must have been since this morning. Normally, these would have been the first words out of her mouth.

"Iris died in the Swiss Alps. I plan to find out exactly what happened to her. Perhaps we can do that from Geneva. Otherwise, we'll rent a car and go there. Sound doable?"

Liv isn't sure, but she's seen Tristan pull strings several times now, so why doubt this plan? "Unless the stalker, or stalkers, has figured out your new alias, it should work. We could start at the main library in Geneva."

"Yes. Agreed." Tristan leans back after checking the time on her phone. "We have another hour before our flight. I'll set the alarm on my cell. We'll need our strength later."

Liv doesn't hesitate but scoots closer and places her left hand on Tristan's thigh. No matter what, she plans to keep at bay the pain the future holds like the sword of Damocles over her head. Tristan may move on to her next persona, to keep Liv safe. Having broken the Amaranthine Law by sharing her true-life story with Liv, Tristan might then be bound to make sure she doesn't break it again. The paragraph forbidding anyone to reconnect with someone from a former existence will mean Tristan would then be gone forever. As much as this possibility makes Liv's heart stop, she refuses to let it discourage her from grabbing every single moment of closeness and, yes, happiness, with Tristan. She presses her lips against the soft, creamy skin of Tristan's neck, just below her hairline.

Tristan sighs and puts her hand on top of Liv's. "Olivia."

Liv doesn't care where they are or that the host might appear at any time to remove their tray. She slides her hand up another few inches and kisses a trail along Tristan's jawline until she finds her mouth.

Tristan is waiting for her. Her lips parted, her eyes half-closed, she studies Liv with fire burning in her blue eyes. Liv squeezes the inside of Tristan's thigh, and the heat under the fabric of Tristan's pants makes her close the distance between their lips. This is what Liv wants, this unrestrained, passion-filled caressing of lips and tongues. That, together with the heat between Tristan's thighs, is dangerous.

Slowly, Liv tries to take the fiery touches down a notch, but it's damn near impossible when she can feel Tristan having the same struggles.

"You are evil," Tristan wheezes against Liv's lips. "Doing this here. In public. Is evil."

"You may have a point," Liv whispers and pulls back enough to minimize the risk of self-combustion on her part. "In my defense, we ignited more forcefully than I thought possible."

"We did." Tristan runs a hand over her face. "And until we're actually alone, now we know better."

Liv gapes but then promptly closes her mouth. Does Tristan really mean that she is ready to let Liv that close when they are alone next time? There is already so much uncertainty because of the Amaranthine Law and the danger they're in. So far, they have indulged only in kisses and caresses. Is Tristan prepared for how she will feel after they make love?

Despite her bravado only a moment ago, Liv isn't sure she'll survive such an emotional hit-and-run.

CHAPTER TWENTY-FIVE

Tristan manages to catch some sleep on the luxurious jet with Olivia next to her. Before she dozes off, it amuses Tristan to see how the three men and one woman who originally chartered the plane all show interest in Olivia—and how oblivious Olivia is. Of course, Olivia is a charismatic, beautiful young woman, so why wouldn't these people notice her? The fact that Olivia keeps Tristan's hand in hers for the duration of the flight seems to finally dawn on the corporate crowd.

After reaching Geneva, they rent an innocuous car at the airport. On the way to the garage, Tristan pulls out her cell phone and hands it to Olivia. "When we get to the car, find us a hotel room for one night. We also need to shop for some clothes."

"And locate the library."

"Yes. Even more important." Tristan stops by the white Toyota Yaris and can't help but sigh inwardly, thinking of her sports car in New York. She places her to-go bag in the backseat while Olivia puts her bag between her feet on the passenger side. Tristan checks the time on the dashboard. "It's too late to head to the library. Let's do the other errands after you find us a hotel."

"I'll put the address into the GPS when I'm done." Olivia is already working on Tristan's phone.

Tristan pulls out of the garage and into traffic. Driving toward the center of Geneva takes all her concentration. The traffic doesn't bother her, but she doesn't know her way around.

"I found the library. Promenade des Bastions 1. There are several hotels not too far away."

"Just pick one."

"All right." Olivia taps at Tristan's phone. "There." She enters the address into the car's built-in GPS.

Relieved at having a goal, Tristan follows the sonorous automatic female voice's directions. "We'll check in and then take care of our errands."

"Gotcha." Olivia gently squeezes Tristan's knee, making her clutch the wheel harder.

The hotel turns out to be a large, anonymous enterprise, geared toward visiting politicians and businesspeople. Tristan relaxes as they weave through the crowd after checking in. Upon reaching the room, she's pleased to find a large enough safe to place her ledger and pouch of documents in. It always irks her to have them out of her sight unless they're in her safe in New York, but this is better than carrying them around all the time. When Tristan steps away from the safe, making a mental note of the code she chose, she flinches as she sees Olivia standing right behind her.

"Olivia?"

Olivia doesn't answer but takes Tristan by the shoulders and tugs her into her arms. Like Tristan, she's taken off her coat, and now she's running her hands up and down Tristan's back.

"Oh, God." Tristan breathes the words in a whisper, as her vocal cords have given in.

Olivia raises her hands until she gently cups Tristan's cheeks. "Alone."

"Excuse me?" Tristan's head is spinning. She clings to Olivia's hips, bunching up the shirt with her fists.

"We said we'd wait until we're alone. We're alone now." Olivia kisses her. Her lips are soft as they explore Tristan's mouth.

"Mm. Yes." The fact that they have errands to run and plans to make fades into a mist when Olivia moves her lips down to her neck. Small, sharp nips and soothing caresses with a quick, agile tongue have Tristan's knees sagging. She shoves her fingers into Olivia's hair. "Jesus…"

Olivia walks Tristan backward until her back is against the wall. There she stops, their bodies not even touching now, but their lips are so close together that an intake of breath will mean they're kissing. Olivia waits. For what?

Tristan raises a hand and whispers her fingertips along Olivia's cheek. "It'll mean broken hearts," she says huskily. "The more I let you in, the greater the pain."

"Too late." Olivia sighs, and her breath is sweet with traces of the coffee from the plane.

Olivia is right. They are in too deep. Yet Olivia doesn't realize there are degrees of how bad "too deep" can become. How it can tear a person apart. It's been more than a hundred and fifty years, but Tristan has stuck to her vow not to go through that pain again. Yet—here she is with Olivia so close, physically and, sweet Jesus, emotionally.

"Yes, it is too late, but it's not too late to minimize collateral damage," Tristan says, and she can hear how hollow her own voice is.

"Collateral damage?" Olivia doesn't move other than tipping her head back to meet Tristan's gaze. "Is that supposed to be me?" She doesn't appear angry, but her eyes are opaque.

"Collateral damage occurs when my actions, or any Amaranthine's, cause pain or injury to someone who is not one of us." Tristan clears her throat. "It's the law. It clearly says I have to protect anyone…normal. 'Do not cause those of normal stature any undue bodily or emotional harm.' "

"That fucking law," Olivia snarls, startling Tristan. "It's not real." She closes the distance between them. "It's not an actual law. And I'd like to remind you that I'm my own person, perfectly capable of judging the risks I take, or choose not to take. I don't subscribe to, or recognize, this law of yours." Her body fully aligned with Tristan's, Olivia kisses her, not angrily, but with a tinge of frustration. She sucks Tristan's lower lip in between hers, and Tristan responds the way she must. The way she has to because Olivia is right. It is too late. Too late to regret anything.

Tristan shoves her hands under Olivia's shirt, finding smooth, warm skin. Growling low in her throat, she takes Olivia's mouth, caresses her tongue with hers, claims this woman, and her heart already begins to shatter. She doesn't care. Right now, all she can feel is Olivia and how this girl, so strong, so loyal, burns against her.

"Oh, God." Tristan whispers the words into Olivia's mouth. "So be it."

CHAPTER TWENTY-SIX

"So be it." Tristan's words, coming as breaths against Liv's lips, leave her trembling.

Liv kisses Tristan again, now slower, taking her time to revel in each caress, each sound, and to memorize how those elegant, strong hands feel against the skin on her back. There is something poignant in the way Tristan lingeringly moves her fingertips as if each new trail is part of a grid search. Knowing that she's fantasizing, Liv imagines being able to distinguish each swirl of Tristan's fingerprints against her. Blunt nails draw patterns, and Liv arches against them, as they don't sting enough. "It's like you're painting me," Liv says, her voice barely audible even to herself.

"In a way I am." Tristan doesn't stray from Liv's back, seeming content, for now, to map out every muscle group, every square inch of her skin. "I think I'm drawing you, even etching you, into my mind."

To not forget her? Liv draws a quick breath. "I have sketched you…on paper, I mean. From memory." She didn't mean to say that.

"May I see? Later?" Tristan nips at Liv's lips, making it impossible to answer until she lets go, but by then, Liv has forgotten what she asked.

"May I?" Tristan repeats.

"Yes." Who was she to deny Tristan anything? She wouldn't even be able to deny Tristan the choice to leave her, should she choose to follow that inhumane Amaranthine Law.

They're still by the wall, but now Tristan pivots them slowly, pressing Liv gently against the forest-green wallpaper. She slides her hands along Liv's sides, tickling her some before she pulls her hands out from under her shirt. "May I?" She tugs at one of the buttons on the front of Liv's shirt.

"Yes." Again, no denying. More than that, Liv's ready to urge Tristan to go much further, to do anything she wants with Liv because she wants it all. Not one to remain inactive, Liv doesn't even ask but undoes the top four buttons of Tristan's shirt. Tristan's wearing a thin tank top underneath, and as the shirt falls open to her waist, Liv can see she doesn't have on a bra. Small nipples, mouthwateringly hard, poke at the fabric.

"Beautiful," Tristan says, making Liv raise her gaze to Tristan's face. Tristan in turn has unbuttoned all of Liv's buttons and now hooks her index finger around her bra, tugging gently. "There's so much I want with you. So much I need."

"Same," Liv manages to say weakly, thinking she sounds entirely inadequate. "I want all of you. For hours. Days. For a long time." For her entire life. Liv's throat closes around the unspoken words, and to her dread, her eyes well up.

"Darling?" Tristan flinches and lets go of Liv's bra.

"No. It's fine. It is. It's just me being silly." She tries to will the tears back into their ducts by blinking, but they roll down her cheeks, fat and seemingly never-ending as they make wet spots on her shirt. Furious at herself, Liv wipes at her cheeks.

"I've never considered you silly." Tristan takes over and uses her thumbs to stroke away Liv's tears. "You are anything but. I can tell that I've already started on the journey of hurting you, and we have barely done more than embrace and kiss. If this causes the tears of a woman like you, so strong and independent, to fall, then what if we let it go further? What if we try to start something that is bound to fail? That is doomed to cause us unimaginable grief if we let it. Do you think so little of me?"

"What do you mean?" Liv sobs quietly, wanting to stop the horrible words from Tristan's lips but, at the same time, needing to know.

"You can't imagine what's in store, but I can. I have lived through something similar to this, though I would argue that this," Tristan says, flicking her fingers back and forth between them, "is far beyond that. You're twenty-four. I have lived as Tristan Kelly for more than twenty years. In another twenty, I would have to leave you behind and move on to my next persona and wipe my past. You'd be a forty-five-year-old woman then, childless and abandoned. And knowing that—it would be unspeakably cruel for me not to follow the part of the law that actually protects *you*. It was written for a reason, by the ones among us who possessed some semblance of a conscience."

Liv wants to slam her palms against something but steels herself. "Why would I be childless?" She is trying to meet Tristan's arguments stemming from that damn law head-on.

"Because I cannot have children. Not just because I'm obviously barren, but because it is something I made my peace with a long time ago. If it is heartbreaking to leave a beloved spouse, how could I leave a child and start anew somewhere else? So, no children. Ever."

Liv is about to object, frustration and sorrow warring inside her at not being given an equal chance to argue, to decide, when Tristan pales and takes two steps back. There are now two feet between them, and there might as well be the entire city of Geneva. "What?" Liv feels the last tears cool the skin on her face as they evaporate. Tristan is white now. "What's wrong? I mean, what did you just think of?" Liv tries to remember Tristan's exact words, which is nearly impossible as she is busy being rejected, again.

"Something about the law being written by people with a conscience." Tristan nods. "Two among us weren't all that big on conscience, but…but they're dead."

A chill runs up Liv's spine. "What about the extreme longevity? How can you be sure?"

Tristan's eyes express nothing, but their shade has changed from icy blue to dark navy. "Because they were executed."

CHAPTER TWENTY-SEVEN

Tristan knows the mood—and, oh God, what an insufficient word to describe the turbulence of feelings—is gone. For now. Olivia's wide eyes speak not of passion, but of shock and confusion at Tristan's words.

"Executed? How? Or, rather, why and by whom?" Olivia walks over to the window that can't boast of much of a view, but she still presses her forehead against it.

"These two women, Caroline and Trudy, were sisters, about ages eight and ten, when we got ill on the ship." Rigid now, so much so her back aches, Tristan turns on the light above the small table, sits down, and pulls the ledger from her bag. "I couldn't even make myself put them on the page of the other ones when I started my ledger. These girls had a mean streak from the beginning—I mean before the plague."

"They were children. Kids can be mean." Olivia turns around and seems to hesitate before she walks over to Tristan. She stops before sitting down and places a hand on the back of Tristan's neck, giving her a quick caress. The touch is soothing.

Feeling ridiculous for wanting to say thank you, Tristan pats the chair next to her. "Let me show you."

Olivia sits down and leans closer, looking down at the page. "These dates are mostly from the late 1800s." She runs her hovering fingertip along the row of dates. "Until September 10, 1888, and September 14, the same year."

"Yes. It was quite the scandal in Philadelphia." Tristan shudders. "As I lived there at the time, I followed the trials from a distance. I felt obligated, but also their actions…I admit I worried about the plague and what it did to us, being the reason for their…megalomania? Insanity? Psychopathy?"

Olivia squeezes Tristan's knee with her free hand. "Well, you know the answer to that question by now. You have neither of those traits."

"No, perhaps not. During some long periods of time I've displayed blatant disrespect for my own life. Knowing your days aren't numbered, that you have days to spare, to waste, if you will, doesn't make for good decisions all the time. It makes you tempt fate, challenge it, in ways most people wouldn't do, as all they know for sure is that they get this one life. And no, I'm not talking about daredevils, adventurers. I mean, downright foolhardy, idiotic, almost death-wish things."

"Oh?" Olivia leans her head in her hand as she rests her elbow against the table. She's entirely concentrated on Tristan, and her determination settles something inside and makes it marginally easier to speak. To explain.

"When we are young, life seems endless, almost. Certainly, old age seems very far away. The older we get, the more people we lose, well, that reminds us of our own inevitable demise. It makes us value each moment—or it should. At least it brings self-preservation to the forefront. Now, enter a bunch of little girls from a ship in 1769. We all get seriously ill. Our parents let the ship's priest give us the last rites. They try every home remedy they can concoct aboard a ship in the middle of the Atlantic, with limited resources. We're dying. And then we're not. All nine girls recover and live on. And on and on. Eventually I, and the other girls, put two and two together, which naturally took us a while, as not a lot changed at first. But then it did, for me. During many decades I was reckless. Perhaps I was testing my 'immortality' in a manner of speaking. I drank too much, I took lovers left and right, I gambled, stole, broke a lot of laws and went to prison. You name it. I disrespected myself and, worse, the people around me." Her voice so raw now, it hurts to speak, Tristan fully expects Olivia to withdraw. She doesn't. "I daresay I broke both the US law and the Amaranthine at the same time."

"What changed?" Olivia asks quietly.

"I reached a crossroads where I needed to once and for all decide what kind of human being I intended to be for this seemingly never-ending life of mine." Tristan sighs. "I could go on being a callous bastard with a cavalier attitude toward life and my place in the world, or I could take stock of what this difference of mine meant, adjust accordingly, and make the best of it. I found out that what was best for others meant solitude and sacrifice for me, eventually. I've come to accept that, until—"

Olivia waits patiently, gives Tristan time, but the words are stuck in her throat. Wrapping her arm around Tristan's shoulders, Olivia pulls her closer. "Yes? Until?"

"Until you." Tristan knows it's a mistake—this honesty, this confession. "Until you, Olivia." Oh, she'll pay the price for this temporary relief in being completely honest. Tristan knows, as this has been her reality for so long, that she'll think back on the two of them, here at this small table in this boring hotel room. Her memory will depict Olivia and the way she looks at Tristan, accepting, with tenderness, and underneath that, the passion…and, Tristan hopes she's wrong, perhaps even with love.

"Tristan." Olivia brushes her lips lightly over hers. "How did you regain your appreciation for life, even after knowing, in your case, it's going to be a long, often lonely, one?" The question, spoken so softly, cuts deeply, as it's prompt and to the point.

"I looked for purpose. Sometimes from a humane angle, but mostly from an artistic point of view. Like my current endeavor. I've built Amaranthine Inc. from nothing to one of the most reputable art-restoring companies in the world. I know"—Tristan shakes her head—"choosing that name was foolish, but in all honesty, I saw it as a way of vanquishing the demons from my past. Nothing untoward had happened for a long time, and when I say long, you better believe I mean long. Apart from having to inevitably change my identity and relocating once I reached a certain age, I suppose I got complacent."

"Because of Rosalee's digital research about what became of the Amaranthine girls?"

"I've thought of that. I was likely targeted before she reached out. Whether she had anything to do with it, or if she's merely doing what I do, trying to stay ahead of the game, I just don't know."

"I met her only very briefly, but to me, she looked like a woman on the verge of collapse," Olivia said, stroking Tristan's back gently. "Thin, no, emaciated, pale as a ghost, and with enough nervous energy to charge a cell phone."

GUN BROOKE

Tristan nods. "Yes. Her fear is real. It still isn't proof that she's not involved, or under someone's thumb."

"True."

"God, I feel we're talking in circles." Tristan pinches the bridge of her nose.

"Perhaps, but you never know when what we say will stir an idea or a revelation." Tugging the ledger closer, Olivia peruses the pages about Caroline and Trudy. "Back to these girls. I suppose they didn't want to conform to the Amaranthine Law?"

"Not even close," Tristan says slowly. "They flaunted their youthfulness, attended balls, courted one man younger than the other. As the rest of us were treated horribly by certain people, especially the churches, Caroline and Trudy made themselves into local celebrities. I don't think most people believed the truth about their birthdates, but enough people knew them from their childhood to suggest there was a tinge of truth about it all."

Tristan can't sit still. She stands, and Olivia's arm falls from her back. "The older they got, the more brazen they became. Trudy especially, who was considered the prettiest. They took such risks, and eventually, it caught up with them. I had no idea at the time that they had resorted to putting their longevity into a horrible system. They married older men, who really were their peers, and even younger, and I'm sure they waited them out in the beginning. You know, waiting for their husbands to die of natural causes. But soon that wasn't enough. They began poisoning their men. Not only did they inherit their money and entire estate, but often they had made the men take out sizable life insurance policies."

"Holy crap." Olivia stood also but walked over to an armchair and curled up in it. "Black widows."

"In a manner of speaking. They were caught eventually and sentenced to death by hanging. I was in town for their trial, but not in the courtroom, as they could have recognized me. Knowing their scruple-free personalities, I couldn't risk it."

"Yet you thought of something before, about Trudy and Caroline. Despite them being dead." Olivia looks up at Tristan, leaning her head against the backrest. "What was that?"

"I was trying to figure out if one of the others could somehow be behind this. As far as I know, only Rosalee and I are still alive. And even if all of them had still been alive, all the others abided by the Amaranthine Law to the best of their ability, and they wouldn't go after us, for they'd have no reason. Caroline and Trudy didn't help write the law and never did follow it or the US law. They spat at the idea since they obviously thought their own method to enrich themselves and social climb was much better."

Olivia nods. "The truly callous, ruthless ones."

Tristan groans softly. She's nervous now, knowing full well she's pushing the boundaries of credibility, of the suspension of Olivia's disbelief. "If you think anything of what I've told you is crazy, you'll think I'm certifiable if I share my theory. I have never discussed it with anyone."

"If you want to, I'm listening." Olivia pats the wide armrest next to her, and Tristan fetches the ledger, gives it to Olivia before she slowly sits down. Olivia takes Tristan's hand and kisses it. Her lips linger. Warmth spreads from the caress to the deep recesses of Tristan's chest. Before Olivia, she always felt cold, thinking it was due to her too-long life. That she was cold because she should have been dead a long time ago. Now, all Olivia has to do is touch her, even in the most innocent of ways, and it is as if heat radiates from the connection.

"It was about fifty-some years ago that this theory gained a foothold with me." Tristan pauses, leans over, and opens the ledger to a new place. "I think I was actually quite drunk, and therefore uninhibited, when I jotted down my notes." She looks down on the page. "See what I mean?"

Olivia's hand trembles as she follows the title of the page with her index finger, reading the words out loud. "Circumstantial Evidence of Resurrection."

CHAPTER TWENTY-EIGHT

Olivia knows they're not going out to buy clothes or anything else this evening. She feels drained after everything that's happened, and damn it all to hell, she needs to process all this. "Resurrection? Surely this is...you said you were drunk?" She turns to Tristan, who still sits on the armrest next to her. "I know. I said I'd keep an open mind, but this...is..." Her voice falters.

"You can accept that I'm more than two hundred and fifty years old, but not this." Tristan moves over to the couch. She's pale, but her eyes burn like blue fire.

"That's just it." Olivia looks at the page before her. "You've had all those years to take things in, little by little, and I have been thrown into it over a few days. I feel like I'm losing my mind!" She flings her hands in the air. "Then there's the fact that I'd much rather jump your freaking bones than try to find who's out to kill you!"

Tristan gapes, and then the corners of her mouth turn up. Chuckling, she slumps against the backrest. "Now, there's a complaint I can understand."

Olivia is appalled at how she just spoke to Tristan, but Tristan's reaction makes her giggle. "This is a bit ridiculous, isn't it? I mean, people talk about May-December romances, but this..." She points at Tristan and then at herself. "This is—"

"Ridiculous." Tristan has stopped laughing, but the smile is still in place. "We approach all this from such different viewpoints. I try to protect you—from myself and those who are out to harm me—and, at the same time, I desperately want you to believe me. To understand. It's all asking too much. I know this."

"I just need some time to grasp things. This, what did you call it, ledger? This ledger is chock-full of journal entries and theories, and facts, and it's like opening a book that leads me into another world. The thing is, I want to be on this journey with you, to help you. My brain just can't keep up, even if my heart does." Olivia grips the ledger harder.

"You did speak of romance. And now your heart," Tristan murmurs. "Do you have any idea how painful the presence of hope is to someone like me?"

"What do you mean?" Olivia can't bear the physical distance between them. She takes the ledger and moves over to the couch as well, sitting down close enough to Tristan for their thighs to touch.

Tristan places a gentle hand on Olivia's knee. "Hope is what we live by. Right? But I stopped taking such chances more than a century ago. I vowed to never fall into the trap of wishing for things that would ultimately shatter me. You see…you must be selfish when you live a life like mine. You have only yourself because, eventually, everyone else dies. And before that happens, when they age in the way I'm supposed to, they see that I don't. They realize that something's wrong, that I've lied about something essential. So, I have to leave them—unable to stay and care for them during the last years of their existence." Only anger and sorrow are written on Tristan's face now.

"Okay, so there's a major difference when it comes to us," Olivia says and rests her head on Tristan's shoulder for a few moments. "I already know. You have informed me more than you've done with anyone in ages. I go into this with my eyes open, even if I admit I don't know every single intricate detail." She opens the ledger to the page about resurrection and begins to read out loud. "August 14, 1959. Circumstantial Evidence of Resurrection."

Tristan grips Olivia's knee more firmly.

"Perhaps it is the booze talking, but all the facts I've collected have put me on a new path when it comes to the sisters Trudy and Caroline. To understand what sets them apart, I have to tell the story of how the plague hit us."

Pausing, Olivia takes Tristan's hand in hers. "Let me know if it gets too much, okay?"

"Very well." Tristan's voice shows little emotion.

"We left London for Liverpool in April 1769, Mother, Father,

Corinne, and I, and I remember it was raining. The stagecoach was a nightmare, as the weather was so poor. The horses had problems on parts of the road that had suffered mudslides, and at one point, Father and another gentleman had to go outside and help push it out of the sludge. It took us one extra day to reach Liverpool, six days instead of five, and everyone was relieved when we finally reached the inn. My parents had taken potential delays into consideration, and we had two days to rest before we were to go aboard the Fortune.

"The ship was crowded with families with children, women, and men. We were assigned small quarters, which really consisted of only a hard bed with a drape for some remnant of privacy. We had to sleep in there, all four of us, but we made do. The journey would end up taking thirty days. In the middle of the Atlantic, the first person became ill. Nobody knew why, or what it was, but soon I heard the adults call it a plague. High fever, a rash, loss of appetite were the first symptoms. The ones who died did so after having been ill for five to seven days. They were all adults or boys. The little girls who got sick, like me, all made it, but it was strange, the adults said, because we were the sickest of everyone. We didn't even seem to breathe. My mother was certain I had passed away on the tenth day. I was rigid, cold, and my eyes wouldn't close. She didn't want me to ever learn of this condition, but Corinne told me after I begged her. So, nine little girls cheat death on the Fortune, *and it slows our aging process.*

"Some facts are indisputable. No girl that had entered puberty was affected this way. Neither was any girl under the age of three either, as far as I know. We all went through the mock-death experience, and in one case it went so far, my father said they had to stop a family from performing a burial at sea for their little girl.

"What if we were in some suspended animation—a fake death— and what if something happened to us then? To our brains? To our entire system? Who knows what type of virus, bacteria, fungus, or parasite this was? Perhaps I could find out if I allowed medical science to draw blood and examine me? The thing is, of course, they'd be much more likely to put me away in a psychiatric ward and throw away the key. I'll be damned if I'm going to spend eternity—quite literally—in such a place."

Olivia stops reading and just stares at the text for a moment, before turning to Tristan. "And now you wonder if Trudy and Caroline might have survived being hanged in much the same way. Being fake dead, and then waking up again? But even so? Why would they come after you—and why now? It's been a while."

"It has. And your questions are valid. These two hated the rest of us. They didn't want to conform, and they apparently blamed us for the fact they were arrested and tried for their crimes. According to the woman who wrote me poste restante, they swore to take us down with them. Back then I thought, what if they meant it? What if that became their agenda—if they survived the hangings?"

"It's a theory. And I don't blame you for grasping at straws." Olivia puts the ledger away and pulls Tristan into her arms. Feeling rigid at first, Tristan then melts into Olivia, pulling her legs up under her. "We'll figure it out. We're going to run our errands in the morning and also visit the library. Why don't we order room service and then catch up on some sleep? It's been a long day."

"It has." Tristan seems reluctant to move. "I don't think I've ever felt this...lost? It's as if I know exactly what to do one minute and start flailing the next."

"I mostly flail. But I do know that we need to eat. Let me order us something." She kisses the top of Tristan's hair and walks over to the desk that holds the binder with the menu and the phone. Tristan sounds uninspired when deciding what she wants, but Olivia's relieved that she's going to eat at all, as it appears Tristan has reached some limit. Hopefully, it's temporary. They'll need to be able to focus tomorrow.

After their meal, Olivia rolls her shoulders, so tired she's aching all over. "I'm going to get a hot shower before bed." She eyes the king-size bed, thinking it's a good thing she's exhausted. That way, she'll fall asleep instantly and not pine for Tristan half the night.

"Go ahead." Tristan is tapping on her burner phone, apparently having regained some of her concentration after the meal.

The bathroom is beige and white. The only pop of color comes from the small bottles holding shampoo, conditioner, body wash, and body lotion. They sit on the counter, a bright aqua. On the opposite wall is a large glass shower stall. She turns on the water, and soon the steam fills the bathroom. After undressing, she washes her underwear with hand soap, removes some towels from the rack, and hangs her bra and panties to dry. Olivia steps into the shower and closes her eyes as the warm water pounds her shoulders. She moans and tips her head back, the spray hitting her face and soaking her hair. She's brought the small bottles with her, and now she lathers her hair. The scent is pleasant, on the fruity side, and she is just about to flip open the lid to the body wash when she hears Tristan's voice.

"I'm exhausted, Olivia. Mind if I join you?"

CHAPTER TWENTY-NINE

Tristan can hear Olivia gasp through the mist in the shower stall. She certainly likes her water quite hot, which Tristan normally doesn't, but right now, she couldn't care less. All she wants is to get out of her clothes, shower, and curl up in bed. At least that's what she tells herself, when Olivia has to clear her voice twice before responding.

"S-sure. Um. If you're certain."

"I am." Was she? Was she really? Tristan undresses, only now noticing Olivia's underwear on the towel rack. Tristan has a couple of changes in her go-bag but still washes her cotton panties and bra as well. It gives her a moment to compose herself.

When she's done, she cautiously opens the door to the shower stall and steps inside.

"Careful," Olivia says huskily and extends a hand. "It's pretty slippery."

Tristan takes the proffered hand, and then she's standing very close to a naked Olivia. Curvaceous, with full breasts, a flat stomach, and beautiful hips, she shimmers from soap and running water. Her long hair is glued to her shoulders and back. "God, you're gorgeous," Tristan says before she even realizes she intends to speak at all.

Olivia's gaze feels like hands as it runs all over Tristan. "You're the most beautiful woman I've ever seen," Olivia murmurs.

Tristan gulps. Stepping into the shower with Olivia is going to be the best—and the worst—thing she's ever done. She frees her hand from Olivia's steadying grip and wraps it around her waist. She tugs Olivia to her, gently, so neither of them slips. She was correct. Olivia is coated with soap, which accentuates every part of her that is now aligned with Tristan. The glorious breasts, soft and firm, with hard, wine-colored nipples, flatten somewhat against her. Olivia's arms are now around Tristan's neck. They both moan as they glide against each other, breasts cushion each other, and stomach muscles tremble where they press together.

Olivia fumbles to her left, and Tristan notices vaguely how she finds a grab bar and anchors them by gripping it. Tristan knows what she needs now, and she cups Olivia's cheeks, finding those full lips with her own. Standing under the spray of water, they kiss as if it's the first time, but also as if they've been starving for each other for years. And perhaps they have because Tristan can't remember ever feeling this way about anyone else. She slips her tongue into Olivia's mouth and is met by its counterpart. The exploration, the caresses make Tristan moan. She nudges Olivia toward the wall where the grab bar is located. "Hold on, darling," she whispers and feels how Olivia moves her free hand to grip the bar.

"What are you going to do?" Olivia says huskily.

"I need to touch you, and I don't want you to fall," Tristan says and runs her hands over Olivia's arms. She maps the skin and then moves up, across the collarbones, and down over Olivia's breasts. Tristan weighs them in her hands, feeling the nipples grow impossibly harder. Olivia tips her head back against the tiled wall, and now it's her turn to whimper.

"Yes." Olivia arches against Tristan. "Oh, yes."

Bending, Tristan takes Olivia's left nipple into her mouth. The water has washed away the soap and left only the clean taste of Olivia. She flattens her tongue against the puckered surface, and it's as if a current goes through Olivia, who jerks and moves as if to push more of herself into Tristan's mouth. Cupping the breast from underneath, Tristan lifts it for easier access. With her other hand, she finds the unattended nipple and rolls it between her fingers.

"Ah!" Olivia cries out and wraps a leg around Tristan's hips. "Oh, God." Her voice echoes in the shower stall.

Taking advantage of Olivia's position, Tristan lets go of the right nipple and slides her hand down between them. Slowly, she pushes it between Olivia's legs, cupping her. "May I?"

"Yes…" Olivia trembles so much now, being in here is really starting to get a bit dangerous, as it is even more slippery. Tristan kisses the nipple she's been licking and lets go of it.

"Will you change your mind if I suggest we continue this where we won't risk our necks?" She draws the tip of her tongue along Olivia's lower lip.

"As long as you don't change your mind…I think I'll die if you do," Olivia says.

"Oh, I won't." She would die too, longevity or not.

Tristan washes her hair and nearly loses her resolve when Olivia spreads body wash over her skin and seems adamant to not miss a single spot. Once they've rinsed and turned off the water, Tristan pulls some bath towels into the shower, wrapping one around Olivia and the other around herself. After kissing Olivia again, she takes a smaller towel and wraps it around Olivia's long hair. She doesn't care about her own.

Tristan is glad she turned off all the lamps but the one on the nightstand before she walked into the bathroom. The dim lighting creates a cozier mood, and though she might have huffed at such a sentiment before, now, with Olivia, it matters.

Olivia reaches the bed first. When Tristan comes closer, Olivia unfolds her bath towel and begins drying Tristan's shoulders. She kisses each part she has just dried, and when she reaches Tristan's breasts, she's aching with need. Settling for kissing them chastely, she avoids the hard, pink nipples, and Tristan groans, sounding aroused and frustrated at the same time. Olivia keeps drying Tristan until she eventually is kneeling before her.

"Spread your legs," Olivia says quietly.

Tristan separates her feet, and Olivia looks hungrily at the sparse tuft of silver strands at the apex of Tristan's thighs. They barely cover the now-swollen folds.

"May I?" Olivia asks, much like Tristan did in the shower.

"Yes." Tristan's voice is barely audible.

Olivia rakes her blunt nails through the pubic hair and lets her fingers follow the swollen folds. The dampness has another viscosity, and Olivia can't hold back a moan at the thought of Tristan being this wet—because of her.

"Why don't you lie down?" Olivia stands. All she can think of now is how she wants Tristan underneath her on the bed—legs spread.

Tristan climbs onto the bed, clearly shaking. It's amazing how they respond to each other. As Olivia quickly squeezes water out of her hair with the towel, she watches how Tristan gracefully moves onto the pillows and bends one leg at the knee, then lets it fall to the side.

"Oh…" Both her towels sliding to the floor, Olivia joins Tristan, parting her legs with hers. She lowers herself down onto her elbows, and now her mouth is all over Tristan's breasts. She moves back and forth between the two nipples, licking, tugging with her lips, and when Tristan whispers, "Bite me," she does just that. Carefully, she tugs at the rigid flesh, and Tristan begins to squirm.

"Yes. Like that," Tristan says between gasps. "With your teeth."

Olivia pushes Tristan's breasts together and is lost in the sensation of licking, kissing, and nipping. When the nipples are more red than pink, she relents, despite Tristan's objections, and continues her exploration after a detour to Tristan's mouth.

Nudging the slender thighs apart, Olivia moves in between them, looking up at Tristan the entire time. Tristan has placed one more pillow underneath her. Olivia parts the glistening folds with her fingers and has time to think, "This is making love," before she lets her tongue plunge inside. Working it up to Tristan's clit and back down to her entrance, she can feel the muscles in Tristan's legs go rigid and tighten around her.

"Olivia!" Tristan is keening her name now. "Olivia, Olivia…"

Olivia wants Tristan to come. She flattens her tongue against the swollen clit after pushing the hood up with her thumb, which makes Tristan push her hips off the bed. Olivia starts flicking her tongue over her clit, faster and faster.

Tristan cries out, pulls her legs up, only to push with her feet against the mattress, raising them both off the bed. Olivia is on her knees, her tongue still against Tristan, still working her.

Shaking, Tristan slumps back, but then Olivia can feel something new happening. Wetness coats Tristan's thighs and Olivia's cheeks when Tristan comes again. Now she whimpers and sounds half panicked, and

Olivia realizes it's her cue to crawl up Tristan's body and take her in her arms.

Tristan hides her face against Olivia's neck, still whimpering, trembling, and gasping for air.

"Shh." Olivia rocks her gently. "That good, huh?"

"L-lethal." Tristan presses firm kisses against Olivia's shoulder. "You're perfectly lethal, Olivia." Her voice is unsteady and she's shaking, but nonetheless, she seems on a mission. Reaching around Olivia, she grabs her ass and squeezes it. Not hard, but hard enough.

"Oh." Olivia raises her hips against Tristan's.

"Beautiful." Tristan moves fast, and Olivia ends up on her stomach with Tristan on top. "Stunning." Massaging Olivia's ass with both hands now, Tristan pushes one knee, then both, between Olivia's legs. "And wet."

So, Tristan talks during sex. Olivia knows she's in trouble. Her clit has been on fire ever since Tristan came. It will probably take only one caress, and she'll go off like a rocket. Olivia doesn't want that, but she can't keep her hips from moving, undulating her pubic area against the mattress.

"Oh, no." Tristan pushes a hand between Olivia's legs, sliding her palm against her and moving it in slow circles. "This is mine. Wouldn't you agree?"

Olivia can only groan something resembling a yes. It's as if she can see herself and Tristan from a distance, and the fact that Tristan is nearly taking her from behind makes Olivia's hips begin to buck against Tristan's slick palm.

"Take me," Olivia whispers huskily. She wants Tristan to fill her up and claim her.

"You're certain?" Now it's Tristan's turn to sound out of breath. And even shocked?

"Yes. Please."

"Then turn around." Tristan moves to the side as Olivia clumsily rolls over.

"And spread your legs for me." Tristan runs a finger down Olivia's right leg.

Hearing how Tristan repeats Olivia's words from when she dried her off makes her moan as she complies.

Tristan moves back in between Olivia's legs. She draws circles with her fingertips along the inside of Olivia's thighs, bypasses her folds, and continues up to her trembling stomach. Olivia tries not to show how desperate she is, but of course, Tristan knows. She smiles down at Olivia as she slowly slides two fingers into the wetness. Her smile fades and her mouth opens. "Oh, fuck. You're so…wet. Where do you need me?"

"In-inside." Olivia gasps.

Tristan doesn't hesitate. She slips at least two fingers into Olivia and immediately curls her fingertips up toward Olivia's stomach. Picking up a steady pace, she firmly caresses that elusive spot. Shocked at how fast her orgasm begins, first as small waves and soon like full-blown convulsions, Olivia fumbles for Tristan.

Tristan, leaning against her elbow, starts to rub herself against Olivia's hip at the same pace as she pushes her fingers. She keeps the same tempo, and the first orgasm morphs into the second.

"Olivia! Oh!" Tristan cries out and pushes her pubic bone hard against Olivia, undulating as she arches. "God…"

Olivia's heart is hammering so hard she can barely hear anything else, but she has her arms around Tristan as the fingers that took her so well slowly withdraw. Olivia pushes the damp, white hair from Tristan's face and kisses her with all the tenderness she feels.

"I don't know about you," Tristan says after clearing her throat, "but I didn't expect that."

"Which part?" Olivia nuzzles Tristan's temple.

"I mean, I thought there'd be passion. I knew that. I didn't know I'd feel as if I'd been dropped into a volcano."

"Is that your way of saying we were on fire?" Olivia smiles.

"Fire is not enough. Lava."

"You have a point. I knew there'd be passion too, but the lava was…a surprise."

"Exactly." Tristan shifts and groans again. "So was finding muscle groups I haven't tapped into before."

Olivia's own muscles ache too. "Mm-hmm."

They settle into an exhausted, content silence, and after a while, Tristan pulls the duvet around them without letting go of Olivia, exhaustion getting the better of them. Olivia closes her eyes and hears Tristan turn off the last lamp.

As Olivia is nearly asleep, she feels Tristan move to lie behind her. Now comfortable, she wraps an arm around Olivia and nuzzles her neck. "Sleep well, Olivia."

"You too." Olivia slurs the words before she falls asleep.

CHAPTER THIRTY

W alking into the vast library on Promenade des Bastions 1 with Olivia, Tristan finds herself doing yet another double take when looking in Olivia's direction. She can't get over the change in her appearance. Gone is the young woman she has made love with repeatedly during the night, as they both completely disregarded how tired they were. Tristan easily confesses that, on her part, it was also both because of a deeply felt need and a knowledge that the night in Olivia's arms will be the only one.

Now, in the early afternoon, after all their errands and a beeline back to the hotel to change into their new clothes, Olivia looks nothing like the girl who applied for an internship a while back. Next to her, dressed in an expensive trouser suit over an emerald-green blouse, carrying a bougie-looking tote bag, walks this auburn-haired beauty, wearing impeccable smoky-eyes makeup.

"You're staring." Olivia smiles but doesn't turn her head.

"Can you blame me? I barely recognize you." Tristan stops by an information board and begins to look for the newspaper archives.

"That's the point, right? And you should talk."

Olivia has a point. Tristan hasn't colored her hair but wears it in an austere, combed-back do. For her clothes, she has changed her style to a more conservative look. Gone are her boots and leather messenger bag. Instead, she too wears a suit and carries a Samsonite briefcase. Where Olivia holds a high-end-brand poncho over her arm, Tristan has settled for merely unbuttoning her trench coat.

A librarian guides them to the area that holds computers and even some of the older microfilm scanners, and they sit down together in the booth, Olivia by the computer and Tristan next to her. She pulls out the ledger and places it next to the computer. Opening the page to the Carmichael page, she turns to Olivia, who has used their temporary guest card to log in.

"This is the latest name I have for Iris. Anneliese Manz." She taps the page.

"When did she die?" Olivia pulls up a list of newspapers.

"When Rosalee told me, it had been twelve days, according to her. Why don't you set the date parameters to between five to three weeks ago?"

Olivia typed fast. "Done. She said an accident, right?"

"A vehicle pileup in the Swiss Alps. She could be mistaken. It might have been a skiing accident for all we know."

"All right. Let's cast a wide net and see what we find." Olivia kept typing and then pressed enter. "Not much reported about skiing, but I would imagine they can't report every time someone breaks a leg. Several vehicular accidents during this time. And...oh. Here. Fifteen days ago there was an avalanche. It surprised the drivers coming out of a tunnel and caused a pileup. Let's check that out."

Tristan leaned closer as Olivia pulled up articles describing the accident that took two lives and injured several others. "Two women died. Does it say what ages? Anything?"

"Hang tight." Scrolling down, Olivia murmured, "One lady was a backseat passenger and a mother of small children. God. The other was alone in her car."

"That could be her." Tristan rubbed her neck.

"Let's look at the obituaries," Olivia said, typing in new commands. "She must've had someone who misses her."

"One would hope." Tristan grips the backrest of Olivia's chair, flooded with unwelcome thoughts of how many times in her life she has wondered if anyone would ever truly miss her—and why. She shakes them off when Olivia stops scrolling and taps the screen.

"Anneliese Manz. The date is correct if it was twelve days ago, plus the four since Rosalee told you. Her burial was...hey, *is* tomorrow." Wide-eyed, Olivia turned to Tristan. "Which we should attend."

Tristan blinks. Her mind has stalled on details in the obituary, and she's not quite able to follow. The obituary speaks of a husband... and a daughter? Iris had a child? It lists several family members and friends. How can this be? How can Iris, sweet and soft as far as Tristan remembered her, have broken the Amaranthine Law like this?

"Tristan?"

"What? Oh. Yes. You're right, of course."

"What's going on in your mind right now? You're pale." Olivia takes Tristan's hand, which is resting on the Carmichael page of the ledger, in hers.

"The details sidetracked me. Her blatant disregard for the rules... the law...we set. Makes me wonder what happened to the timid young girl who was the last to protest or stand her ground. See? Married. Family." Realizing she sounds stark and offended, Tristan squeezes Olivia's hand too hard, but Olivia doesn't even blink.

"She may have fallen head over heels. Or she may have felt enough time had passed. That she felt safe enough."

"And clearly that was an error in judgment." Tristan lets go of Olivia. "I'm sorry."

Olivia captures Tristan's hand and kisses it gently. "This is hard for you."

Tristan nearly chuckles at the understatement but settles for nodding. "You're right. Is there a number for the funeral home?"

Olivia holds her gaze for a moment but then finds the phone number at the bottom of the obituary. Tristan finds her burner cell and dials. A male voice answers politely in German. Tristan replies in the same language, telling him her name and that she would like to attend the services.

The man in charge of the funeral arrangements is polite and asks a few follow-up questions about how many are in Tristan's party and if they will take part in the gathering after the funeral, which is taking place at the Manz residence. Tristan tells him there will be two of them and that they indeed want to join the family gathering. She takes notes of the time and the addresses to the church and Iris's home, feeling a pang of guilt while doing so, but tells herself that Iris would have understood.

"I don't speak much German, but I got the gist of it," Olivia says after Tristan disconnects.

"We are expected tomorrow and are welcome to the reception at the Manz estate." Tristan puts down her pen before her trembling fingers send it to the floor.

"Feels weird to crash a funeral like this, but I don't see what other choice we have." Leaning back in her chair, Olivia sighs. "I can tell you feel the same way."

Tristan merely nods.

"I do think there was foul play behind her death." Olivia chews her lower lip. "I mean, the timing is suspect, if nothing else."

"I do. Not sure how, or why, or even if this idea of Trudy and Caroline somehow surviving the hanging can be applied to this situation, but we have to figure it out."

"It makes my head spin to even contemplate them being alive— and carrying on with their evil ways all this time. I hope I'm wrong. I really do. After my reckless years, I did turn my life around, but if Trudy and Caroline are alive...I doubt they have."

"What changed for you?" Olivia asks quietly. "You never quite said."

"It wasn't just one thing. It started when I found out my sister had passed at the age of eighty-three. She had lived a full life and left four children, sixteen grandchildren, and fifty-two great-grandchildren. This information made me take stock. What did I have to show for my eternal youth? I was seventy-five and looked twenty. I attended her funeral, and her oldest son, Laurence, somehow realized who I was. I was ready to bolt, but his reaction wasn't based on fear, anger, or hatred, but rooted in compassion. He pulled me aside and told me how much Corinne had protested how the village treated me—and the rest of the girls—everything that took place when it became obvious we weren't aging. Among her children, he was the one she had confided in, trusted him to know the truth, I suppose. He begged me to stay in touch." Tristan swallows, hating the tears filling her eyes, threatening to spill over. "I did until he passed away, eighteen years later. He was my last link to my family."

Olivia's tears are even less obedient than Tristan's, flowing freely down her cheeks as she patiently waits for the rest of the story.

"Those decades, corresponding with Laurence, confirmed and became the basis for how I've lived my different lives since then. Carefully, consistently, and always looking over my shoulder."

Olivia doesn't offer any platitudes or sticky comments of attempted comfort, which is a relief. She merely runs gentle fingertips against the back of Tristan's hand, showing she's listening intently.

"I don't know the exact inner journey for the other girls from the ship, but it is safe to say that for Trudy and Caroline, they never considered their own safety nor that of others. They notoriously flaunted their eternal youth, and there should be old newspaper articles about them because of that type of behavior."

"But do you really think they can have survived the hangings? It sounds impossible. But so does a lot when it comes to your life, so who am I to argue? It clearly isn't impossible." Olivia wipes her own tears away, and then she gently brushes her thumbs against Tristan's cheekbones. "So, we have to dig deeper when we return to the US." Olivia lowers her leg and then presses her lips to Tristan's cheek. Lingers. Warmth spreads from that caress to the deep niches of Tristan's chest. Before Olivia, she was always cold. Now, all Olivia has to do is touch her, even in the most innocent of ways, and this happens.

Tristan understands fully now that Olivia won't back down when they go home to New York. She's adamant about seeing this through with Tristan. Looking down at her ledger, Tristan reminds herself of the Amaranthine Law. She's managed to heed it for so many years by never straying from it, and when it comes to Olivia, she has to become even stronger in her resolve. For centuries, she has abided by it to save herself from unspeakable pain, but now, nothing is more important to her than protecting this woman.

CHAPTER THIRTY-ONE

That evening, Liv immerses herself in the ledger. She merely places her hand on the embossed leather cover and looks over at Tristan, who doesn't even hesitate, but nods. Tristan is by the small table, poring over a map that she got from the hotel concierge and going online on her burner phone. Watching Tristan squint at the phone, Liv stops on her way to the couch.

"Tristan, I'm an idiot."

Tristan snaps her head up, frowning. "Excuse me?"

"You're killing your eyes trying to read everything off the phone. Why don't you log onto the hotel Wi-Fi—"

"It's not safe, darling."

The term of endearment nearly makes Liv lose her train of thought, but she manages to remain collected. "I realize that. But you can borrow my VPN server. It's one of the best. Anyway, that means you can use your tablet without the hassle of using your phone as a hotspot."

Tristan smiles now. "I'll gladly accept." She pulls out her ten-inch tablet and boots it. Liv walks over and enters her password.

"There. You should automatically be logged in as soon as you have Wi-Fi access."

"Oh, this is better." Tristan goes into a browser and seems to forget about Liv standing right next to her. As Liv picks up the ledger again, Tristan's hand shoots out and takes Liv's by the wrist. "Thank you."

Liv bends and kisses the top of Tristan's head before walking over to the couch. Curling up in the corner closest to the window, she opens the ledger to the journal section. The handwriting changes slowly as the narrative progresses, and when Liv reaches the time during the hanging of Trudy and Caroline, it is far easier to read. She only skims over the passages about Caroline and Trudy's executions, as she has already reviewed that event, but as she turns the fragile pages, she comes upon another entry that catches her eye. Here, the ink is smudged in some places. Liv's chest caves in. Perhaps Tristan cried while writing.

Philadelphia, December 24, 1888

I picture them, my nieces and nephews, and their children and grandchildren, especially the small ones, as they eagerly look forward to Christmas Day. Many of my memories of childhood are hazy, or distant, as if they belong to someone else who kindly retold them to me. I do, however, remember my excitement on this day, Christmas Eve, when I knew my parents were being deliberately secretive to heighten my and Corinne's anticipation. I could barely sleep, even if I tried very hard, to make the night go faster. I listened to every footstep making the floorboards creak, as one of my parents put them out during the night. This was before the tradition of Christmas stockings or the Christmas tree, of course. My parents placed our presents beside the fireplace, and that's where Corinne and I sat in the morning and opened them, while having our oatmeal and hot tea. Mother would, on this special morning, put extra sugar in our oatmeal and, if she could find it in the mercantile, some cinnamon sticks, for flavor.

My most precious present as a little girl, and this was our first Christmas in the log cabin our father built with the help of neighbors, was a doll my mother made. Her body was sewn of scrap fabric and, I found out later, one of Mother's blouses that she cut to pieces for the doll's dress and undergarments. Her hair was made of yarn, which I believe came from one of my father's old socks that she pulled apart, attached to the doll's head, and combed until it looked like angel hair. Mother worked on the doll, whom I named Clarice, in the poor light from the candles as soon as I was in bed. At the same time, she sewed a new dress for Corinne, also from an old dress of her own.

I loved Clarice. She proved to me that my strict and sarcastically inclined mother loved me. Not that I truly doubted it, but after the incident with the illness on the ship, I harbored a fear that my parents' feelings toward me would change. They did, to a degree, but not in a way that truly mattered. They never berated me for the slow progression of my aging. They defended me against anyone who ventured a hostile opinion. And it was because of that attitude, as they grew older, that I had to leave. I had to protect them from the onslaught of accusations and questions about me, their youngest daughter.

I didn't tell anyone except Mother of my plans. She gave me money she had set aside for this purpose, which she claimed she always knew would come. Together with my own savings, I had enough to take the stagecoach to New York, where I planned to disappear into the anonymous crowd. I left Father and Corinne a letter each—I'm afraid rather lengthy and nostalgic letters that might have upset, rather than reassured, them. I hoped Mother would be able to explain why it had to be this way.

Now the only family member who knew the truth about me has been dead and gone for more than a quarter of a century. Why does it strike me tonight, this year when so much time has gone by? Is it because, for the first time since we arrived in America, to our supposedly new and bright shining future, two of us girls have died? The sisters, Trudy and Caroline, were hanged earlier this year, only weeks apart, and I was there, far back in the crowd, to witness their hanging. Now here I sit on Christmas Eve, coming close to wishing it was me who was laid to rest next to my parents, my sister, and her oldest, Laurence. I do, however, leave that up to my maker. This is a private vow that I've once and for all made. I will not take my own life.

Again, my thoughts drift to the small group of families that protect Corinne's loved ones. They're hardworking, good people, but I don't know them. If they come across any of my letters to Laurence, though I implored him to burn them,

I hope they think they're the ramblings of some stranger. I doubt anyone in that small Massachusetts town remembers me, or the rumors about me.

Here, there's an ink spot that makes Liv think Tristan stopped, her quill resting on the paper, to consider her words.

But there is also a risk that if they do, they'll make the connection with the rumors about Trudy and Caroline Jenkins. It's enough of a risk, at least, to make me stay away. And what could I possibly say that makes sense to them should I attempt a visit? Perhaps one day, once the speculations about the sisters have died down, I might visit my hometown incognito.

And now it has just dawned on me. If I wait long enough, I can go back under my original name, Sarah Duncan, and nobody will be the wiser. The undeniable fact is, I am once and for all erased from history in a way that's even more efficient than death.

Liv can barely breathe at the anguish and fatigue in the words Tristan once wrote. She wants to rush over and reassure her this is no longer true. That it never was. A voice inside keeps her from moving, telling her to calm down. They have more urgent matters to handle than this subject right now.

After another hour, Liv stretches, having to almost shake her head to shift out of the world Tristan's journal has taken her to. Reading about her struggles and triumphs has been inspirational and heartbreaking. Liv thinks the red thread throughout this part of the ledger is how resilient and passionate Tristan has remained amidst loneliness and bouts of depression.

"I'm done," Tristan says from the table, putting down her tablet. "Are you hungry?"

"Not really. I ate too much when we ordered room service." Liv stands up. "But I need a break. I've read a lot, and I need to…process."

"Oh?" Tristan pushes the chair away from the table and leans back. "Something in particular?"

"Why don't I mull it over before we discuss it?" Liv walks over to Tristan and steps between her and the table, leaning against it. "You ready for bed?" she murmurs.

Tristan colors faintly and stands. Stepping in between Liv's legs, she cups her cheeks and kisses her lips. "I've been ready for quite some time."

Liv's own cheeks warm now, and Tristan chuckles quietly, deep in her throat. Then she slides her lips along Liv's neck, nipping lightly only to soothe the almost-sharp sensation with her tongue. "If you only knew how much I've thought of doing this. Despite everything, this…" Tristan captures Liv's earlobe and tugs at it gently with her teeth. "Like this. Tasting you."

Liv eventually regains control of her muscles and wraps her arms around Tristan. "Glad it's not just me." Thank goodness, despite her words at the library, Tristan's not rejecting her. Yet. Forcing that last little word out of her mind, as thinking about it will surely be a slide down a chute to perpetual heartbreak, Liv wraps her legs around Tristan and kisses her. Deep, probing, the kisses are of the best kind. She simply wants to taste, caress, and lose herself in the sensation of being the sole focus of this amazing, beautiful woman.

"Liv…" Tristan's voice offers a benediction, so soft, husky, and filled with enough pent-up emotions to bring far too much hope to Liv. Hope that Tristan will realize how amazing and unique this feeling between them is.

"I'm here." Liv parts her legs, and Tristan's hand is there, right at the junction, cupping her. "Ah!" Liv tips her head back, arching against Tristan, who bends and closes her teeth around Liv's left nipple through the thin layers of fabric.

Tristan moans, and the reverberations travel through Liv's entire body. Suddenly, her clothes are stifling her. Her skin is as sensitive as if flames are licking her, and Liv is grateful when agile fingers unbutton the blouse and pull it off her. Tristan then unzips Liv's suit slacks and wraps an arm around Liv's waist, tugging her up enough to shove the slacks down. Liv kicks them off her stocking-clad feet, glad she's wearing thigh-highs.

"Sweet Jesus," Tristan gasps, and her hands are back between Liv's thighs. "So hot."

"Right…there." Liv leans back on her hands, her legs spread wide. She's still wearing her panties, but that doesn't stop Tristan, who eases them aside. She slides one hand under Liv's bra and merely pushes it up above her breasts. At the same time, the fingers of her other hand find their way between Liv's folds, searching for and finding her clit.

"Yes. There." Tristan's eyes narrow as she locks her gaze on Liv while starting maddening caresses. She fondles Liv's breasts, one at a time, tormenting her erect nipples until they're a deep red and screaming for Tristan's mouth. Liv can hardly breathe when the fingers of Tristan's other hand roll her clitoris, then dip into the moisture, only to return and start all over again. Over and over, she does this, keeping Liv on the precipice until she's sobbing.

"Please…" Liv can barely speak. Her arms can't hold her up much longer.

"You never have to beg with me. Just tell me what you want," Tristan says, breathing so fast now, she's trembling.

"I'm so close." Liv tries to put her need into words. "Go…inside."

Tristan shifts her stance and moves closer. "Hold on to me." She abandons Liv's oversensitized breasts and wraps her arm around Liv's shoulders. Positioning her fingers at Liv's entrance, she slowly moves inside with enough fingers to make it burn in the best of ways. Liv wraps her arms and legs around Tristan, grateful to change position, and the closeness is really all it takes. Chest to chest, Tristan fully clothed and Liv in complete disarray, they kiss as Tristan starts thrusting her hand faster and faster. She's hitting all the right nerve endings, and her thumb intermittently strokes Liv's clit. Liv's world shrinks to hosting only her and Tristan and how they're feeling right now. The pleasure, the way they move against each other, taste each other…nothing can compare to this.

And then she comes. Liv clings to Tristan and hides her scream against the damp, fragrant skin on her neck. She convulses, jerks, and inside her, the contractions pull Tristan's fingers farther in until Liv is spent.

"My God," Tristan gasps, holding Liv tight. It's impossible to judge who's doing most of the trembling. They're both shaking, and Liv can see, as she slowly calms down a little, that Tristan is so turned on, sweat is beading on her temples and upper lip.

"So good," Liv manages to say as her breathing is less labored. "And…my turn."

"What?" Tristan looks up, glassy-eyed and clearly unable to let go.

Liv shifts and turns them around. She makes sure Tristan is perched against the table, since there is simply no time for them to move to the bedroom, yet. Unzipping Tristan's slacks, she does what Tristan did earlier and pushes them off her. She kneels before Tristan and helps her out of her shoes and slacks. Single-mindedly, Liv pulls off Tristan's panties and tosses them onto the chair next to her.

Still kneeling, Liv smiles up at Tristan. "Open your legs for me." She doesn't make it an order, despite the words, more of a strongly desired request, but Tristan responds immediately and does as Liv asks. Without hesitation, Liv parts the folds with her hands and clamps her mouth over the swollen clit that protrudes enough for her to wrap her lips around it. Caressing Tristan's thighs gently, Liv makes sure Tristan knows she's not going to stop until Tristan has come—or tells her to—whichever happens first.

"Olivia!" Tristan buries her fingers in Liv's hair. She undulates against Liv, keening unintelligible words until she grows rigid. "Oh!"

Liv feels the pulsations and softens the way her tongue glides and flicks over Tristan's rock-hard clit. Eventually, as Tristan's knees look like they're losing cohesion, she stands, finding herself rather wobbly as well, and hugs Tristan close. "I have you."

"You...sure do," Tristan says, clutching Liv. "Don't let go."

The last words pierce Liv's soul and also fill her with tenderness. "I won't," she whispers and wonders if Tristan hears the resolve and sacred promise in her voice. "I won't let go."

CHAPTER THIRTY-TWO

The drive to the funeral, held on the north side of Lac Léman on the way to Montreux, takes exactly one hour and forty-seven minutes. Tristan knows this as Olivia's driving, and she has very little else to do but check the time. Around them, the beautiful scenery of the lake and the Swiss landscape should attract some of her attention, but her mind goes only inward right now.

Tristan remembers the shy little girl that was Iris. How she clung to her mother's skirts. How the raucous laughter of the men aboard the ship made her shrink and hide. How this child, later an ethereally beautiful woman, could survive the illness that tore through small bodies as if they were set aflame. But she did. She lived on to be almost two hundred and fifty years old, only to have her life snuffed out by a car crash caused by an avalanche. Tristan balls her hands into fists, forcing herself to breathe calmly.

Apparently, this mood doesn't escape Olivia, who places a hand on Tristan's left. "You're nervous?"

"No." Tristan wills the muscles around her jaws to relax enough to make it possible for her to speak. "Furious."

"About?"

"How Iris died. I've been injured in my life, on a few occasions, so badly, the physicians predicted it impossible for me to recover. How can a car crash injure her so drastically that she doesn't recover? Trust me, we're not easy to kill, we girls from the ship."

"What does it take?" Olivia asks quietly, her hand shaking now.

Tristan loathes this subject but realizes that going to a funeral for someone who is her peer brings it center stage. "As there are only two of us left, that we know of, obviously death is possible. Decapitation. Exsanguination. Generally depriving the brain of blood for an extended time, so, in theory, strangulation. And gorier imagery that I won't disgust you with."

"I can...imagine." Olivia swallows audibly but keeps her hand on Tristan's. "Is this why you think hanging may not have been enough when it comes to Trudy and Caroline?"

"It's a theory."

They continue in silence for the next few miles. Then Olivia squeezes Tristan's hand and runs her thumb over her knuckles. "Did you mean it...last night?"

Tristan blinks as the question takes her off guard, and she's not sure what Olivia means. "Excuse me?"

"Did you mean it when you asked me not to let go? Or was that... sort of in the moment?" Olivia's tone is matter-of-fact, but the fine tremors in her hand show she's not.

Tristan doesn't know how to respond. No, that's not correct. She knows exactly how she wants to reply to Olivia's brave question, but that's not the same thing. A quick glance at the stunning, temporarily auburn-haired woman next to her makes it impossible to lie. "I shouldn't mean it." Tristan's not prepared to say more, but she can tell from how the tension around Olivia's mouth relaxes that she understands. Does Olivia also realize that it's a non-answer? Probably.

They locate the church, which is beautiful and ornate, and parking doesn't pose a problem. Together with Olivia, Tristan enters the building, and they find seats among the multitude of attendees. In front of the altar sits Iris's casket, white and adorned with white carnations, pink baby's breath, and peach tulips. The color scheme is springlike, rather than wintry, which perhaps speaks of her taste, or maybe of her family's preferences.

After a while, the organist starts playing, and the ceremony commences. Tristan listens to the priest while stealthily scanning the faces in the crowd. She doesn't recognize anyone, but she's on edge, and she trusts the instincts that she's honed for so many years.

The priest pauses and motions toward the first pew. "And now we'll hear some words from Anneliese's daughter, Camille."

A woman in her mid-twenties walks up to the podium to the right of the casket. She is pale, her eyes watery, but she manages a wobbly smile as she smooths out a wrinkled paper before her. She gently clears her throat. "My mother, Anneliese, has to have had the gentlest soul, the kindest spirit. She never met anyone she didn't like, or who didn't end up adoring her. Mother could come off as very shy at first, but once you got to know her, she ended up being your best friend. Losing her has changed my life, and that of my family's, forever, and…the loss is irreparable."

Camille continues to talk about Iris, of her accomplishments, her humanity, and how she and her father had a long road ahead of them, learning to live without her.

As Camille returns to her seat and the priest takes over, Olivia turns to Tristan. "Biological daughter?" she mouths.

"Adopted?" Tristan whispers back.

The ceremony takes a little less than an hour, and then the family and close friends begin walking out of the church. Tristan and Olivia follow among the last ones, and as they do, a man bumps into Tristan, making her stumble.

The man apologizes but also grabs her arm rather brusquely.

Tristan yanks her arm free and glares at the man who dares to touch her, no matter the reason. She goes cold. This face is familiar. She can't say exactly where she's seen him before, but she has. Her mind is racing, but she stays composed as she moves along with the rest of the funeral attendees. "It's quite all right," she replies in French. "Think nothing of it."

Olivia is by Tristan's side, and if looks could kill, the man would self-combust from the way Olivia's gaze singes him.

They get out of the church without any further incident and watch as Iris's casket is loaded into the hearse. Springtime flowers adorn it too. Most obvious among the mourners, a tall, salt-and-pepper-haired man stands with his arm around Camille. She's weeping softly against his shoulder, and he kisses the top of her head. This must be Iris's husband. From the obituary, she knows his name is Mikael Manz.

Watching the hearse move to ready itself for the caravan of cars with mourners, Tristan takes Olivia's hand. "We'll go to the cemetery but keep our distance. It's enough that we intend to infringe on this family at the house later."

"Agreed."

They walk back to the parking lot among the other people and wait until all the cars have left before Olivia pulls out. Only then does Tristan realize that yet another car, a black BMW, has waited and is now right behind them. She pulls up a compact and directs the mirror to the back over her shoulder.

"I see them," Olivia says calmly. "They drove slowly, as if to let everyone else pass. I was going to let them pass, but they stopped."

"Unsurprisingly, the man who stepped into me at the church is behind the wheel." Tristan snaps the compact closed. "I suggest we keep a little nearer the mourners than we originally planned. We can't risk finding ourselves alone with our potential stalker."

"Stalkers. Plural. If it's that guy, he's got two others with him in the car." Olivia thuds the back of her head against the seat. "Did we walk straight into a trap by coming here?"

Tristan sighs. "Perhaps."

CHAPTER THIRTY-THREE

After shivering in the outer ring of the mourners around Iris's grave, it is a relief to be indoors. The Manz residence is in a wealthy neighborhood, and with its Scandinavian interior configuration, it speaks of an interest in modern design. A fire in the double-sided fireplace warms Liv, who stands to the side, watching Tristan exchange niceties with some of the other guests.

"Are you a friend of my wife?" a pleasant baritone voice asks in German, making Liv jump. She turns, clinging to her cup of coffee. Of course. Iris's husband. For a startling second, Liv's mind is blank, but then she manages a smile. "Herr Manz." Changing to English, Liv continues. "I'm so sorry for your loss. And no, I didn't have the pleasure of knowing your wife, but my friend over there did." She motions to where Tristan stands, noticing her slight alarm.

"I see." Manz looks at Tristan, who now is walking toward them.

"You must be Mikael," Tristan says easily in German. "I'm Tory Kline. I'm so sorry for your loss. I had hoped to one day make your acquaintance under much more pleasant circumstances."

"Tory Kline?" Mikael blinks as he takes her in, his gaze stopping at her briefcase. "I'm sorry, but I don't think Anneliese ever mentioned you."

"Our contact was sporadic, at best, but when we spoke, it was like no time had passed at all. I guess that can be the case when you've known each other for so many years."

"You were childhood friends?" Mikael goes rigid, a light in his eyes that wasn't there before. "This is amazing."

Liv can't figure out what this interchange means. She keeps her attention on the nuances and undertones of what is being said, not wanting to miss a thing.

"How so?" Tristan asks gently.

"My Anneliese was a very private woman. The kindest, most gentle person I've ever met, but…secretive. To learn of a childhood friend…I have so many questions!" Mikael gestures to a door to the left of the fireplace. "Can I persuade you to join me in the library? Just for a moment. I've greeted all the guests, and to be honest, I need a little break." He did look exhausted, and the blue semicircles under his eyes spoke of sleepless nights and tears.

"But of course. Is it all right if my partner joins us?"

"Certainly." Mikael motions for them to follow him. As they enter the library, Liv is impressed with the floor-to-ceiling bookshelves that line all the walls, even framing the windows. "Please. Have a seat."

Four armchairs sit in front of the fireplace, which is built to be enjoyed from either side of the wall. Liv sits down to Tristan's left, which puts her directly in front of Mikael Manz.

"Where did you meet Anneliese? Was it already in the US?" Mikael kindly provides Tristan with a clue about what Iris may already have told her husband.

"Yes. In a small village on the East Coast. We weren't neighbors but saw each other often," Tristan says softly. "We went to church with our families and the same with picnics and church outings. And to school of course. We belonged to the same group of friends. She was very intelligent if you took the time to know her. She was shy already back then."

"Oh, my poor darling. Yes, she was. I had to ask her out four times before she said yes, twelve years ago. She always used to say I wore her down. I suppose that's right. It's just…after I met her, there couldn't be anyone else." Mikael wipes at the corners of his eyes. "When did she leave for Europe?"

Liv holds her breath, wondering what Tristan will say. "The last time I saw her, we spoke of our futures and what we'd end up doing." Speaking easily, Tristan uses a tone that tells Liv there is some truth to what she's saying. "I think Anneliese left the US when she was barely of age. She was set on finding a new life—supporting herself, working toward a career before anything else."

"That's what I thought when I met her. She owned a set of art galleries, and I visited one with my daughter, Camille. Camille's mother and I divorced when she was only two, and after that it was the two of us until we met Anneliese. I think Camille fell in love with her at the same moment I did. And once Anneliese dared to trust me, she returned the feelings. She and Camille were inseparable." Mikael reaches for a pack of tissues in his pocket and wipes his nose and eyes. "What was she like as a young girl?"

"As you say, shy. Painfully so, at times. Her father could be very strict, and I know that frightened her."

"This correlates with how she was as a grown woman. I always wondered if she had an authoritative person in her past. Even some trauma. I suppose I may have been a coward for not asking, but it was as if she had this invisible wall around her. She gave so much of herself in other ways, I felt disrespectful and presumptuous about asking for more."

"I'm so sorry you lost her through this horrible accident, Mikael," Liv said softly.

His face changes as his mouth turns into a grimace. "Accident," he growled. "I could have lived with it being an accident."

Liv flinched. "I'm sorry. It wasn't?"

"The police say it was, but it's a ridiculous assumption, and I finally reached out to my friend in Geneva who is a forensic expert. I demanded he examine her body before the funeral, and he did so two days ago. He claims there is no way her seat belt could have strangled her the way it did without it being manipulated." Mikael lowers his voice into a whisper. "She was murdered, and my friend is going to help me force the local police to finally start investigating."

"Father." Camille steps into the room. She's tall, her hair a golden blond, perfectly coiffed. "Please, not today."

"But, Camille, you know it's true. Your mother deserves justice." Mikael's eyes fill with tears.

"I know, but come out and join our guests. They want to talk to you, be of what comfort they can." Camille tugs at his hand.

"All right, darling. Of course." Mikael wipes at his eyes with his wrinkled tissue and then tosses it into a bin. "Thank you, Tory, for talking to me. And you, Olivia. I'm glad at least one of Anneliese's friends cared enough about her to come all this way." He squares his shoulders and walks back to his guests.

"He's right." Camille's lips are tense, pale. "Mother wasn't hit by the avalanche. A car behind hers slammed into hers, pushing it into the one before her, but it wasn't a high-impact collision. Yet the seat belt was found looped around her neck and…it was too late."

Tristan nods slowly. "Can you think of anyone who might want to harm her?"

"My mother had no enemies." Camille's eyes harden. "But I think she had a stalker."

Liv forces herself not to let her reaction show, but Tristan's hands jerk. "Did Anneliese say something about that also?"

Camille sits down, and it is as if she has waited to talk about the matter of her mother's death to someone. Perhaps it is easier for her, as Liv and Tristan are strangers. "She didn't. And if she knew about it, she wouldn't have. My mother kept many secrets, far more than my father ever knew."

"But you know." Tristan's voice is softer yet.

"I made it my business to know." Setting her jaw in a clear challenge, Camille looks firmly at them. "Before we met Anneliese, it was just my father and me. I love him, and he did his best for me, but I missed my mother…or, perhaps I should say, I missed what she could have been." She sighed. "You know when you do a jigsaw puzzle and you're missing just one piece, the one that will make everything make sense and fit perfectly. That was Anneliese. She fit perfectly with my father and, even more, I think, with me. I made it my business from the age of eight to protect her."

Liv's heart ached for the eight-year-old, and for the young woman sitting in front of them. She knew about parents not being what you need and wish. In her case, they lived in Boston, alive and well, but not ready to accept her sexual orientation or career choice. Some days Liv wasn't sure which hurt the most. Now she saw her pain mirrored and emphasized in Camille's eyes.

"What led you to believe she was stalked?" Tristan asked, leaning forward.

Camille seemed relieved. Most likely because neither of them scoffed at her words.

"Someone vandalized her art here in Montreux at one point. They didn't steal anything, but they ransacked her office. After that, she became what Father considered paranoid. She bought stuff to protect herself with. You know. Pepper spray. An alarm for her keychain that could scream bloody murder if you pulled the pin. She upgraded the house alarm and insisted we should always park our respective cars in the garage, etc. I figured that if she was this frightened, she must have a reason. Yes, my mother had an aura of being frail, but she was no fool. On the contrary."

"And where was she going when the avalanche hit?" Tristan locks her gaze on Camille.

"Mother was on her way home from a client. She called as she was leaving, and she was unusually angry…or irritated, maybe that's a better word. After driving all the way up into the Alps, taking the client several paintings to choose from, as he wanted to make the selection in his home to get it right, he wasn't there. She couldn't reach him on the phone and eventually decided to drive back home."

"And then the 'accident' happened?"

"Yes." Now the tears spill over for Camille. Liv can't take it and rounds Tristan's chair, crouching next to Camille.

"Thank you for telling us. We believe you. We believe your father. Just so you know." She gently strokes Camille's arm.

"Thank you. Both Father and I have felt as if we're going crazy. Especially since the police ruled it an accident so quickly. That is insane, as a witness told the press they'd heard a rifle go off just before the avalanche. And the person who hit Mother with his car was nowhere to be found. The police spoke of how common it is for people to be so shocked after an accident that they simply walk home. In the middle of nowhere in the Alps, where an avalanche had just happened?"

"Ridiculous," Tristan says. "Your mother's death sounds highly suspicious. And whether there's a new investigation or not, please take it all seriously. Keep up your mother's safety measures, and don't go anywhere alone as she did. That's my best advice."

Camilla gapes. "Who are you two? I mean, who are you *really*?"

"I did grow up near your mother. We're as eager as you to discover why and how she died. I can't tell you more than that. I'm sorry." Tristan shakes her head.

Camille stands. "All right. So, you've shared a few things but also created more questions. More secrets. Will I ever find out the whole truth about Mother?" She looks so forlorn and hurt, Liv wants to hug her.

Tristan is quiet for a few beats but then clears her throat. "If I feel the danger is over and the time's right, I'll return and speak with you and your father and answer as many questions as I can. This will entail the two of you keeping an open mind, but if this is what you truly want…I'll try to accommodate you."

Camille nods slowly and then extends her hand. "Thank you for coming, Tory. Olivia." She shakes Liv's hand as well. "I suppose it's my turn to tell you to be safe as well."

"We'll do our best," Tristan says and then makes her way out of the library and through the throng of mourners. They say good-bye to Mikael as they pass him on their way toward the hallway. There, she pulls on her coat and gloves before turning to Liv. "Now we just have to make sure we shake the men in the BMW. I wouldn't be surprised if they're circling this area."

Liv follows Tristan out the door, the crisp air from the mountains filling her lungs instantly, making her gasp. "And if they catch up with us?"

"A BMW against our rental car? Let's hope we can outsmart them, because we sure can't outrun them. You ready to keep driving, or should I?"

Liv pulls out the keys and is just about to hand them over when she detects fine tremors in Tristan's hand. "I'll drive. I need you on the map. You're far better at that than I am."

Tristan grips her briefcase harder. "All right. Shotgun it is."

CHAPTER THIRTY-FOUR

They drive back toward Geneva but soon realize they need to stop and eat somewhere. The roadside taverna is in open terrain enough for them to feel secure, and Olivia pulls into the parking lot. Tristan has begun to loathe carrying around her heavy briefcase but brings it with her, as she refuses to leave her ledger in the car.

Choosing sandwiches to save time, they opt for a booth in the far corner. Tristan makes sure she can see everyone coming and going, and she can tell Olivia is just as wary.

"Camille is a fantastic young woman," Tristan says after eating in silence for a few moments. "Strong and observant. I wonder how much she truly knows."

"Did you get the impression she was holding something back?" Olivia pulls a thick slice of cheese from her sandwich and puts it aside before taking a bite.

"I could be wrong, but I did get how incredibly close she was to Iris. It was as if she was the dream stepmother, a fulfillment of a little girl's desire for a mother. I doubt Iris broke any of the Amaranthine Laws by telling her the truth, but the girl's not stupid. She could have sensed something was, well, if not off, then at least different."

Olivia stops eating, her eyes darkening. "Do you think the stalkers will go after Mikael or Camille?"

Tristan considers the possibility but then shakes her head. "What would they gain? The damage is done, whether it was a homicide or not. Iris is gone, which means they succeeded, if that was their goal. Still, I'm glad I urged them to be careful."

"Do you believe that's the stalkers' goal for you? Death?" Olivia clenches her utensils, still wrapped in a napkin, and Tristan doesn't think she's aware of her action.

"Depends on who they are. The spookier the theory, the more dire the consequences, maybe." Finishing her subpar sandwich, having settled for fixing the hunger rather than having a culinary experience, Tristan pulls out her burner phone to check the time. "We have to return to the US. Flights may still be available if we're lucky. Here in Europe, we have only Iris, who's dead, and Rosalee, who's in hiding. If we go back home, we can try to search through records and find out how the rest of the more recent deaths happened. Before Iris, two more passed away in modern times, and by that, I mean after World War One."

"You don't think we can find more useful information if we remain here, or go back to London, or even Paris?" Olivia pushes her plate away, leaving a third of her sandwich.

"I can't be sure, but logically, it seems safer there as well." Safer for Olivia, which mattered more than anything else.

"All right. Back to Geneva first, then. Will you get us tickets while we drive?"

"I'd prefer to buy them at the last moment, in case they have a way of tracking bookings, but that will mean being vulnerable while waiting around at an airport." Tristan takes her briefcase and tucks her phone into her pocket.

When they reach the car, they both study the parking lot, but it's impossible to judge which one of several dark BMWs could be the one they saw in Montreux. After starting the car, Olivia pulls out before either of them is fully strapped in.

Back on the road, Tristan shifts in her seat, sitting half-turned toward Olivia. This way, she can keep an eye on who's behind them. She sees no BMW, but after a short while, she frowns as another type of car, a silver metallic Mercedes, keeps a consistent distance two cars behind them.

"Change lanes and pass a few cars." Tristan doesn't take her eyes off the Mercedes.

Olivia complies and weaves in and out between a few cars, speeding up. Tristan glances at the speedometer, hoping Olivia's not pushing it too far and thus attracting unwanted attention from traffic cops.

"I'm ten kilometers above the limit. I'll slow down once I pass this truck." Olivia is calm and collected, and now Tristan sees the Mercedes mirror their maneuver.

"That them?" Olivia asks after glancing in the outer rearview mirror. "Silver car. Mercedes?"

"Perhaps. It's either that or they fancy your driving style and want to mimic it."

"What's our plan?"

"If we take the highway all the way into Geneva and to the airport, we tip our hand. If we exit at the nearest ramp, if it's them, they'll follow, and we might be able to lose them. Unless there are more of them, and they have additional units waiting to spot us along the highway, once we get back on again."

"Can you find an alternative route to the airport? Or are they just as likely to have posted some lookout there? Fuck. We don't know if this is a two-man job or if they're utilizing an entire army."

Tristan smiles wryly. "Probably not an army, but perhaps more personnel than we realize."

"We won't reach Geneva for an hour or so. Perhaps less." Olivia overtakes another tractor-trailer truck. So does the Mercedes and several other cars, but as some of the other cars overtake Olivia when she is back in the right lane, the Mercedes moves in behind them, again, two cars back.

Tristan accesses the map function of her phone, rather than messing with the in-car GPS. "A dense residential area is coming up in a few miles. From what I see, it's quite the labyrinth. If we're going to be able to shake them, that's it. Once we feel we've lost them, we can double back and go around the lake on the other side." She's annoyed at herself for not thinking of this option sooner. It's unimaginative to use the same route back, and this choice makes her and Olivia sitting ducks for those trying to catch them. "It's not this exit, but the next one."

"Should I speed up and get to it quicker?" Olivia glances over at Tristan. She's gripping the wheel harder than normal but sounds calm.

"No. Keep the same pace, and if it's safe, turn onto the ramp at the very last second. If they're lulled into thinking we don't know they're there, they might just be too slow to react, which will buy us time."

"All right. Be ready, then."

They keep driving down the highway at the allowed speed,

Tristan peering around the corner of her neck rest to keep an eye on the Mercedes.

"Coming up now. There's one car in the exit lane, but they're pretty far back. Here we go!" Olivia turns the wheel when they've already gone a bit too far, hitting the white paint picturing a chevron triangle on the asphalt. The wheels clatter loudly against the uneven surface.

Tristan is prepared but still finds herself tossed toward Olivia. Not wanting to grab Olivia's arm and knock her off balance, she turns and clings to the driver's-seat neck rest with both hands, pushing herself away from it.

"They still there? Did we lose them?" Olivia gasps as she struggles to curb a skid. Behind them, several drivers honk, understandably upset at their dangerous driving.

"Wait. I can't see." Tristan straightens and turns to look. Behind them is a large SUV with a couple in the front seat, gesturing wildly at them in an unmistakable, universal way of saying "are you people insane?" The SUV obscures the ramp behind it, and Tristan turns to try to look past the big vehicle in the right-outer-rearview mirror. "I can't see them, but the way the ramp curves, I can't be sure. Can you see anything in your mirror?"

"No. From my perspective, it's us and the upset people behind us."

Tristan begins to slowly relax and rights herself in her seat. "Take a right at the top of the ramp. No matter what, that's the direction we need to go—back north, for now."

After another hundred yards, they reach an intersection, and as Olivia speeds up after turning right, a silver-tinted shadow passes them on screaming wheels and then cuts them off. Not having a chance to stop in time, Olivia drives right into the Mercedes's passenger door.

CHAPTER THIRTY-FIVE

Liv can't see. Something is in her eyes, and she wipes furiously at them. A sharp sound follows the loud crash when she plowed into the Mercedes, and white dust now fills the air.

"Airbags," she murmurs and coughs. She blinks and sees a half-deflated airbag hanging from the wheel. To her left, other airbags have deployed from the seat and in front of the side window like a curtain. Flinching, she turns to Tristan, and the movement makes her neck smart. She wasn't wearing a seat belt. A look at Tristan's slumped figure shows neither was she.

"Tristan!" Liv pulls her own legs up and out from under the wheel, glad she isn't stuck. Kneeling on her seat, she bends over Tristan. "Can you hear me?" Airbags have deployed around Tristan as well, and Liv can't see any blood. She feels along Tristan's legs, but she doesn't seem to be stuck either. Then Tristan moans and tips her head back.

"Careful," Liv says and puts her arms around Tristan. Her own heart is thundering, and her teeth are clattering. "We hit the other car."

"Mm. I...know. We need to get out of here," Tristan says and then moans. "Fuck. My neck."

"M-mine too. Careful." Liv peers through the window and sees the two people in the car she hit trying to exit it. She has struck the passenger door and, as it turns out, pushed the other car into a lamppost, which blocks the driver's door as well. As it was a two-door sports car, they can't open either one.

Tristan pulls at her door handle, and to Liv's relief, it opens. Tristan falls sideways toward the asphalt, but Liv grabs her arm. Tristan rights herself, moves her legs out, and manages to stand. "My briefcase," she says, holding her neck with one hand and supporting herself against the door with the other.

"Got it." Grabbing both their bags, Liv crawls out next to Tristan and hands her the briefcase. She glances at the Mercedes and sees one of the men, the one from the church, trying to push himself through the sunroof. "We've got to get out of here. Can you walk or, better, run?"

"I'm sure as hell going to try." Tristan steps up onto the road and begins moving in the direction they meant to go.

Liv looks across the road. "The residential area is just over that divider." She points at a raised, snow-covered area between this road and the local one. "It gives us a chance to hide. They'll catch us in no time if we're out in the open."

"All right. Let's try that." Tristan begins walking, but she's obviously dizzy.

Liv takes her arm. "Lean on me and move as fast as you can." She pulls Tristan along, feeling horrible for yanking at her, but when the men in the Mercedes get out, they won't stand a chance. They need to get as far away from the crashed cars as possible.

They reach the raised snowy bank and begin climbing over it. Their boots don't gain much traction against the slippery surface, and Tristan falls onto her knees twice. The second time, she can barely get up, and Liv has to drag her over the top so they can slide down on the other side. The snow sends chills through Liv's slacks, and she's shivering. Her hands are already numb from the cold and perhaps from the shock of the collision. After a few frantic attempts, she manages to help Tristan to her feet. Stumbling onto the local street, Liv keeps a firm grip on Tristan's waist and ruthlessly tugs her along.

"I…can't…" Tristan gasps after another fifty yards, grabbing for the narrow trunk of one of the trees lining the street with her free hand. She's clasping the handle of her briefcase with her right.

"You have to," Liv says. "Just a little longer so we can turn a corner and get out of sight. Please!"

"Oh, God." Tristan stumbles along for a few moments longer, but then she's down on her knees again.

"Tristan!" Liv cries out and tries to pull her up, but it's as if Tristan's legs have given in completely. "Please. Just a few more yards. Just a little longer." Tears of frustration and fear slide down Liv's cheek.

The sound of a car pulling up and stopping next to them makes

Liv push Tristan behind her, while still crouching. She stares up at the large, dark SUV, trembling in from what she realizes is mostly rage. If they've come to hurt Tristan, she's not going to let them near her without a fight.

The front passenger door opens, and a middle-aged woman jumps out. She's tall, lanky, and dressed in workout clothes.

The woman speaks quickly in German as she kneels next to them. Her eyes are wide, and she, like Liv, is looking back to where she and the SUV were coming from.

"Do you speak English?" Liv stands and tries to get her arms around Tristan to help her up.

"I do. My God. We saw them swerve in right in front of you!" The woman moves closer, and with her help, Tristan manages to get her legs under her and stand.

Tristan clings to Liv's arm and clutches her briefcase. "Thank you," she manages to say between gasps. "Are they coming? Do you see anyone after us, Olivia?"

Liv glances behind the SUV. "I don't think so."

"If you're talking about the men in the other car, I think one of them was stuck." The woman frowns. "I suggest you get in the backseat. You're shivering, both of you." The woman opens the back passenger door. A dog, a golden retriever, is bouncing on the seat. "Waldo! Move over!" the woman orders the dog in a firm voice, and the exuberant Waldo backs up, wagging his tail.

They help Tristan inside, and Waldo licks her cheek. Liv jumps in after Tristan, and the woman closes the door behind them. When she's back in her seat, the man at the wheel drives off, speaking in German to the woman.

Tristan straightens and tries to turn around to look behind them. Instead, she flinches and stops in midmotion. "Damn. My neck. Can you see if anyone's following?"

Liv manages, despite her sore neck, to look out the back window. Two cars are in the street, but they aren't hurrying. She can't see the two men from the Mercedes either. "I think we're good." She turns forward again. "Thank you," she says to the people in front. "You have no idea how grateful we are that you stopped."

"We saw you pull that stunt on the highway first, and I admit, Ulrich here cursed up a storm. Then the Mercedes overtook us, nearly forcing us off the road." The woman shakes her head. "Ulrich said it was two men, and one was holding what looked like a weapon. To be honest, I thought he was seeing things. When we came far enough to see you two speed off back north, suddenly, that same Mercedes was there again, cutting you off. It looked like a deliberate action, if you ask me. You were obviously trying to get away, endangering yourselves by crossing the road, despite being hurt, so, we had to see if you needed help."

"Again, thank you." Tristan sounds calmer now, and she is patting the dog next to her. "I'm Tory. This is Olivia."

"As I mentioned, this is my husband Ulrich, and my name's Naomi. The old boy slobbering all over you is Waldo. He's also sharing his fur with you, as you can tell." Naomi shakes her head. "He's never met a woman he didn't love."

Tristan smiles wanly at the adoring dog. "He's lovely."

Liv sighs, trying to think of a new plan on the fly. "Naomi? Could we possibly impose on you to drive us to the nearest car rental or a hotel?" She turns to Tristan. "Or should we try for an Uber or taxi?"

"You need a hospital, or at least, a doctor," Naomi says, and her less-talkative husband nods. "I suggest you come home with us, and I'll look you over."

"Are you a doctor?" Liv asks.

"A vet." Naomi grins. "But being a vet is my second career. I started out as a chiropractor."

"We can't impose, and as you may have guessed, some not-so-nice people are following us." Liv doesn't care if she gives away too many details. She isn't going to let their good Samaritans get into trouble because of Tristan and her.

"They were nowhere near when we picked you up. We have changed direction twice already, and nobody is following us. Right, Ulrich?" Naomi doesn't give her husband time to respond. "We have a guest room with its own bathroom. And a washing machine and tumble dryer. You can clean up and rest while we wash your clothes."

Liv looks at Tristan. "You do need rest, and if Naomi is a chiropractor, she can maybe take a look at your neck and mine too."

"I absolutely can." Naomi nods briskly. "That's settled, then. We're only five minutes from our house by now."

Knowing for certain that they have just dodged a bullet again,

Liv feels Tristan lean against her as Ulrich drives on. She wraps her arm around Tristan's shoulders, feels something warm and wet on it, and smiles, knowing without looking that Waldo has just given her his stamp of approval.

CHAPTER THIRTY-SIX

The guest room is rustic, pine the predominant material. A queen-size bed sits in the corner, and a blue-white fabric is draped around it. A rag rug in the same color scheme covers part of the pine floor. Two closets, a small desk, two chairs, and a bedside table make up the rest of the furniture, and everything is pine.

"Like a sauna," Tristan murmurs when Naomi has left the room with their slacks and jackets. She looks bemusedly at the two well-worn terrycloth robes on the bed. "It's not that I'm not grateful. I am. I'm just so…" She sits down on the bed with a groan. "Tired."

"Naomi will be back to examine your neck. Then you can rest." Olivia removes her shirt and puts on one of the robes. The red-and-black plaid actually looks becoming on her. Tristan glares at the bright pink-and-white striped one. Brilliant.

Tristan unbuttons her shirt, but when she moves her arms to pull it off, a sharp pain shoots through her neck and out her shoulders. "Fuck!"

"Let me." Olivia peels the shirt off Tristan's arms. "Careful. Yes. Like that. Can you stand up?"

Half offended by the question, Tristan stands, albeit on unsteady legs, as Olivia holds up the monstrosity of a robe. Grudgingly, Tristan concedes that the fabric warms her. When Olivia tucks a knitted blanket around her legs, Tristan manages to lean forward and kiss her cheek. "Thank you," she says huskily.

Olivia turns to Tristan, cups her cheek gently, and kisses her on the lips. It's not like the passionate, all-overwhelming, erotic kisses they shared just yesterday, but one of true affection and reassurance.

Something inside Tristan manages to connect to this difference, to Olivia, and it helps keep the shock from the crash manageable.

Sitting down next to Tristan, Olivia takes a deep breath and expels it. "Now, that was a little too exciting if you ask me. When I hit that car, I thought we were going to die. Truly."

"I'm sorry this is happening to you. I really am." Can Olivia guess that apologies are not her strong suit? Tristan has always found them counterproductive and—if she's being honest—a source of too much vulnerability. After spending her first "lifetime" apologizing and asking forgiveness for what she'd become, yet never receiving any absolution from anyone, Tristan gave up trying. Watching Olivia's horror as the Mercedes overtook them and caused the crash is, however, something she'd never want to repeat. Somehow, she has to find a way to return Olivia to the US safely. Even if it means staying behind in Europe and putting the plan for the transfer of ownership of Amaranthine Inc. in motion. Even if it means saying good-bye forever.

The agony that thought causes is worse than the throbbing, stabbing pain in her neck. Tristan shudders, which of course makes Olivia cautiously put her arms around her.

A knock on the door interrupts the attempt at soothing, but Olivia doesn't remove her arms when she calls out, "Come in!"

Naomi enters, carrying a small bag and a folded-up massage table. "Tory first?" She beams, making Tristan wonder if this woman is in a constant good mood. Not sure if she can manage to remain polite toward such a person, since too much glitter like that rubs her the wrong way, Tristan lets Olivia carry on the conversation.

"Absolutely. I'm not bad off at all." Olivia gestures toward Tristan.

"All right. Here goes, then." Naomi flips open the table and puts it in the center of the floor, draping towels over it. "I don't want you to get cold, Tory, so keep your clothes on, and just slip the robe off your shoulders, okay?"

"Sure." Tristan moves over to sit on the massage table and lets the robe slide down. "That all right?"

"Perfecto!" Again, Naomi sounds too chirpy, but her fingertips are gentle as they probe the sore spots. "You normally tense up here, am I right?" Naomi now sounds calmer, as if she's pulled on a professional persona when she started her examination. "I can feel knots and tension. No wonder the impact of the collision hurt your neck." Naomi lowers the table and begins working on Tristan's muscles. Olivia sneaks the blanket around Tristan again, giving her thigh an encouraging squeeze in the process.

"All right," Naomi says after a while. "I've worked on the knots, and I'll do a gentle adjustment. As we have no X-rays of potential injuries, I can't go full force—I might make things worse, but this, together with some painkillers, should provide you with some relief until you can reach your family doctor."

"I have everything I need when it comes to medication," Tristan says, surprised at how she slurs the consonants of her words. "Carry on, please."

"Just relax then." Naomi has Tristan lie down, with Olivia's help, and starts working on her neck. It doesn't hurt, but the cracking sound is unsettling. When Naomi finishes, Tristan uses the bathroom and then simply crawls into bed. Unable to muster the energy to talk, she rolls into the corner and falls asleep facing the wall.

❖

"She's exhausted," Olivia says as she climbs onto the massage table. "How bad is her neck?"

"It's not unstable, but she may have some damage to the muscle tissues around it. Was she facing forward during the crash?" Naomi starts probing Olivia's neck while she talks.

"No. Sideways, as she was facing me. No seat belts." Olivia holds up her a hand. "I know, I know. We were foolish, but when I thought of them, we were already being followed." Unsure how much she can share, Olivia quietens. Naomi keeps working on her sore neck, and even if Olivia can't relax fully, her muscles begin to. And they also ache more, but in a less sharp way. "You know your stuff."

"I used to work on people, but then I became a vet and specialized also as a chiropractor for animals. Dogs, cats, horses, mainly." Naomi pulls the robe up around Olivia's shoulders. "You need to rest as well. When you wake up, we'll have dinner for you."

"You're so incredibly generous." Olivia stands and fastens the belt around her waist again. "You must realize an element of danger might spill over on you and Ulrich." Olivia must be honest.

"I do. And so does Ulrich. He's the strong, silent type, despite being in his early sixties, and he also knows how to keep us safe. In his youth, he belonged to the French Foreign Legion. I met him twenty-seven years ago, and I suppose you could say we're joined at the hip."

Olivia sees the tender humor reflected on Naomi's features. This woman obviously loves her husband.

"But I do have one question," Naomi asks.

Tensing, Olivia nods. "Sure." She hopes she'll be able to answer.

"Can Waldo stay in here with you? He's been patiently patrolling the hallway between here and the kitchen. I don't know why, but he's taken a liking to your partner. He's always very friendly, but to see him whimper outside the door is rather heartbreaking."

Olivia grins, a completely authentic smile this time. "He can be here if he wants to. I'll let him back out if he gets tired of us."

"But you promise to rest too? Your clothes will be done when you wake up." Naomi folds the table. "And I'll take another look at your necks later, just to make sure."

"I'll rest. And thank you. I have no words, Naomi, for how grateful we are." Tears burn along Olivia's eyelashes. "Honestly."

"Aw, but of course. You remind me of my daughter, Olivia. I would like to think that someone would help her if she was in trouble."

"You have kids?" Olivia sat down on the bed.

"Two. A boy, Max, who's twenty. Tanya is twenty-two. You'll meet Max tonight if you want. Tanya lives in Geneva. Now, enough talking. Rest up." Naomi walks over to the door, and as soon as she opens it, Waldo slips inside and hurries over to Olivia.

Placing his head on her lap, he looks up at her and then shifts his gaze to Tristan behind her. After he does this several times, it is obvious what he wants. Naomi has closed the door behind her, and Olivia isn't going to ask if Waldo is allowed up on the bed. She figures they'll both feel safer to have a guard dog of sorts close.

"All right, sweet boy. Up you go." Olivia pats the mattress, and it takes only two seconds for Waldo to curl up at Tristan's feet.

"What the hell…?" Tristan stirs but doesn't turn her head, which Olivia is grateful for.

"Just your second biggest fan. Waldo." Olivia takes off the robe and crawls into bed behind Tristan. Hoping Tristan isn't against spooning, she slides closer and places her hand on her hip.

Tristan hums, a sound that seems approving.

"This okay?" Olivia whispers. She isn't slurring as badly as Tristan did earlier, but fatigue is taking over, and she supposes the shock is easing up.

Waldo shifts at their feet and uses some strange dog variety of an army-crawl to worm himself up between their legs. There, he buries his nose into the thick duvet and sighs contentedly.

"You're kidding." Tristan snorts softly but then pats the head nestled behind her. "Just don't kick me."

"Talking to me or Waldo?" Olivia says sleepily.

"Both." Tristan rests her hand on top of Olivia's, and that is the last Olivia remembers as sleep claims her.

CHAPTER THIRTY-SEVEN

Dinner with Naomi and her family is a pleasant experience, and to Tristan's surprise, it is easy to smile and participate in the slightly irreverent conversation. She sits next to Olivia, and on her other side sits Max, a handsome young man with a mop of blond hair, which he keeps flicking away from his eyes with a practiced toss of his head. He mercilessly teases his parents and seems genuinely intrigued by her and Olivia.

"You were chased down the highway?" Max's eyes glitter with excitement. "Like in a James Bond movie? Or *The Fast and the Furious*! Did the police get involved?"

Tristan is fully aware that they might be on the police's radar after fleeing an accident, but their rental is in a name she doesn't intend to use ever again. It isn't as if the men pursuing them stuck around to explain how it happened.

"How understanding of you, my son." Naomi groans as she passes around yet another bowl, this one containing a mix of steamed vegetables. "Tory and Olivia have been through such an ordeal, and it was certainly not to entertain you, you movie freak."

"I get that," Max says with a self-deprecating smile. "It just has to be the most interesting thing that's happened in our town for ages. And to think that my parents were involved in the rescue. You've had zero coolness factor for the last few decades, Dad, but things are looking up. Like your old times, *nicht*?"

"Dear God." Ulrich sits opposite Olivia and looks at his son mournfully. "We failed at bringing you up. I apologize for this boy having no manners. I think military school...or perhaps my old stomping grounds...might be in his near future."

Max merely beams and pats Tristan's hand. "Don't listen to them. They use that line a lot, and I'm not going anywhere. Except to college next year, in the US."

"Really?" Olivia leans forward to look at Max, past Tristan, who can't help being charmed by the boy. "Where?"

"I have applied for scholarships and hope to be accepted to Yale."

Tristan listens to Max talk about his hopes and plans while his parents exchange smiles. The ambiance is one of acceptance and warmth, and underneath the table, Waldo has his head on her feet. She has no idea what the deal is with this dog, but he's clearly decided to adopt her and Olivia into his family unit, which makes Tristan's heart clench harder with each beat.

"So, Tory, what do you do?" Naomi asks as Max's comments about education die down. "I'm curious, and we have a right to know a little about what was going on back at the highway ramp. Those men were clearly chasing you, and they obviously didn't mind risking other people's lives in the process, the way they drove." Naomi's glance is kind but direct in a way Tristan understands and respects. And she's right. This family deserves as much of an explanation as she and Olivia can provide.

"We have been investigating a crime that has to do with my past," she says quietly. "Olivia's not involved. She's been helping me and, by doing so, gotten far too tangled up in the repercussions of these men's criminal actions—obviously through no fault of her own. We plan to return home to New York as soon as possible and contact the authorities if we can't resolve this situation any other way." This is mostly the truth, and when Tristan looks back and forth between Naomi and Ulrich, Naomi nods, but Ulrich's expression is stern.

"I can protect my family—and you two—if it comes to that," he says darkly. "I will, however, insist on involving the authorities if the situation gets out of hand. My wife and son come first."

"As it should be," Olivia says calmly. "We do realize that our presence here is placing you in danger, but we fully expect to be on our way tomorrow, and you'll never have to deal with our...baggage again."

Ulrich's shoulders relax, and the conversation moves on to other topics as they finish the meal. Once they leave the dinner table and settle down in the living room, Tristan sits on the smaller of the two couches with Olivia. Fatigue washes over her again. If she wasn't so sure she wouldn't be able to sleep during the night if she went back to bed now, she would have excused herself in an instant.

"You okay?" Olivia murmurs and runs her hand along Tristan's leg.

"Yes. Just tired." It's all she can confess at this point. She hears a buzzing in her ears, and her vision is blurry.

"Hm. You're awfully pale still." Olivia slides closer. "Lean on me. I think we're in for a movie night. You can just chill."

Ulrich begins browsing one of their streaming services, and soon their hosts have selected a movie. Tristan is grateful it isn't an action film, or something with loud music or flickering lights. The romantic period drama isn't catching her interest, but at least it isn't assaulting her senses. She leans against Olivia's shoulder, letting her head rest there.

Once the movie ends, Ulrich and Max take Waldo out for his evening stroll.

Tristan is about to close the door to the guest room when she hears the men come back. She can't make out their words, but something in their tone makes her return to the center of the house. "Something wrong?"

Ulrich is unfastening Waldo's harness and frowns. "A car's driving slowly along the streets."

"When they passed us, they slowed down and lowered the right front window." Max takes over as he hangs his jacket away. "Dad doesn't agree, but I could swear I saw a gun, or perhaps a Taser. Something black and shiny. The guy wore a black knitted hat that seemed very thick around his forehead. I can picture him pulling it down like a balaclava." Max seems half excited, half spooked.

"Did you recognize them?" Tristan turns to Ulrich just as Olivia joins them.

"Is it them?" Olivia's lips are tense.

Tristan ignores her headache and keeps her gaze locked on Ulrich. "Did you?"

"No. Too dark. Besides, Naomi was the one who got a good look at them earlier today. I was driving and cursing you and didn't pay as much attention as she did." Ulrich sighs. "Either way, they didn't follow us home, just drove slowly in the opposite direction. No need to panic."

Tristan admired the man's aplomb. "That's admirable of you, but we're endangering you by remaining here." She clenches her hands.

"If you go outside, you'll be exposed. If you stay indoors, you'll be fine, and so will we," Naomi says calmly. "We'll set the alarm like we always do. If something happens, against all odds, the private security company we use will be here in less than five minutes."

Tristan looks over her shoulder toward Olivia. "What do you think?"

"Going out in the middle of the night will absolutely attract more attention than slipping away in rush-hour traffic," Olivia says. "Let's get some more rest and leave early tomorrow morning. It's our best chance."

"All right." Tristan has to put a hand on the wall. "I do need a few more hours of sleep." This fact bothers her more than she's let on. Normally, if she's injured, Tristan's healing qualities make her bounce back a lot faster than this. The fact that the whiplash injury is affecting her still, and like this, is disconcerting. She certainly doesn't like it.

"Can we rent a car around here fairly early in the morning?" Olivia asks their hosts, who shake their heads, all three of them.

"What about Kleine Berta?" Max asks.

"Who's Berta?" Tristan frowned.

"It's Mom's old Volkswagen, from the late sixties but completely restored. She sits in the garage mostly, but Mom takes her out once every two weeks to get her juices going." Max places a hand on Naomi's shoulder. "Why don't we lend it to them, and they can just call us and let us know where they leave it once they arrange another ride?"

The expression in Naomi's eyes grows soft. She leans in and kisses Max's cheek. "We must have done something right while bringing up you and your sister. A brilliant idea."

"We can't take your car!" Tristan has to stop this family before they start pulling money out of their accounts to donate to her and Olivia, or something equally insane.

"Of course not. We fully expect to get her back in mint condition," Naomi says, as if it is the most obvious thing in the world. "Whether you drive it to a car rental, and for God's sake don't pick one close by if you do, as they might have it under surveillance, or to an airport, just pay enough for parking for twenty-four hours. I think that's logical."

"How is it logical?" Olivia asked, sounding taken aback.

"You say you don't want to risk our safety, something I appreciate, and us driving you somewhere can connect the dots between us, so to speak. Also, if you need our help again at one point, you'll have burned that bridge if they do make the connection." Naomi nods with emphasis.

"Mom's fond of all kinds of crime and secret agent movies, if you can't tell." Max smiles, but he looks serious. "And she's right. So am I."

"Ulrich?" Tristan looks over at the soft-spoken man who has just finished wiping off Waldo's paws.

"Naomi is right." Ulrich grunted as he stood. "And Max. You'll take Kleine Berta tomorrow morning and some extra clothes to wear. You can leave them in the car when you reach where you're going."

Olivia's tears overflow without warning. Tristan hears a sob behind her and turns in time to see Olivia hide her face in her hands.

"Darling." Tristan wraps her arms around Olivia. "This can work. It'll work."

"I know," Olivia manages to say. "It's just…they're so kind…and I'm so tired."

"Poor thing." Naomi takes charge, which Tristan knows is in her nature. "Take the girl to bed, and Waldo too. I'll set the alarm and make sure we're all up in time."

"I'll go double-check Kleine Berta before I'm off to bed, to make sure it starts. I know it has a full tank of gas." Max pats Olivia awkwardly on the back. "It'll be okay."

"It will. We'll make the most of the sleep in your wonderful guest bed. Thank you." Mustering the last of her energy, Tristan nods gratefully to their hosts and walks back to the guest room with Olivia, who is now wiping her cheeks and collecting herself.

"I'm sorry. It's just…it got to me." Sitting down on the edge of the bed, Olivia sighs. "I'm supposed to help you, to be of use to you, and yet—"

"And you are. You're more than that. From day one, you've stood by me and taken all these risks when you don't have to." Tristan enfolds Olivia in her arms. "Do you still need to use the bathroom?"

"Uh-uh." Olivia shakes her head a little against Tristan's neck, and even though Tristan is aching all over and so tired she can barely see, the sensation of Olivia's lips against her skin makes her shiver.

"Then go to bed and I'll be right there—now what?" A scratching sound at the door makes them both flinch.

"Waldo," Olivia says, and now she chuckles, which makes Tristan like the sweet boy even more. "Go get ready, and I'll let him in."

Tristan kisses the top of Olivia's head and walks into the bathroom. As she brushes her teeth, she studies her reflection, recognizing the look. Eyes a cold, pale blue, lips a thin line, she has her jaw set so firmly, her teeth grind hard together. This is the look she has met in mirrors every time she's expected trouble and gone in guns blazing, metaphorically speaking for the most part. This time, she wishes she still had her weapon, but she doesn't.

Mentally reviewing plans A, B, and C, she tries not to think of the option that includes leaving Olivia behind, but it may well come to that. As she returns to the guest room, she finds Olivia fast asleep, facing the wall, with Waldo nestled behind her bent knees. So much for properly spooning. Tristan climbs into bed, turns off the light, and manages to find a position where she can wrap her arm around Olivia and still not crowd the dog. As soon as she's settled, a long, lanky, and decidedly furry leg ends up curled around Tristan's ankles. She smiles just as she drifts off to sleep.

Tristan isn't sure what wakes her, just that her heart's pounding— and Waldo is growling.

CHAPTER THIRTY-EIGHT

Liv gasps as someone, Tristan, shakes her brusquely. "What? What's happening?" She sits up so fast, her lower back smarts.

"Shh. Listen." Tristan places a finger against Liv's lips.

Liv blinks against the darkness of the room. Only a faint light from the crack in the door to the bathroom makes it possible for her to make out the contours of the furniture. Then she hears the unfamiliar rumbling between them where Waldo is sitting up, growling softly.

"He hears something. I doubt this dog growls for no reason." Tristan slips out of bed, groaning as she pulls on one of the robes. "Don't turn on the light. Put something on."

"All right." Liv nudges Waldo, who is already sliding off the bed, and joins Tristan over by the door.

Liv finds the second robe and puts it on, tightening the belt so hard, she has to loosen it to breathe. She joins Tristan by the door just as she opens it a small crack.

"*Ruhe*, Waldo!" Tristan says to the dog that's nudging at the back of their legs, trying to pass them.

Liv pats the dog's head, hoping he won't bark. She can feel his lips are even pulled back, which means he's truly growling, not just making noise at some mind ghost.

"Think someone's in the house?" Liv whispers, the hairs on her arms rising at the thought of them all being in danger.

"Not sure. I would think Waldo would be even more agitated if that were the case."

"Should we let him out?" Liv is torn. If someone's managed to get inside, the dog might be injured or killed if he attacks them. But he might also alert his owners enough for them to save themselves. Trembling, Liv tugs at Tristan's sleeve. "Let me by. I'll just sneak up to the living room and have a peek."

"I should do it," Tristan objects, predictably.

"You're still not well. Let me." Liv knows this irks Tristan, but she can feel how unsteady Tristan is. She doesn't wait but pushes both Tristan and Waldo out of the way and slips out into the hallway. Here, some faint moonlight creates unfamiliar shadows, but it also provides enough light for her to make out where to step. She keeps away from the wall, even if she'd rather press her back to it, as she remembers the many paintings and knickknacks the family has an affinity for. Slowly, she inches through the narrow space, half expecting to hear the floor creaking or someone breathing. When nothing stirs as Liv reaches the corner where the hallway does a ninety-degree turn, she rests her hand against a small dresser and leans forward to peer around the corner.

A dark form takes her shoulders and pulls her forward. It happens so fast, Liv doesn't even have time to scream. Her heart pounding hard, she yanks back, hands raised and feet apart in a practiced maneuver, ready to attack whoever's threatening them.

"It's me. It's Max," someone hisses in her ear. "Calm down. It's just me."

"M-Max?" Liv whispers. "What are you...? Waldo's growling. Someone might be here—"

"I know. I saw the silhouette of someone against my blinds." Max whispers too. "Waldo never growls. He can sense them."

"We have to get him and Tri—Tory." Now Liv yanks Max's arm. "Wake your parents, but quietly."

"Got it."

They separate, and Liv walks back toward their room. When she reaches the door, she raps her nails against it, to alert Tristan. "It's me." She pushes the handle down, and Waldo zooms past her out into the hallway. Tristan is standing in the middle of the room, putting on her slacks. "Get dressed. I saw someone outside."

"So did Max." Liv tears off the robe and pajamas, putting on her clothes. With their small backpacks and jackets over their arms, they exit the room. Liv looks at the old-fashioned alarm clock by the bed. Three a.m.

In the windowless hallway, Naomi and Ulrich are waiting with Max and Waldo.

"We're so sorry," Tristan whispers. "Unless this is a common burglar, I think whoever is after us might be investigating the homes one by one here. Perhaps they saw you passing them and took note of your SUV."

"And it's parked in the driveway." Ulrich sighs. "That was shortsighted."

Liv shakes her head. "You couldn't possibly know."

"We must leave. No way am I going to be responsible for any of you getting hurt." Tristan takes Naomi's hand. "If you give us the keys to the Volkswagen, we'll wait about fifteen minutes and then go."

"What makes you think you can leave without them following you?" Ulrich doesn't sound convinced.

"They're gone." Liv points to Waldo, who is now lying between them, yawning. "Waldo's stopped growling. We just have to give them a little more time to get farther away from the house."

"All right. But I don't have to like this." Naomi presses her lips together. "I'll worry."

"She hates worrying." Max puts his arm around his mother. "I have a feeling Liv and Tory can normally take care of themselves quite well."

"I know. Still." Naomi sighs. "Anyone want anything from the kitchen?"

"Two bottles of water, maybe?" Liv follows Naomi to the kitchen door but doesn't step inside. The kitchen windows don't have any blinds, and even if the moon doesn't show any dark figures lurking outside, she must be careful.

Naomi hands her four bottles of water, some bananas, and a small box of protein bars. "Here. Just in case."

"Thank you, Naomi. You're amazing. The same goes for Ulrich and Max. And Waldo."

Naomi hugs Liv fiercely. "Be safe. Promise me that."

"I promise. We'll be in touch about the car."

Merely nodding, Naomi follows Liv back to the others. Tristan is crouching next to Waldo, scratching his ears. She gets up, moving somewhat easier than last evening, and expresses her thanks to their hosts one more time. Then she looks over at Liv, her eyes flat.

"I know," Liv says quietly. "It's time to go."

❖

The driveway is lit by only two old-fashioned sconces, one next to the front door to the house, and the other by the garage door. Stopping just outside the door, Liv listens for footsteps on the gravel, but the night around them is quiet. She steps off the small wooden step, and the crunching sound her feet make against the gravel makes her freeze.

"Just keep going," Ulrich says behind Liv and Tristan. "When you're halfway to the garage, I'll open it with the remote."

"All right," Tristan murmurs.

Liv reaches back and squeezes Tristan's hand quickly. "Let's go." She hurries across the yard to the garage, relieved when the door slides up much quieter than she's feared. Clutching the keys to the Volkswagen, which turns out to be bright yellow, she aims for the driver's door. She tosses her small backpack and her own jacket into the backseat and slips inside. On the other side of the car, Tristan opens the passenger door. She steps inside and places her bag between her feet and her coat in the backseat. Saying a silent prayer, Liv buckles up and makes sure Tristan has done the same before she turns the key in the ignition. Glad she remembers to push the clutch down, she hears the old engine whirr for a few seconds and then turn. Pushing the stick into first gear, Liv eases up the clutch. It catches much closer to the floor than she expects, and the small car virtually jumps out of the garage.

"Whoops. Sorry," Liv mutters, hearing Tristan draw in a breath between her teeth. She accelerates only briefly and then puts it in second gear, this time with a much smoother result. "There. I assume back to the highway."

"Yes. But go back north, as we said."

"Got it. Keep a lookout." Liv knows she doesn't have to remind Tristan, but she's going to have her hands full driving a stick shift, as it has been a while. She makes a left turn after looking for traffic on the residential street. Nobody is out at this hour, and if they are, their presence is suspicious.

"No one in sight," Tristan says. "Keep going."

Liv speeds up until she can slip the transmission into fourth gear. The car is well-kept, like Max had said, and faster than she thought. "Remind me. It's right and then an immediate left, correct?"

"Yes." Tristan looks back over her shoulder. "Still no one. If we can make a few turns without seeing anyone, we'll have a good chance."

"Yes. I doubt anyone will recognize us in these clothes and hats, even if they pass us." Liv chuckles. "Never thought I'd see you in a Cossack-style fur hat and pink jacket."

"That makes two of us." Tristan snorts softly. "You look quite fetching in that baseball cap with a built-in blond ponytail. Not to mention the paisley-patterned down jacket."

"Ha. Sure." Liv quiets, as their first turn is coming up. She shifts gears and lets the VW take the turn a bit faster than is advisable. Tristan supports herself against the dashboard and Liv's seat as she keeps looking over her shoulder but doesn't say anything. Turning left immediately, Liv spots the sign showing how to drive toward the highway, just like Ulrich told them. She finally dares to relax, if only marginally, as Tristan still hasn't alerted her to any other car in the vicinity.

"How far are we going before we ditch this car and find something else?" Liv asks as she makes another turn, now actually seeing the highway in the distance.

"Let's go back to Montreux, find a car rental, and drive back to Geneva. We'll find standby tickets at the airport. What do you think?" Tristan cupped Liv's neck.

"All right. They won't expect that. I think they'll assume we're either still hiding or, if we're on the move, we're heading the same direction we were going yesterday. I agree." Liv wants to object when Tristan removes her hand.

"There's another option," Tristan says, her voice huskier now. "We can put you on a plane to the US tomorrow, and I'll catch a flight back to France. I really should take this on my own from now. It's what I've always done before."

"You weren't chased by homicidal stalkers before! Or were you?"

"Well, no, but—"

"There you go." Liv grips the wheel harder. "You need me. You can't expect me to abandon you when I know that." She turns onto the highway, speeding down the ramp and making sure she keeps the same pace as the few cars that are on the road this early in the morning. "I'm not going anywhere without you."

Tristan is quiet for a moment but then reaches out and places her hand under Liv's fake ponytail again. "All right, Olivia." Liv hears sadness in her voice, but also something else she interprets as relief. "All right."

CHAPTER THIRTY-NINE

Tristan lets Olivia keep driving. They continue back to Montreux, where they find a rental. They change cars in a long-term parking lot, paying for Kleine Berta to remain two more days. Olivia places a call to Naomi from the nearest gas station, letting her know where to pick up her car and how grateful they are to her and her family. They change back into their own clothes in the gas station's restroom.

Deciding to drive toward Geneva along the south side of Lac Léman, they find the silence in the car thick with emotions. Tristan keeps shifting her gaze between the rearview mirror and the passing scenery. She barely notices that it's a beautiful journey. Her mind is simply too fragmented after their ordeal yesterday and the threat hanging over them.

"It felt sad to say good-bye to Naomi and her family, again, over the phone." Olivia flips her hair back over her shoulders with one hand. "At least their car is in good condition and with a full tank."

"Without them, those men would have taken us," Tristan says, her voice stark. "They still might, but at least I'm doing better, and you—you're nothing short of amazing." She runs the back of her curled fingers along Olivia's cheek.

Olivia smiles but doesn't say anything.

"When we reach Geneva, we must risk going straight to the airport. There, we'll be vulnerable until we're past security. At least I hope these people will think twice about attacking someone in the departure lounge. Then again, they've done things that don't make sense before."

"We do recognize them by now. We'll be able to spot them." Olivia sends Tristan a quick glance. "Right?"

"I get the feeling that whoever's behind this has goons on retainer. I can't swear that the man in the church was any of the ones chasing us in London. He was the passenger in the car that cut us off. That, I'm sure of."

"Me too. So, you mean he may not be *the* one? What the hell? Who's doing this? And goddamn it—why are they doing it in the first place?"

"They're taking us out. Us as in the girls who survived the 'plague' on the ship heading for America. One by one. It feels personal because it is deeply personal."

"Are you still thinking about Trudy and Caroline? That they might have survived their execution?" Olivia sounds dubious. "I mean, anything's possible, but so far, we haven't seen any women being part of this chase."

"True…and yet…what else would make sense? Who else than those two might hold such a grudge on what has to be a personal level? They did swear to haunt us, to come back to destroy our lives for not rescuing them from the gallows." Tristan looks down at her bag but knows better than to pull out something that requires reading. She's prone to motion sickness as it is, and no matter how much she wants to confirm facts from her ledger, just thinking about reading makes her queasy.

They stop at a roadside restaurant and manage to get a booth in a corner, overlooking all the exits. Tristan brings her ledger but, truly hungry for the first time since her presumed concussion, wolfs down her toast. Olivia stops eating and stares at her.

"That's a first," Olivia says, winking. "Never seen you literally pull a lawnmower over your plate like that. Wow."

"Funny." Tristan sips her mineral water and merely raises her eyebrows.

"I'll say. Usually, I'm through half an hour before you." Olivia eats the rest of her yogurt and muesli. "There. That'll hold us for a while."

After Olivia finishes, Tristan orders two lattes and pulls out her ledger. "I'm not sure when we'll find the time or opportunity to catch up with this, so unless you're against it, can we have a look?" She gazes around them as she waits for Olivia's reply. Nobody is close by or paying them any sort of attention.

"Sure." Olivia moves to Tristan's side, sliding close. The warmth of her leg against Tristan's sends a pleasant tremor through her. "Where did we leave off?"

"Well, we've skipped around a lot, so I'm not sure about the journal part. I was thinking of what I learned about the two deaths before Iris's, which was a while ago."

"How long exactly? When you say a while, it's usually an understatement." Olivia winks at Tristan and nudges her shoulder gently.

"True enough." Tristan pulls up the pages she had in mind. "This is the one who died before Iris. 1988. I knew her as Eileen. She died under another name, which we can look up under her list of aliases." Tristan pushes the ledger over so they both can read.

Toronto, Canada, July 5, 1988

Good thing we all try to keep track of all the name changes, or we might have missed that little Eileen is dead. I think of her as little, because she was...there on the ship. Not the youngest, but the one who seemed paper-thin and who everyone was certain would not make it, that she'd lose her fight with the illness first. In fact, instead, she recovered first. And now she's gone.

I flew to Toronto at once. This is where she lived, and I needed to know how she died. I can't believe it. The cops say she took her own life. I refuse to believe it. Among all of us, she was the most resilient, the one I could have sworn would be around the longest, no matter what. To think she rolled her car into a lake. I can't fathom it. I just can't.

Iris is equal parts anxious and upset. Rosalee is, much like me, filled with disbelief. The police don't think it was foul play, and neither did the coroner. But what if?

Now I find myself wondering how long my life will end up being. I don't let myself dwell on it, normally, but after today, I'm thinking, what if this seemingly endless life really did become too much for Eileen? Could that be a reason for her to commit suicide—something none of us has ever brought up among us before? Such thoughts are dangerous. We all know that.

Now it's the three of us, and we live in different countries.
Only fifty years ago, traveling between Europe and the US
was a long journey. Expensive. Nowadays, anyone can skip
the Atlantic, and we could meet up at some point. It's a nice
thought but not advisable. It would be a mistake.
I know I'll have to revisit these thoughts, but preferably
not for a long time.

"You felt it already back then. Or hinted at it, at least." Olivia puts
an arm around Tristan. "Just like with Iris."

"Yes, but I had no idea it could become a pattern. I hope Rosalee
is safe where she is. But I'm not going to try to find her and end up
leading whoever is after me, well, us, to her." Tristan tensed.

"The person who died before Eileen. What happened to her?"

Tristan closes her eyes briefly. "Mariette. She lived in Cartagena,
Colombia. I already know she was killed but never thought it had
anything to do with her past. She and her husband got in the way of
some war between drug lords. She died in 1979." Tristan flips over
to another page, where only a few sentences show what happened
to Mariette. "I could have made more of an effort to find out about
her existence. What if they weren't killed because of drug lords, but
because of…whatever this is?"

Olivia pulls her in for a hug. "Don't do this to yourself," she
murmurs in Tristan's ear. "You've got enough on your plate right now
without adding to it like this. Once we've figured out who's stalking
you and dealt with it, perhaps we can revisit Mariette's past. Who
knows? But for now, just let that go."

Tristan allows herself to press her face into Olivia's neck,
inhaling her scent and absorbing her warmth. Olivia is right, of course.
Misplaced guilt is counterproductive when they need to stay sharp. "All
right." She kisses Olivia's cheek. "Good point. And on that note, it's
time to get going. We have another hour before we reach Geneva, and I
need to try to find us tickets. Perhaps we can avoid being on standby."

"Then let's go." Olivia stands, putting on her coat and hoisting her
bag over her shoulder. She too scans the room through slitted eyes, and
it pains Tristan that an open, warm woman like Olivia now is forced to
regard the world through a filter of suspicion and caution.

They make their way back to the car. The parking lot is half full, but no one seems even vaguely interested in them. A soft whirring sound makes Tristan look around one more time, but she can't find the source. "What's that noise?" She remains with the passenger door open, looking over the roof of the sedan at Olivia.

"That buzzing noise? Look there. Someone's playing with a drone." Olivia points up and to the side.

Tristan turns and sees a small black drone hovering about twenty yards from them. Who would play with a drone in a parking lot next to a busy road? Was it even legal? "Just get into the car and take us back to the main road quickly. It could be nothing—but I don't like it." Tristan gets in, and soon Olivia speeds out into traffic, where Tristan prays their anonymous-looking rental car will be one of many going to Geneva. They can't reach the airport fast enough.

Chapter Forty

Turning in the rental car at the airport went smoothly, but Liv can't relax. Ever since Tristan freaked out about the drone, her own paranoia has surged. Now she stands with her back to Tristan, who is using her passport as Tory Kline for the last time while buying their tickets. Now she plans to switch to her last one, where her name will be Tracy Kovac.

"We're in luck. They had five seats available," Tristan murmurs when she turns from the counter. "Hey, you're trembling. Something wrong?"

"Nah. Just my stupid nerves." Liv regards Tristan and determines that if she barely recognizes her with the knitted hat covering her white-blond hair, perhaps the stalkers won't either.

"You have every right to be on edge. This is hardly a normal situation." Tristan hooks her arm around Liv's. "Now, let's find our check-in counter. I want to be on the other side of security as soon as possible."

Tristan is obviously rattled too. "Over there." She has already spotted it. "I can't believe you managed to get us first-class tickets."

"Only ones available. We'll both get a good night's rest, as we don't know what to expect when we reach Boston."

Liv wasn't entirely surprised when Tristan didn't buy tickets to New York, as she had expected, but instead chose Boston. Big enough of a city to disappear in, but also unexpected for an outsider. In Boston, another rental will be waiting for them.

The woman behind the counter doesn't pay them any more attention than she does the other passengers in line, which is reassuring.

She pulls Tristan's fake passport through the computer, which accepts it without a hitch. Liv adjusts her facial expression to not look relieved.

As they don't have any checked luggage, and both are returning US citizens, they go through the check-in procedure quicker than normal. Hoisting their carry-on bags, they move through the crowds toward security. As they stand in line, Liv casually lets her gaze run up and down the lines leading to the X-ray machines and metal detectors. Too many dark-haired men of the right age. Too hard to see.

Pulling out their phones and tablets and placing them in the bins, Liv empties her pockets and watches her items go through the X-ray. She steps through the metal detector and then the scanner that will show if she is wearing explosives or weapons. She is cleared and keeps her eyes on Tristan as she puts her belongings back where they should be.

"Remove your hat, madame," the officer manning the metal detector says. "It needs to go through the X-ray machine."

"All right." Tristan tosses her knitted hat into the bin holding her bag with the ledger. She steps through the different machines without a problem and then joins Liv, who is ready to help her.

"We have to look in your bag, madame. It contains some metal objects we can't identify," a woman on the other side of security says. "This way." She takes Tristan's bin and walks over to the table.

"Did you forget to take something out?" Liv whispers to Tristan.

"No. I can't imagine what it might be."

The woman opens the bag and pulls out the ledger and some pieces of underwear. "Ah, there's the culprit." She taps the ledger's metal corners that keep the leather from fraying. "An antique?" She lifts the front cover carefully. "Perhaps it's better if you flip through the pages so I don't rip it by accident."

Tristan sets her jaw but turns the pages carefully.

"Thank you," the woman says. She then scans the cover with a wand that squeaks when it passes the metal corners. "Ah, yes. That'll do it."

"May I put it down now, before it gets, um, contaminated?" Tristan clearly does her best to sound polite, but from Liv's point of view, she looks ready to launch at the woman for delaying them.

"By all means. Thank you for your cooperation." The woman waves them on as if she is doing them a favor.

After Tristan has safely stowed the book that is the only proof of her past, they walk toward the busy area, where shops and restaurants compete for customers and patrons.

"We need to get new clothes again," Tristan says, putting her hat back on. "We're not going to change here, or on the plane, but when we land in Boston. If someone's following us, or if someone's waiting for us at Logan, at least we won't look the same as now."

"Guess we're reinventing ourselves again, then." Liv squeezes Tristan's arm. "Let's find a store that caters to all kinds of tastes."

Tristan stops walking and regards Liv with eyes that clearly search for something.

"What?" Liv asks gently.

"You just go along with every insane plan, or cloak-and-dagger method, no questions asked. I'm…even after our time together so far, I'm just not sure…" She shakes her head, clearly at a loss for words.

"Hey." Liv doesn't care that they're standing in the middle of a massive throng of people hurrying in both directions around them. She pulls Tristan close and kisses her on the lips. "You know why."

"Perhaps." Tristan presses her face against Liv's shoulder for a few, precious moments. "And you're right. An eclectic store is exactly what we need."

They find what they're looking for in a small boutique tucked away in a corner. The woman behind the counter is beyond helpful, though looking a bit confused, as Liv and Tristan choose such diametrically different outfits compared to what they're currently wearing. Liv picks an ankle-long country-western-inspired denim skirt and a knitted off-white sweater. A denim jacket completes the look. She figures it all goes with her boots, and she will also be able to move unhindered in the wide skirt. Tristan chooses black leggings, a luxurious, knitted shirt that reaches halfway down her thighs, and a colorful, silky poncho to go with it. All very high-end. All very chic.

Leaving the boutique with their large bags, they make their way to a restaurant, and after finishing their quick meal, they walk to their gate. Liv keeps a lookout for any men she might recognize. Dark hair. Pale complexion. Goatee on one. The other clean shaved. They wore elegant, dark overcoats the last time she saw them, but, naturally, they too could easily change their appearance.

Aboard the plane to Boston, Liv finds they're shown to a booth with double seats that they'll be able to lower into a bed when it's time to sleep. The flight attendant tells them she'll be taking care of their every need during the flight. She returns with a menu and offers them their choice of beverage. Liv asks for water and so does Tristan, plus a double whiskey.

Liv wants to ask Tristan if it's advisable for her to drink alcohol so soon after a head trauma but reels herself in. Tristan doesn't need her to hover. Or, at least, she won't appreciate it.

"I'm going to savor it, I promise," Tristan says softly, taking Liv's hand. "I'm no fool. I know I shouldn't." She raises Liv's hand to her lips and kisses it. "You can always have a few sips and save me from myself."

Liv smiles and rests her head against Tristan's shoulder. The flight attendant comes with the water bottles and Tristan's whiskey. She points out a few features, among them a privacy screen that they can use once they settle down. Liv's cheeks warm, and she hides her face in the fabric of Tristan's shirt.

"She has us pegged, I think," Tristan says, chuckling before she sips her drink.

"I'll say."

"I'm sure she's just as nice to everybody, but the way she winked when she mentioned the privacy screen…spoke volumes." Tristan runs her hand through Liv's hair.

Liv begins to laugh. "So, we're that obvious, even to a stranger?"

"Well, I'd assume that flight attendants, like so many others working in service professions, are used to reading people. But yes. Perhaps we're obvious." Something in Tristan's voice softens, no, *melts*, and she tips Liv's head back and captures her mouth. Slowly, she deepens the kiss, and the way she tastes, very faintly of expensive whiskey, but mostly like her unique self, makes Liv tremble. "I haven't had the time, or the energy, to truly look at you, let alone touch you, the way I want, since the funeral. And despite everything, nothing seems more important. This. With you."

Liv cups Tristan's cheeks, tilts her head to the perfect angle. She kisses Tristan back, runs her tongue along her lower lip, over and over. Nobody has ever made her feel like this. Nobody else ever will.

The sign for fastening seat belts comes on, the captain greets her passengers over the speaker, and the plane starts moving across the tarmac—but all Liv knows is how amazingly wonderful it is to be in Tristan's arms.

CHAPTER FORTY-ONE

Logan International Airport is buzzing with people, which is both a good and a bad thing. Tristan steers them to the closest ladies' room and then watches Olivia disappear into a stall before she enters the one next to it. After using the toilet, she pulls the clothes they bought in Geneva from her bag and hangs them from the hook on the door. The garments are rumpled, but not too badly. After putting them on, she bunches the old ones together and shoves them into the shopping bag. Stepping out of the stall, Tristan makes her way to the row of sinks and washes her hands while waiting for Olivia.

She barely recognizes the luxuriously and eclectically dressed young woman that emerges from Olivia's stall. With her hair tucked under the hat, Olivia approaches the mirrors, where she completes her transformation by darkening her eyebrows and adding kohl to her eyes. Dramatic and beautiful and, if you looked into the cognac-brown eyes, certainly still Olivia.

"You look lovely, *Tracy*," Olivia says, winking at her.

"Thank you. Likewise." Tristan wipes her hands and checks her face. Deciding she needs to alter her features more, she digs into her messenger bag for her small makeup pouch. Adding some contouring and lots of mascara, but leaving her lips bare, she is happy to not look too much like herself. She ties the long, narrow scarf she initially put around her neck, around her hair instead, letting the ends fall down her back, which completes the look. "Ready?" she asks and runs a finger along Olivia's cheek.

Grabbing Tristan's hand, Olivia pulls it toward her full lips and kisses the palm gently. "Yeah."

As they stride through the airport, Tristan is acutely aware of one mistake they've made. They have changed their looks dramatically, but they still carry the same bags. Not that any of their bags stood out, but it is a rookie error. They sail through customs, and nobody has an issue with Tristan's passport. On their way to the part of the arrival area where the car-rental companies are lined up, Tristan grips her bag harder and keeps scanning the crowd for anyone suspicious.

In the arrival hall, Tristan rents a small, plain sedan. Silver metallic, it looks like any other car, which she knows doesn't guarantee they won't be spotted, but at least anonymous enough to make it harder for their stalkers. She recalls their escape in the Volkswagen and has to smile. What a ridiculous getaway car—but it worked. She prays their luck won't run out before they unravel the mystery of who's behind it all.

"I have to stock up on burner phones," Tristan says and looks around the shops for the closest tech store. She ends up buying four different brands of phones and SIM cards. Starting one immediately while Olivia carries her bag, she dials Graham from memory.

"I'm not interested in whatever you're selling," a sullen Graham says in lieu of a hello.

"Graham. It's me." Tristan's heart aches at the sound of his voice. She misses everyone at the art-restoration workshop, especially Graham.

"Trist—"

"Listen." Tristan interrupts Graham's incredulous voice. "I'm all right. So is my assistant." Tristan sent Olivia a quick glance.

"Your assis—oh, right." Graham exhales loudly. "I'm so glad you called. I was in touch with the Louvre, and they said you both up and left days ago. Where are you?"

"It's better if you don't know. We're trying to figure out a few things, and I wanted to touch base and let you know we're still here." Tristan keeps walking to the exit, and Olivia walks right next to her, clearly as vigilant about their surroundings as she is.

"What can I do?" Graham asks.

"Pay attention. In my safe, you'll find documents that give you, Marlena, and Dana full power of attorney to run the company until we return. And if we don't, there's also a will that in time will divide the company among the three of you. You'll find the combination where you stash your tobacco." Tristan snorts. Graham sometimes smokes a pipe, and he probably never knew she is aware of his hidden stash of tobacco in his workshop.

"What? What are you talking about? You're scaring me, Tristan." Graham's voice betrays his distress. "What have you gotten yourselves into?"

"I will explain when I can, Graham. I promise. Right now, the less you know, the better. And I can't do this over the phone. Please, trust me."

The extended silence from Graham's end makes Tristan grip the cheap cell phone harder. "Graham?"

"Will you truly call me again?" he asks huskily. "I need to know that you're safe. Both of you."

"I will. I've already promised. Now, listen. You can't return my call on this cell. I'm getting rid of it. Do you understand?" Tristan hopes he does.

"No. But yes." The cryptic remark settles something in Tristan. Graham understands that this is how it has to be, for now, at least.

"Thank you, my friend. Stay safe, and be mindful of new, unexpected customers. All right?" Tristan says. "If someone approaches the firm, and you're wary of them, make sure their faces end up on the surveillance tapes, and then dismiss them."

"Got it, Boss." Sounding more composed, Graham clears his throat. "Say hi to Liv from me."

"I will. She's right here. And I'll be in touch." Repeating her words, this feels very much like a good-bye, an event she's lived through too many times in her life. Tristan's throat constricts, and she disconnects the call. She removes the SIM card as they approach the car, letting it fall next to a gutter. The phone stealthily ends up in a bin.

Olivia slips in behind the wheel after tossing their bags into the backseat. She waits until Tristan has buckled up and then leans over and cups the back of Tristan's neck.

Surprised, Tristan snaps her head up and looks over at Olivia. "Yes?"

"It's all right to miss them. I know you're good at being stoic, but it's okay, you know." Olivia slides the back of her fingers along Tristan's neck.

"I know you mean well, but I can't—I just can't afford to

acknowledge all these damn emotions. Not right now. I can't allow it. I've never been able to." Tristan knows she isn't being entirely truthful, but the depth of Olivia's feelings is reflected in her eyes, and Tristan feels, or fears, she might drown if she gives in. They have no time for that.

"Things are different now. No matter what happens, things are coming to an end," Olivia says, sounding remarkably calm.

Tristan stares at Olivia. "Are you truly that fatalistic? Or optimistic?"

"Well, the way I see it, either they get ahold of us or we of them. Finding out the truth about the stalkers is the only way to deal with this situation, and I have faith in us. And in Graham and the rest of the staff to keep your business afloat until we can return with you as Tristan Kelly, and nobody else." Olivia kisses Tristan lightly. "That said, I'm not naive. We're ahead right now, as there's a chance they don't know exactly where we are. Considering their talent for tracking us down when we were in Europe, though, I'm not holding my breath. They'll find us again, but we'll be ready for them. We might even find them first. So, where to?"

Tristan tries to process Olivia's words, but her brain is still fatigued after their crash. "Plymouth. I'll book a hotel room there in my new name. Tomorrow we'll go to my hometown and examine the census records. I know they were sketchy in the late 1700s and early 1800s, but the churches kept records." Tristan tries to speak matter-of-factly, but the lingering feeling of Olivia's lips against hers distracts her. "What do you think?" She really isn't used to checking with anyone else about her decisions, but as Olivia constantly risks her very life to help her, to be with her, it's only fair.

"Good plan. I've never been to Plymouth." Olivia checks the rearview mirrors and over her shoulder before she pulls out into the busy airport traffic. "And either way, I'll be very interested to see your hometown."

"My memories from my childhood home are mixed, but with you by my side, perhaps I can better endure revisiting the area." Tristan shrugs. "Either way, it's the best I can come up with. I'll be able to compare notes with my ledger, and if we're lucky, a name might pop up."

"That'd be great." Olivia nods. "Also, I wish we could check in with Rosalee. To see she's okay still, and if she's found out something we haven't."

"We might find a way. She's somewhere in the French countryside, or perhaps the Netherlands or Belgium, but I bet she still reads *Le Monde,* when possible, to stay connected to what's going on. We could take out an ad and see what happens."

"Wow. An encrypted ad like in old spy movies. Cool." Olivia winks at Tristan and then changes lanes. "Okay. How long's our drive?"

"It's not very far. About forty-five minutes. Just keep going south on MA-3." Tristan leans back against the neck rest. "If you see some unassuming shopping center on the way, pull over so we can buy some normal clothes."

"All right." Olivia briefly touches Tristan's knee. "Just relax. I've got this."

Tristan normally would have scoffed at the "just relax" comment, but now she feels that it's entirely possible for her to do just that with Olivia at the wheel. She can hand over responsibility and let someone else take the lead for a bit.

Huh. Imagine that.

CHAPTER FORTY-TWO

After the short drive, Liv pulls into the small parking lot of a hotel clearly designed to resemble an old inn. She manages to find a free spot where the car can't be seen from the street, no longer amazed at how thoroughly she's adopted the mindset of a fugitive. She just goes with it.

The receptionist is overly enthusiastic to the point where Liv fears Tristan's going to pull him over the counter by the collar and snarl in his face. It's not high season, and perhaps the hotel has a lot of vacancies, which might become boring to a young desk clerk.

"Your room has the best view of all!" the young man hollers after them as they walk to the elevator. Tristan growls under her breath, and Liv places her free hand at the small of her back, ushering her into the elevator before an incident occurs. Pressing the button for the third floor, Liv makes sure she has the keycard ready. Tristan's had it for now, and frankly, so has she, even if she has more energy left to hide her fatigue.

Their room is at the end of the corridor, and as they enter, Liv has to agree with the guy at the desk. The view over Cape Cod Bay is beautiful. She can imagine how it looks during the summer when sails dot the water.

"I need a shower," Tristan says, her tone short. She simply drops her bags onto the bed and heads for the bathroom. At the door, she stops and looks back over her shoulder. "Do you need to use the bathroom first? I might be a while."

"No. I'm fine. Go ahead." Liv flicks her fingers, and Tristan disappears through the door, closing it halfway behind her. The water starts running instantly.

Staying by the window for a few moments, Liv pulls off her new jacket. They stopped at a shopping center halfway between Boston and Plymouth to buy new clothes, and Tristan paid from her perpetual stash of cash. Even that is something Liv has stopped fretting about.

Kicking off the sneakers, Liv then pulls off her blue jeans, white shirt, and white socks. She walks over to the bathroom door and peers inside. Tristan is in the shower, and all she can hear is the water gushing steadily. This means Tristan's just standing there, very still, under the spray. If she were washing her hair or body, the water would slosh around. Without hesitation, Liv steps inside and, as she does, pulls off her sports bra and panties, letting them stay on the floor. Naked now, she's pleased that this bathroom has a shower stall rather than a slippery tub.

Liv pushes the sliding door open just enough to slip inside. If Tristan hears her, she doesn't let on. "Want me to leave?" Liv murmurs as she stops just behind Tristan, their bodies close but not touching.

"Never." Tristan has her hands on the tiles, and now she lifts her head as she pushes back against Liv until their curves have meshed. "Thank you."

"For what?" Liv wraps her arms around Tristan's waist and holds her in place.

"For this. For everything."

Liv runs her lips along Tristan's left shoulder and kisses her way over to the other one. She repeats this journey several times, humming lightly as the sensation of Tristan's skin against her lips makes her heart race. She carefully pushes one leg in between Tristan's and secures their position by grabbing a safety handle on the wall.

"Oh, God, Liv." Tristan tips her head back and turns it, searching for Liv's lips. "Kiss me."

As if Tristan ever has to ask. Liv parts Tristan's lips, deepens the kiss from the moment they touch, and now Tristan pivots in her arms. Pushing one arm around Liv's waist and the other around her neck, Tristan devours her. There's no other word to describe the way Tristan explores every part of Liv's mouth and lips.

Liv needs to taste more of Tristan, and she can't wait. Almost regretfully, she moves her mouth from Tristan's and traces down her neck. Nibbling, nipping, licking, she tastes the silken skin, and to her joy, she hears Tristan whimper and call her name again.

"Don't stop…" Tristan's voice is husky.

"Never." Liv cups one breast and lifts it to her lips. Sucking it into her mouth, she massages and flicks it with her tongue, and then she has to hold on harder to Tristan, as this kiss appears to do things to her knees. She tugs gently at the rigid nipple with her teeth, pulling and then soothing it by drawing her tongue around it over and over.

Tristan's hands shift and are pushed into Liv's hair, holding her close. "Yes. Yes."

Liv moves to the other breast, treating it just as lovingly, and after repeating it all twice, Tristan is keening and slides down the tiles.

Liv reaches over and turns off the water. Pulling a stumbling Tristan along, she manages to just reach the bed before Tristan's legs do give in and she falls onto her back, her legs hanging off the side of the bed. Perfect.

Dragging a decorative pillow off the bed, Liv kneels on it and parts Tristan's legs. She kisses the skin on the inside of her damp thighs, licking droplets of water off the velvety flesh. "This all right?" she murmurs, knowing that her words are vibrating against Tristan, increasing her tremors.

"Mm. Uh, yes." Tristan attempts to get up on her elbows, but clearly, that's too much of an effort, and she slumps back against the bed again. "God…"

Liv can't wait. She wants this so much, wants this woman so much, that it's all she can think of. Parting the slick, no, drenched, folds, she flattens her tongue and starts her exploration. It's Liv's turn to whimper as she feels herself grow wetter when she tastes the woman she loves. Flickering her tongue over Tristan's swollen clit, she uses the fingers of one hand to circle the opening.

"Jesus!" Tristan's back arches off the bed. "Oh…Liv. Inside. You have to…inside…" She's grabbing fistfuls of the bedspread and pulling her knees up and out.

Liv is eager to please and can't think of anything she'd rather do right now than make Tristan this way. She pushes two fingers inside and lets her tongue work the clit even harder—and that is all it takes.

Tristan cries out, slaps a hand over her mouth to quiet herself, and starts convulsing. Liv's on fire too, feeling every part of Tristan's orgasm as she moves her fingers in and out, faster, harder. As it begins to subside, she slows her caresses. Once Tristan goes still, panting for air, Liv climbs onto the bed, helping Tristan get her legs up as well, then straddles the tousled woman before her.

"You're beautiful," Liv says and kisses Tristan. "And I need you more than I've needed a single soul in my life."

"Good." Tristan can barely speak, she's so hoarse, but she runs her hand over Liv's back and cups her ass. "Tell me what you want. I'll do anything, anything at all."

"Oh, fuck…" Liv's field of vision shrinks, going blurry at the edges. "I need to be yours. I need you to take me…"

"Like you took me." It's not a question, but Liv nods. Tristan rolls them, obviously recuperating fast. "My pleasure." She grins wickedly as she pulls Liv's left leg up. "Wrap this gorgeous leg around me. Give me access."

"Ohh." Liv complies eagerly.

Slipping her hand between them, Tristan cups Liv's swollen folds. "Damn, you're wet." Without hesitation, Tristan slips her finger through them and finds Liv's clit. "And hard." She regards Liv intently as she rubs it in a circular motion. Somehow, what she sees on Liv's face makes her do it perfectly. Liv panics.

"I'm going to come. I'm too close." Liv tries to squirm, but her body is on a path now and just wants to be pleasured.

"I'm sure you'll be fine," Tristan says and bends down to kiss her. At the same time, she enters Liv with several fingers and keeps her thumb locked on her clit. It takes only a few thrusts of Tristan's strong fingers and the insistent pressure of her thumb for the contractions to start, but it's when Liv looks up at the bright blue eyes gazing down at her that she's pushed over the edge.

From here on, it's just them. She knows only that she belongs to Tristan, that it's about them and this immense pleasure. When she sees Tristan's face contort and realizes that she's coming again, just from making love to Liv, her vision blurs, and tears run into her already wet hair.

If she ever had a single trepidation about how she feels about

Tristan Kelly, making love like this, giving themselves over like this, has proved one thing. No matter what happens, no matter if she'll be a fugitive for the rest of her life, she loves Tristan and will never abandon her.

CHAPTER FORTY-THREE

Tristan can't allow herself to think too much about the afternoon and night she's just spent with Olivia in the Plymouth hotel room. Taking a break only to order room service, they had turned to each other again and again and made love as if it would have to last them a lifetime. Who knew—it just might, and in her case, it might mean forever.

Now Tristan sits at the foot of the bed, pulling on her boots and smoothing the jeans over them. She glances furtively at Olivia, who is already putting on her jacket. Otherwise, she's similarly dressed in jeans, button-down shirt, sweater, and jacket. Tristan shudders. They don't know what the day's going to bring, which means that no matter how much they prepare, it might not be enough.

"Yes?" Olivia asks, saunters over to Tristan, and sits down next to her on the bed.

"What do you mean?" Tristan pulls on the second boot and repeats the smoothing down of the jeans, thus avoiding Olivia's gaze.

"You looked at me as if you were trying to decide something." Olivia takes Tristan in her arms. "Please. After last night, we shouldn't have any more barriers between us. You know more about me than anyone, and I daresay the same is true the other way around."

"If I looked at you that way, it was because I was trying to decide what I need to focus on today to not get us killed, rather than the fact that I'd love to drag you back to bed and order in more room service," Tristan says, and her throat actually hurts since she's trying to keep her tone light.

"Same. But we'll be back here later, and then I'm at your beck and call." Olivia kisses her, slowly, but without deepening the caress. "As I said last night, I'll do anything for you."

Tristan closes her eyes briefly. *God.* "Likewise," she says, her voice still strained. "And that entails keeping you out of harm's way if I can help it. We better get going."

"Agreed. The sooner we resolve this situation, the sooner I'll have you to myself as a free woman, rather than having someone hunt us down like prey." Olivia stands and holds out her hand. Normally, Tristan would scoff at the idea of being pulled to her feet, but this is Olivia.

"All right. Let's drive to my hometown, though it wasn't a town when I lived there as a child. It was rural and more of a settlement." As they make their way to the car, Tristan gives Olivia more details. "When we reached Plymouth, I remember how the other passengers regarded us, the little girls, with suspicious glances. I could see in my mother's small mirror how pale I was. Wraith pale. The other girls had the same pallor, as if we hadn't seen either sun or moon for weeks or months. My lips looked blood red, and my eyes seemed to have sunk deep into my skull and radiated an almost violet hue. My sister teased me mercilessly until Mother told her to stop. And when my parents and sister saw how people treated us, as if we were indeed cursed, my sister became very protective and my strongest ally." Tristan doesn't even suggest that she should drive. Instead, she's happy to slip into the front passenger seat and tell her story. "We were among a few families that settled just southwest of Plymouth, about a two-hour drive with a horse and cart. There awaited the prospect of owning land and finding work. Mother and Father dreamed of both."

"How did it turn out? It must have been hard to uproot a family and settle in America. So many unknowns."

"More than you can possibly imagine. As a child, of course, I went where my parents and sister did. I didn't question decisions. It didn't even occur to me. Mother taught my sister and me to read and do numbers. She was an unusual woman for her time and in her social bracket. Illiteracy was more common than not, but she would have none of that. Father worked hard with the land and hunted. He also worked shifts at the mill. I admit my memories of a lot of things are very fuzzy. What I do remember is being loved—and feared."

Olivia is quiet but places her hand on Tristan's arm briefly. Grateful that Olivia isn't offering pity, just quiet sympathy, Tristan loosens her grip on her messenger bag.

"Was it the same for Rosalee and the other girls?"

"I'm sure it was. Rosalee and her family moved farther inland at first, but when her mother passed, not sure why, they returned and lived near us. A few other families from our voyage across the Atlantic did the same, and eventually our small community became a village called Greenfield. It's a town now, of course, but the last time I was there, our house was part of a protected area. You know, saved for posterity from a historic point of view."

"Like Colonial Williamsburg?" Olivia asks.

Tristan snorts. "Nothing that grand, but in principle, yes, I suppose so. A moment of history preserved." She goes quiet and then shakes her head, snorting softly. "Like me."

Olivia snaps her gaze to Tristan's for a second. "Hey, it's not like you belong in a museum."

"No, but perhaps in a laboratory?"

Olivia groans. "That's not funny."

"A little funny, when you think about it." Tristan feels strangely better. Perhaps there's something to be said about gallows humor after all.

"Hm." Olivia still doesn't seem amused. "Laboratory." She huffs the last word. "Cute."

Tristan sees the exit to Greenfield come up and points it out to Olivia. She grips the sides of the seat with both hands, her short bout of dry humor erased. They're here, and she is certain that their visit to this place that holds the memories of her childhood, also of relentless persecution and ostracization, will bring them the answers they seek, even if the outcome is uncertain.

The small town hall turns out to be fully digitized. A proud clerk shows them to a room where a row of four computers sits along with a desk, divided into partitions. Liv has a sense of déjà vu from their research in Geneva but sits down at the keyboard, realizing she will be doing the typing. Tristan is so on edge, it seems she will shatter if Liv so much as touches her.

"All right. We need the year when you and your family arrived." Liv tries to sound matter-of-fact, which seems to be the best course of action right now.

"To this area? In 1770. I doubt the census records go back that far." Next to Liv, Tristan is rigid, but who can blame her?

"Let's just do a search for the names. Sarah Stuart and Corinne Stuart. Let's see. What were your parents' names?" Liv looks up from the screen.

"Clara and Neville." Tristan's tone is short, but she moves her hand and lets it rest on Liv's knee.

Liv nods and keeps typing. She finds nothing about the parents, but Corinne's name shows up. "Look, Tristan," Liv says. "See?" She reads in a low voice in case Tristan doesn't see the short note.

"Corinne Stuart, born 1753, married John Granger in 1772, four children, oldest son Laurence born in 1786. Sounds like your sister." Liv squeezes Tristan's hand.

"It's her."

"And here you are. And...no official death date." Liv's stomach clenches. "It says..." She squints at the faded, digitalized document on the screen. "I can't make it out."

"Probably that my fate is unknown. That I moved away and never returned." Tristan sighs. "I see my parents' names. My nieces and nephews."

Liv has scrolled but now stops and goes back a few rows. "Caroline. Trudy. There." She presses a trembling fingertip against the screen. "And here it clearly states that they died within days of each other, just like the dates in your ledger, in September 1888."

"They're listed here? I've never seen that before." Tristan straightens. "Then again, I haven't been back in years. The digitization happened after I visited last."

"Most likely. These are faded old documents. They might have been locked away because of their frailty." Liv keeps scrolling but can't find anything else about Caroline and Trudy. "Seems that we've hit a dead end after the church records. Any ideas?"

"I'm not sure, but something tells me we should visit the old church not far from my childhood home. We might find documents there that the town hall archives weren't interested in."

Liv nods. "All right. Let me just print some of what we found.

We should keep those documents in the ledger." Realizing that she is suggesting things about Tristan's very private notes, Liv stops in mid-motion. "If you think that's a good idea."

"I do." Tristan gives a quick smile.

Liv prints double copies of the documents, and soon they're back at the car. As Liv gets in behind the wheel, she thinks of something. "Did you know that Caroline and Trudy lived around here? I can't remember if you told me that."

"I did, but it wasn't for long. My memory isn't very clear from that time, but I want to say it was only a few months. I can't even remember who the priest was who must've entered them, and their parents, into the church books. I just hope he found it prudent to include more information in other documents. We must find out more to have a chance to solve this mystery."

"We will." Liv stops at the parking lot exit. "Right or left?"

"Oh. Right." Tristan puts on her seat belt. "It's not far."

Tristan hasn't exaggerated. After less than ten minutes, she guides Liv through a wooden portal where a sign says *Greenfield Old Town*.

"The church is outside of Old Town, but we can park here." Tristan unbuckles her seat belt again and grabs her bag.

"Want to see your old house?" Liv asks carefully as she exits the vehicle and locks it.

"No." Tristan stops, perhaps regretting her curt tone. "Not this time," she adds softly. "One day, perhaps."

"Of course." Liv kisses Tristan's temple quickly before they start walking toward the old church on the outside of the fence.

Tall and well kept, considering that it's more than two hundred and twenty years old, the white wooden structure pushes its humble steeple toward the sky. Around them, snowflakes have begun to fall, making the neighborhood look rather romantic. Liv knows that's a ridiculous idea, as the settlers lived under anything but romantic conditions, but the scene of the trees lining the path up to the church door looks idyllic.

"There's a light on," Tristan says. "That's good. Someone might at least be able to point us in the right direction."

"I hope so." Smiling, Liv climbs the stairs first and tries the double door. It opens on well-oiled hinges, and they step inside.

"It looks so much like it used to back then, just smaller," Tristan murmurs. "Even the pews."

"It's beautiful in a rustic sort of way," Liv says.

Afterward, she can't say what she notices first, the still legs sticking out behind the pew closest to the altar or the sound of the door slamming shut behind them.

Perhaps both.

CHAPTER FORTY-FOUR

Tristan swivels the moment the door closes behind them. She hears Olivia give a short scream, and at the same time, she sees two men standing inside the heavy door. Recognizing them, she steps in front of Olivia to shield her.

"Told you," the man to the left says with a smirk. "After all the cloak-and-dagger, these bitches are too predictable." He snorts and pushes his fist against the other man's shoulder.

"Yeah, but who knew it'd be this easy?" The other man shakes his head.

Looking to be in their late thirties, early forties, the men are both dressed in three-piece suits and overcoats as if they're on their way to an office on Wall Street rather than ready to attack two women in a church.

"Tristan," Olivia whispers and moves to stand next to her. "I think they hurt, perhaps even killed, someone over by the altar." Her voice is trembling, but Tristan can't decide whether it's from fear or fury.

Tristan dares to glance behind them, and her heart sinks when she sees the legs sticking out. Whoever it is, he's not moving.

"What have you done to him?" Tristan snarls as she whips her head back around.

"Oh, don't get all upset. He's just out cold. It's amazing what a little good old-fashioned chloroform can do. Who needs all these new, fancy drugs?" The man to the left, who seems to be the dominant of the two, takes a few steps forward.

Tristan and Olivia back up to keep the same distance. Tristan sees no sign of any weapons, but these are tall and quite burly men, and

Tristan figures their only chance is to keep their distance as they try to find a way to escape.

"Why?" Olivia asks, and now Tristan can tell that it's rage in her voice. Good. "Why are you stalking Tristan? What possible reason can you have? She's no threat to you."

"Does your little *friend* here know?" The left man ignores Olivia's question and instead stares at Tristan, his demeanor scornful. "You must have told her, right? Why would she help you if you haven't given her a good reason?" He returns his attention to Olivia. "I bet she hasn't disclosed that she's not much better than a murderer."

"Bullshit." Olivia spits the word. "That's a word you should be careful with, considering Anneliese Manz's fate." She clenches her fists, looking ready to launch.

"Anneliese Manz," the man to the right says, sneering. "You mean Iris Schmidt."

Tristan winces. She can't help it. These men know. They have to know. "Whatever," she says, hoping she sounds as assertive as she needs to be. "She's dead, and you two have everything to do with that. You were in the church in Montreux."

"Brilliant deduction, old woman. *Very* old woman. Or, should we say, the last woman standing." The man to the left raises his chin as he pulls off his scarf, wrapping the ends of it around his large hands.

"What have you done to Rosalee?" Tristan realizes they don't need to pretend they don't all know the entire truth.

"Nothing. But our associates found her after some extensive digging." The man to the left chuckles. "And, as we're being quite transparent, she's down for the count, but not out just yet. But when our associates get access to the hospital in Antwerp, it'll be quick and easy. Unfortunately painless, as she's comatose."

"God." Olivia covers her mouth.

"Hardly. The divine has abandoned our kind a long time ago. What do you say, Sarah…or do you prefer Tristan?" The man to the right performs a mock bow. "Call me Damon."

More like "demon." Tristan shifts her foot in her right boot, feeling the knife against her ankle. What she wouldn't give to bury it in Damon's neck right this second. "And you? Who are you?" She turns to the other man.

"Tyrone." The man steps closer to his cohort in crime.

"Related? You look alike." Tristan wants to know, but she's also stalling. The men seem to have an innate desire to gloat, to explain. Huge egos, no doubt.

"Cousins," Tyrone says merrily. "Keeping it in the family, you could say."

"You didn't answer," Olivia says, her tone insistent, even challenging. "Why Tristan?"

"She's the last one of the girls from the ship, not counting Ms. Comatose. It's a sad situation, but she has to go. And as you're her, well, what are you really…assistant, companion, or *lover*? Anyway, you're collateral damage. A pity, but that's what comes from these women being utterly selfish from the moment they stepped off the ship. They had the chance to be more, but they didn't take it, and that's why we're here." Damon shrugs.

Tristan frowns. He doesn't make sense. "What are you talking about exactly? You need to explain in more detail. You said it yourself. I'm an old woman."

Tyrone tosses his head back and laughs. "Oh, that's really funny, Tristan. Had no idea you had a sense of humor. Very funny." His eyes suddenly go from gray to black. "But this is not funny. I suggest you keep your ill-advised humor to yourself."

"Why would I do that? You're intent on killing us both no matter what. Why shouldn't I have a little fun at your expense?" Using her low, lethal voice that has been known to make grown men and women tremble and cry, Tristan allows a smirk to form on her lips.

Taken aback, if only for a second, Tyrone takes another step toward them. Grabbing Olivia's hand, Tristan pulls her back farther, and now they are almost at the first pew. When Tristan looks back over her shoulder, she sees that the man on the floor is silver-haired and elderly. To her relief, he's breathing.

"He's alive," Olivia mouths, and Tristan nods.

"If you think you can escape by inching away like that, you're mistaken. We borrowed these from the old geezer." Damon holds up a large, old-fashioned key ring. Large keys hang from it, looking as old as the church.

Tristan's mind races. They have to get help, but how? And Olivia has to survive this death trap, even if Tristan doubts the same will happen for herself. She decides to draw the men's attention again.

"Then tell me what I did wrong? Who am I supposed to have killed?" She looks at Tyrone.

"Think back to your past. You're not that old. For being over two hundred and sixty years of age, you're remarkably well preserved." Tyrone snickers.

Damon isn't snickering. His eyes blaze with rage—or is it madness? "So, think back on all those years and confess your *sins!*" The last words come out as a roar as he launches forward toward Olivia. Wrapping an arm around her neck, he pulls her back.

In horror, Tristan watches Olivia fight the much stronger man. She launches sharp blows with her elbows, and the heels of her boots slam into his shins, making him groan and strengthen his grip. Olivia pushes her hands up and over her head and nearly finds his eyes. Only his quick reflexes keep him out of her reach.

"Let her go!" Tristan moves a step closer, her heart suddenly cold as if filled with sharp ice cubes. "She has nothing to do with this. Let her go." She's addressing Damon, but her eyes don't move away from Olivia, who now has begun to slump as she struggles to breathe.

"I think not. You have to confess to your sin, your crimes, and then our sentence will be passed." Damon is starting to sound like a fired-up preacher, and she can see the whites of his eyes.

"All right. I just have no fucking idea what you're talking about. I've never met you before, nor your cousin. I don't know what you want me to say!" Tristan is working herself up into a panic, as she can tell that Olivia's color is darkening. "You're choking her."

"She's fine." Damon drags Olivia back another step. "Aren't you, sweetheart? Very fine, now that I see you up close. A bit young for that abomination of a woman over there, though."

Olivia manages to grab hold of the backrest of one of the pews. "You're insane if you think either of you will get away with this." She's wheezing, fighting against the suffocating arm locked around her neck.

"Oh, don't worry yourself, dear." Tyrone leans his hip against the pew on the opposite side of the aisle, folding his arms over his chest. "We're fully prepared for any possible outcome. So, Tristan, what's it going to be?"

"I still don't know what you want from me." Tristan forces herself to shift her attention from Damon's grip on Olivia and meets Tyrone's slightly deranged gaze head-on.

"We want fucking justice!" Damon roars. "You know it!"

"I think Tristan's telling the truth." Tyrone shakes his head, sounding marginally calmer. "It's obvious she cares for this girl, and who can blame her?"

"Don't let her fool you," Damon snaps. "She has no heart. If she had…"

"Calm down." Tyrone raises his hand to Damon. "All right, Tristan. Are you claiming that you can't think of one single person whose blood is on your hands, whether from your action or inaction?"

"Inaction?" Even more confused than before and growing increasingly desperate as Olivia has lost her grip on the backrest and is beginning to slump—where the hell are her martial-art skills—Tristan flings her hands up. "What are you talking about?"

"I'm your victim, and so is he!" Damon shouts, making Tristan flinch.

"What? You're my victims? I've never seen you before! Who the hell are you?" Tristan yells back, which hurts her throat.

Tyrone steps closer, and she doesn't move. "I'm Tyrone Rhys, and this is my cousin, Damon Rhys. You stood by and did nothing when our mothers, Caroline and Trudy, were murdered."

CHAPTER FORTY-FIVE

Liv feels Damon's arm around her neck loosen slightly as he moans at his cousin's words. The moan turns into a frenzied keening sound, which makes her shudder. These men are unstable, and the one with his arm locked around her neck is about to lose it—she can feel it.

Watching Tristan stagger at the words, the incredible, unfathomable statement that they're the children of Caroline and Trudy, Liv tries to catch her gaze. They need to stay connected, to stay strong.

"You're lying," Tristan says, her voice stark. "None of us ever had children. We were all barren!"

"Wrong again!" Damon shouts, and now his keening sounds turn into a strange chortle.

Tyrone gives a polite smile. "I was born in 1875, Damon two years later." His smile disappears, and his eyes turn opaque. "I knew Caroline, my mother, for thirteen years, and when the authorities murdered both her and Trudy, I took care of my younger cousin. We always knew the facts about our mothers, about their longevity."

"What about your fathers?" Tristan asks. To Liv's relief, Tristan has straightened, and some color has returned to her cheeks. This change gives her hope.

"Father. Singular. Our mothers shared everything, including their men, and especially Isiah Brown. He's our father, which, of course, makes Damon my brother as well as a cousin."

"Keeping it in the family, huh?" Liv says, not liking how Tyrone is inching toward Tristan.

Tyrone turns to Liv, his lips pulled back into a snarl. "And the little girl toy speaks," he says. "If she causes you trouble, just get rid of her." The last words are for his brother/cousin.

Apparently taking advantage of Tyrone turning away for a moment, Tristan bends down fast, and when she straightens, she holds a long dagger in her hand. Where did she keep that? In her boot? Without hesitation, Tristan throws herself at Tyrone and shoves the dagger up under his chin, grabbing a fistful of his hair with her other hand. Pulling his head back with unexpected force, she growls as she pushes the blade up farther. "Let Olivia go." Blood begins to trickle down Tyrone's exposed neck. "And then you're going to explain further. If you were so sure the rest of the girls from the boat failed your mothers, why wait this long?"

It's clear that Tyrone is straining to talk, but Tristan is relentless. "We didn't wait this long. We have picked you off, one by one, since the day I turned twenty and found my mother's journal. I was thirteen years old, and I thought I knew all about her long life, but then I found her diaries, and that's when it became clear. My mother was a goddess, and so was her sister. They should have gone on to live forever, revered, not ostracized, and certainly not murdered by people inferior to them. Damon and I were there at the trials, and we listened to the lies about our mothers. We watched their executions." He spits the words out, obvious agony mixed with something else, hatred most likely, in his voice.

"Tyrone!" Damon calls out, his voice shrill. "Don't talk about that." He's trembling against Liv.

Tyrone merely shakes his head and continues. "We lived on the streets for years. As it turned out, I had a gift for conning people out of their money. Soon I bankrolled my own little empire, and when I was twenty, I told Damon we had the funds, that it was time to start our search. Our mothers always talked about the other seven girls on the boat who had received eternal life the same as them. I knew it was time to start paying them a visit."

"And they were all bitches." Damon's voice is shrill.

"It took us several years to find the first one." Tyrone's speaking slowly, his eyes vacant as if he's reliving everything. Liv doesn't dare take her eyes off him and Tristan. Blood stains the white collar of his shirt, but he doesn't seem to notice. "You all became so good at hiding your tracks. When we found the first woman, we honestly thought she'd receive us with open arms. Instead, she said that we were never supposed to exist. She went on and on about the Amaranthine Law and how our mothers had broken it, over and over. Calling our mothers criminals and murderers was the last thing she ever did. They never did find out exactly how she died."

The madness glows in Tyrone's eyes as he recounts how he and Damon tracked the women they hated one by one for more than a century.

"What took you so long to find me?" Tristan asks through clenched teeth.

"Sometimes our other business meant we had to spend a few years or decades in remote locations. When we realized that we had inherited our mothers' divine longevity, we had to be careful." Tyrone snickers. "But you should know by now that we never give up, and we always reach our goals eventually. You may think you have the upper hand now, but I promise you, today will happen just as it was meant to. You and the others abiding by the Amaranthine Law did nothing to help our mothers, and you did nothing but show contempt each time Damon and I found one of you. He and I are the only true deserving immortals."

Liv can see that Tyrone's words shock Tristan. The hand holding the dagger is trembling. Acting to draw Tyrone's attention from this fact, Liv raises her voice. "I think that sounds more like a God complex than anything else. You're not immortal. You're delusional!"

"Shut up!" Tyrone shouts, growing rigid. "Cut the little bitch!"

"But—" Damon, clearly the weaker of the two men, is shifting restlessly against Liv's back. His grip is hard, but not as hard as it was moments ago. Thinking fast, Liv keeps her eyes trained on Tristan to try to judge her intentions. She doesn't doubt that Tristan is ready to slit Tyrone's throat for all he's just confessed to.

"Let her *go!*" Tristan roars and pushes the dagger harder against Tyrone's neck, making him wince. "Now."

"Ty," Damon says pleadingly. "She's cutting you."

"Shut up," Tyrone says, the left side of his face now flattened against a pillar next to the pews, clearly trying to get away from the dagger.

Liv squirms in Damon's hold. He doesn't seem to notice, and his grip around her waist and neck is loosening.

GUN BROOKE

"You have three seconds to let her go, Damon, or I end your brother," Tristan hisses. "One."

Liv can see Tyrone's eyes are bugging out, and he's struggling to breathe. The dagger must be razor-sharp, as blood is now running, rather than trickling, down his neck.

"Two." Tristan doesn't take her eyes off Tyrone. They're about the same height, and only the knife gives her the upper hand, as he far outweighs her when it comes to raw muscle power. Liv is readying herself for a fight with Damon in case Tyrone slips out of Tristan's grip. She knows these men intend to kill them no matter what, which means that she and Tristan have no choice. They must fight.

A loud groan from the altar makes everyone but Tristan turn their head toward the unexpected sound. Liv knows this is her only chance. She breaks halfway out of Damon's grip and rams her elbow into his solar plexus. She is stronger than normal because of the adrenaline rush flooding her system. His grip loosens further as he gasps for the air that seems to have left his lungs. Pivoting, Liv then jumps back far enough to send her foot out to contact Damon's chest. He staggers back, and she follows up with a good old-fashioned kick to his groin. Doubling over, he moans, low and guttural. Liv keeps far enough away for her third kick to find his chin. His head flies back, and he goes down, hitting his temple against the flagstone floor with a sickening crack. He doesn't move after that.

Liv turns in time to see Tristan and Tyrone fighting. Tristan grips the knife and is forcing it toward him, adding her full body weight, while Tyrone has managed to get an arm in between them.

"You treacherous bitch," Tyrone growls as he manages to half turn toward Tristan. "We should have gone for you first when we decided to track the last three of you at the same time. Iris was easy pickings. She thought we were there to help her after the avalanche we set off. We were smart enough to outsource dealing with Rosalee."

"If you hadn't been stupid enough to send threatening letters and photos after Rosalee, you might have been more successful." Tristan snarls the words into Tyrone's face. "But now your brother is rendered harmless, and you—you're done."

"I cannot die! I'm an immortal like my mother." He screams as Tristan pushes the tip of the dagger farther into his skin just below his chin. He jerks, still cursing, but now in a gurgling voice. "I'm going to kill you," he says, spitting drops of blood onto Tristan's face.

"Wrong. This is when you die, and it's all on you," Tristan says and drives the dagger home.

Tyrone goes rigid, jerks more than once against Tristan, and then slumps to the floor. Tristan staggers back, gasping for air.

"Tristan." Liv hurries over to her. "Oh, my God." She's shaking as she grabs Tristan by the arm. "You...he's..."

"He's dead." Tristan's voice is hollow. Her hands are covered in blood. "Call 9-1-1."

"What?" Liv feels dazed but then tries to gather her scattered thoughts and block the images of Tristan pushing a dagger to the hilt into Tyrone's throat. "Right. Yes, of course." She finds one of the burner phones in Tristan's coat pocket.

"The man by the altar," Tristan whispers and leans against the pew behind her.

Liv winces. "Let me go check. Tell me if Damon comes to." She hurries over to the elderly man, who is now sitting up, holding his head. "Sir? Are you all right?" She's dialing 9-1-1 as she bends over him. "I'm getting help."

"What's going on?" the man whispers. "There was screaming..."

"I know, but I'll get us all help. Just hang in there, okay?" Liv stands as the dispatcher answers. "I need police and paramedics at the old church in Greenfield," she says as she turns to check on Tristan. When she sees her sitting on the floor, ghostly white, Liv's heart nearly stops. Hurrying over, she throws herself to her knees, barely making out what the dispatcher is asking. "Tristan? What's wrong, what—" Staring at the blood on the floor, at first Liv thinks it's Tyrone's, but he has his own large pool of blood over by the column.

"You're bleeding," Liv says, whimpering. "What the hell?"

"Ma'am? Are you saying someone's bleeding? Tell me what's happened, ma'am?" The dispatcher tries to get Liv's attention, but all she can see is the life running out of Tristan. *One of the things that can actually kill us is exsanguination.* The words echo in Liv's mind.

"Yes," she barks into the cell phone after managing to tap the symbol for speakerphone. "I have a woman bleeding out before me and an older man with a head injury. Please, you must get here fast.

You need to send a helicopter. We were attacked." Shaking, she helps Tristan lie down, looking frantically for the source of all the blood. It takes her a while, but peeling back Tristan's coat and the blood-soaked shirt sends a thin-bladed knife clattering to the floor. Apparently, Tristan wasn't the only one with hidden weapons. Tyrone must have had a knife too. "No, Tristan. No." Finding the wound just below Tristan's rib cage on her left side, Liv rips off her scarf and presses the bunched-up fabric against it. She dares to look back at the unconscious Damon. "One of the men attacking us is unconscious, the other one most likely dead." Liv can barely speak. Her throat is locked in panic, but she needs the dispatcher to know. "Please get us help. My...my friend is dying!"

"We have the police and paramedics on their way. Local police are close by and will be with you in minutes." The man on the phone sounds calm and efficient. "Can I have your name, ma'am?"

"Olivia Bryce. Liv." Sobbing now as Tristan's eyes are glazing over and starting to close, Liv pushes the fabric harder against the wound. "Tristan. Open your eyes. Look at me. Please. Look at me."

Tristan's eyes flutter open, just a bit, but the movement signals that she hears Liv.

"You should let me go," Tristan whispers, blood coloring her lips. "But I don't want you to. I want to be with you. I love you...I'm selfish that way."

"You're not selfish. You belong with me. And I need to be with you. I love you more than anything, so you just hold on and fight, goddamn it! Don't you dare die on me."

"I don't think it's up to me. And I *am* selfish. Asking...for this, for love, after all the years I've lived on this earth...is too much." Tristan raises a hand but lowers it again before touching Liv's face. "Don't want his blood on you..."

Liv's weeping now. A movement next to her makes her flinch and cry out, but it's only the older man that Damon and Tyrone attacked.

"That's it," he says in a husky voice. "Keep an even pressure on it. These men do that to her?"

"Yes." Liv is shaking and so cold now, her teeth clatter.

A sound by the door makes all three of them flinch, and Tristan cries out. Liv sees a man and a woman in uniform enter, guns drawn.

"Over here!" she calls out. "We need help. Where's the ambulance?"

"On its way." The female police officer approaches and takes in the scene. "Philip," she says to her colleague while holstering her sidearm, "we need backup. This is a major crime scene."

Liv jerks with her chin in Damon's direction. "That one's alive. He attacked my friend and me, and this gentleman. The other one's dead, I think."

"Roy! That you?" The male cop approaches the older man. "That's a nasty gash on your scalp."

"Philip. These men attacked me and then the girls." Roy, obviously known to the cops, says calmly, "I'm all right, but this woman needs a medevac."

"She's getting one. Only minutes out now." The female cop kneels next to Liv after cuffing Tyrone and checking on Damon. "You're doing great. I'd offer to take over, but you shouldn't let go." She places a gentle hand on Liv's shoulder. "Dispatch gave me the name Liv Bryce. That you?"

"Yes, I'm Liv." Liv can't see because of the tears streaming down her face. "Tristan. Tell me. Is she still breathing?"

"She is," the cop says.

After what seems like an eternity, more people flood the aisle, taking care of Tristan and Roy. They push Liv aside, and she ends up with her back against the opposite pew. She wraps her arms around her pulled-up knees, shaking so hard she can barely breathe. She watches them work on Tristan, attaching pads to her chest, starting IVs, and bandaging her wound.

It's when the rescuers have finally strapped Damon onto a gurney that it happens. Liv watches how they start to wheel him toward the exit, feeling only numbness, when a movement catches her attention.

Unfathomably, Tyrone is on his feet, roaring. His eyes are mad with fury and what has to be bloodlust as he throws the policeman in front of him out of the way. Liv screams in terror when he launches toward Tristan. Taking the paramedics by complete surprise, he shoves them out of the way and lands on Tristan, who is now unconscious. He wraps his hands around her neck and squeezes, shouting how she killed his mother, how she has to die, over and over.

Liv is on her feet, but before she can reach Tristan, the cops are dragging Tyrone off the woman she loves. He roars insults and obscenities at the cops, only to suddenly slump between them as what looks like the last of his blood leaves his system. They still cuff him.

Throwing herself down next to Tristan, Liv feels for a pulse but can't find any. Hands tug at her, and she crumples as the paramedics engage the defibrillator.

CHAPTER FORTY-SIX

Lights. Flickering. Eye piercing. Unendurable lights. Then darkness. Blissful, velvety darkness with no pain, no anguish. Somewhere behind the blackness are voices. Low, murmuring, they're sometimes cut off by a pinging noise. Tristan is certain she hears the words code blue. Who's ill? Who's dying? She can't remember. More darkness. Barely any light. Too exhausted to care.

Her throat is sore to a point where it feels as if someone's shoved a cheese grater all the way down to her larynx. She tries to clear her throat, but she's too tired. Different colors play behind her eyelids. Shapes move and wobble, making her dizzy. Is she underwater? No. She can breathe. Her chest hurts, but she's breathing on her own.

"Tristan?" a gentle male voice asks quietly. "Are you awake?" She hears hope in that voice.

Tristan does her best to pry her eyelids open, but it's hard. After a while, she manages to open them in a tiny slit, but it takes a few moments before the world comes back into focus. Above her hangs a couple of infusion bags, half empty. The ceiling seems very far away. Slowly turning her head, she sees a familiar face by the side of the bed.

"Graham," she tries to say, but manages only to mouth the name.

"Hey. Look at you." Fat tears fall from Graham's eyes and follow brand-new lines on his pale face. He looks exhausted and his smile trembles. "You're awake."

"Wh-what…?" Tristan is trying to remember what's going on, why she's here, clearly in some hospital.

"You're okay. You'll be fine," Graham says hurriedly. "I'm going to call the nurse." He reaches for the button, but she weakly raises her hand. "What?"

"Why?"

"They need to know you're fully awake, finally." Graham wipes at his cheeks.

"No. Why here?" Tristan's voice sounds finally just above a whisper.

"What do you remember?" Graham sits down, clearly hesitant, taking her hand.

"I—I'm not sure." Her brain feels as if it's filled with cotton. "An accident? The smell of blood…"

"I need to wake Liv." Graham squeezes Tristan's hand, but that's not what makes her flinch.

Liv. Olivia…Olivia! The images flicker through Tristan's brain so fast, she's starting to tremble. "Olivia. Where…is…she…" She needs one new breath for each word. "Where's…Olivia?"

"Let me get her. She went for a nap in a room for next-of-kin down the corridor. Please stay awake so I have time to get her." Graham lets go of Tristan's hand and leaves. The room is lit only by the light next to the bed, but the half-open door lets more light in, and through the drumming of her heart, she can hear Graham calling for a nurse.

Where is Olivia? Sleeping in some room? What is going on? Tristan tries to move, to sit up, but something on fire in her side makes her whimper and break into a full body sweat. She grips the rails on either side of the bed when more dizziness hits.

A nurse enters and leans over her. "Good to see you awake, Tristan. Welcome back."

"Where's Olivia? Is she all right?" Tristan desperately wants the nurse to move out of the way so she can see the door.

"Who? Oh, Olivia? She's—" Running footfalls in the corridor interrupt the nurse, and then Olivia rounds the bed to reach Tristan from the other side. Her face is pale, her hair matted and tousled, but she's still the only one Tristan cares about in this instant.

"Tristan!" Olivia lowers the rail with a practiced move. "You're awake. Truly awake. Oh, my God." She buries her face into Tristan's neck and holds her gently. Tristan wants to wrap her arms around Olivia, cling to her and make sure she's all right, but she's too weak.

"Tristan's vitals are still good," the nurse says kindly. "Why don't I arrange for some coffee for you in the dayroom, Graham? These two have some catching up to do, I think."

"Good idea," Graham says from the doorway.

Tristan looks at him over Olivia's head, mouthing "thank you" before he leaves.

"I'll be back later, okay?" Graham nods and closes the door behind him.

"He's been great. They all have." Olivia sits up, wiping at her eyes.

"What do you mean, they all have?" Tristan whispers. Her voice simply doesn't want to carry yet.

"Graham, Dana, Marlena, and the others. They've taken turns sitting here with us." Pushing at Tristan's bangs, Olivia gives an unsteady smile.

"How long?"

"Eight days. Five days in the ICU after your surgery. Three days on this ward. Jacinda, the nurse, has been on duty all three of those nights. She's a gem."

Tristan is still trying to capture the fleeting memories. "The church. The men."

"Tyrone is dead. Damon is in custody. Roy is recuperating like you, but at home with his wife." Olivia takes Tristan's hands. "And now that you're awake, I think I can finally breathe."

"He had a knife. Tyrone. I missed it." Tristan remembers how Tyrone suddenly drew a narrow blade and shoved it into her side only moments before she ended him. "I'm sorry you were there, that you saw all that."

"Hey. We came through it. Last I heard, the cops are rounding up Damon's and Tyrone's cohorts. Turns out they were running quite a successful operation with at least ten other guys. Part of organized crime, specializing in artifacts, etcetera."

Tristan has so many questions, but she's fading. Shuffling to the side, not bothering with the pain from her wound, she pats the bed. "Join me. Please."

"Sure thing." Olivia lies down next to Tristan and slides her arm under her neck. "That okay?"

"Yes." Finally able to relax, Tristan closes her eyes. "How can I be so tired? Slept for eight days."

"You're healing, and it's taking time and energy." Olivia kisses her temple.

Tristan opens her eyes again. "What do you mean?"

"Your stab wound. The cuts and bruises, not to mention the two cracked ribs. It's going to take a while, Tristan." Olivia runs her hand up and down Tristan's left arm.

Tristan closes her eyes again, her mind whirling. She has been severely injured before. More times than she can count. The worst wound was also from a knife at a seedy establishment in Boston where Tristan was trying to persuade the owner to let two young girls go and not be part of his group of prostitutes. The barkeep drew a knife and buried it in her shoulder. Despite the blood loss that time, the wound almost healed in five days. Holding up her arm, where dark bruises mar her pale skin, where someone has stitched her up, Tristan regards the injury, feeling her eyes grow wide. After eight days in the hospital, she should at least have seen the injuries go to yellow or green by now. Some should be gone. Stealthily, she lifts her covers and feels the large bandage along her side. Her wound is painful, and she yanks her fingertips away. It hurts as if it's just begun to heal. This doesn't make sense.

"Can you tell me what happened when I got to the hospital?" Tristan whispers.

"They took you into surgery as soon as they had stabilized you in the ER. You had to have the mother of all blood transfusions, the surgeon said. She claimed they exchanged almost your entire blood volume before they were done, since Tyrone did such damage with that serrated knife." Olivia shudders. "When I finally was able to sit with you, you were whiter than anyone I've ever seen. They weren't optimistic, but I kept thinking that your special physique would kick in since your blood count was climbing."

But not with her own blood. Tristan blinks. She turns her head and nuzzles Olivia's hair. It smells of hospital soap, but the underlying scent is Olivia's own. "I love you," Tristan murmurs. "More than I can say."

Olivia gets up on her elbow without removing her arm from under Tristan's neck. "And I love you." She kisses Tristan's lips gently. "That reminds me. If any of the staff happens to mention that we're engaged, that's the lie I had to tell to be able to be in your hospital room. Graham backed me up. So did the others."

Tristan's heart skips a beat. With her insides melting at the thought of being engaged to Olivia, she can't help but smile. "I think since I know now, and have no objections whatsoever, let's make it official." Holding her breath, Tristan looks up into the amber eyes above her.

"Yeah?" Olivia smiles, and the smile transforms her pale face into a completely different expression. She simply glows, and her cheeks are infused with some much-needed color.

"Yes."

This time the kiss isn't careful. Olivia parts Tristan's lips and deepens it instantly. Only when Tristan has to cough do they part, and Olivia makes sure she's all right before they settle back down on the bed.

Tristan knows her body has had enough for now. She's falling back asleep, but now without anxiety, and with hope that she may have a future with Olivia after all.

❖

Two weeks later, on a Friday afternoon, Amaranthine Inc. looks the same as when they left. Liv steps out of the cab and holds out her hand to Tristan. After raising her eyebrow pointedly, Tristan smiles and accepts it, holding on to Liv as she exits the car. The driver pulls away, and they stand on the sidewalk, looking up at the old warehouse that Tristan once transformed to fit her business and to live in.

"We're back," Liv says and sighs contentedly.

"We are." Tristan moves with care as she reaches for her briefcase, but Liv beats her to it.

"Don't even try," Liv says lightly and takes it. Hoisting their backpack onto her shoulder, she flinches when the door opens, and all Tristan's employees flood the sidewalk.

"Allow me," Graham says and grabs both the backpack and the briefcase. "Step inside, ladies. We're ready for you."

Not sure what to expect and surprised at how hard Tristan is clutching her hand, Liv looks questioningly at Dana and Marlena. "What's going on?"

"It's a surprise." Dana shakes her head. "And if I told you, it wouldn't be, would it?" Dana's warm tone contradicts her acerbic words.

"True." Liv walks hand in hand with Tristan through the door. Inside, Graham points to the workshop.

"In there." He rubs his hands.

Inside the workshop, the staff has put two large work surfaces together and set a fantastic table with white linen tablecloths and napkins, crystalware, and silver utensils. Along the closest wall, Tristan's colleagues have arranged an impressive buffet.

"I know you're tired, both of you, but you've got to eat." Graham points to the two chairs in the middle of the table. "Why don't you sit down and let us wait on you hand and foot?"

"You really must've missed us." Tristan blinks repeatedly, and Liv knows that her tears aren't far away. She also knows how Tristan will loathe for them to fall among her staff.

"What's not to miss?" Liv asks lightly. "I for one can see this happen on a weekly basis." She winks at Graham and Dana, who nod.

"Dream on," Dana says but smiles.

As they sit down and everyone fills their plate, Tristan seems content to listen to the conversation around them about painting and other pieces of art, what everyone has been up to since the last time they were together. Nobody asks Liv or Tristan why they were gone and where. Some junior employees seem to be under the impression that they've been working in Paris all this time and that Tristan was in an accident. This shows how loyal Tristan's senior staff is and what friends she, and now also Liv, have in them.

Once the celebration ends, Graham accompanies Liv and Tristan to the condo on the third floor. He stops outside the door, handing Tristan a stack of letters while Liv unlocks it. "These came during the time you were gone. The newest ones are on the top."

"Thank you, Graham." Tristan pulls him in and kisses his cheek. "For everything."

"Always," Graham says, returning the caress. He gently cups Liv's cheek. "Take care of each other, and I'll see you Monday." He winks at them and hurries down the stairs.

Liv enters the condo, looking around. Dana has arranged for a cleaning service to go over it, and it's immaculate. A lot of dark wood, leather, and almost masculine in its decor, it suits Tristan. A cozy fireplace under a large LCD screen on the wall is the focal point in the living room.

"It just dawned on me that you've never been up here." Tristan stands in the center of the floor. "Do you like it?"

"I do. A lot." Liv joins Tristan and wraps an arm around her waist.

"Can you see yourself living here? We can change anything you want." Tristan pulls Liv in for a hug. When she doesn't let go, Liv tips her head back to look at Tristan's face.

"I've stayed with you in so many different places, from luxurious to quaint, and this"—she motions around them—"your space is beautiful. I really like it. What few things I've collected will fit in nicely."

"It's bigger than at first glance. I even had a studio built that I never use. You can breathe life into that if you want." Sounding eager now, and with a new sparkle in her eyes, Tristan gestures toward the back of the living room, where Liv sees a narrow doorway.

"Sounds like a great idea." Liv kisses Tristan. "As long as you're here, I'll be happy."

"Likewise." Tristan manages to infuse so much love into the single word that Liv simply melts. "Want to just come and sit on the couch with me? I'm starting to feel the effect of the journey back here, which is a new sensation for me."

"Of course. Here. Bring your mail." Liv picks up the envelopes and gives them to Tristan.

Tristan starts going through the letters. "By the way, what was that call about earlier, from the cops? You were about to tell me when we pulled up to the lovely greetings."

"I talked to that cop who came to the church. She has a contact among the feds. They don't think Damon is fit to stand trial. He might not be as resilient as the girls from the ship, as his brain injury may cause him long-term problems. That, along with him ranting about his brother having his immortality stolen and how inferior mortals murdered his goddess of a mother, resulted in a psych evaluation. The feds are more interested in rounding up the people that worked for him and Tyrone at this point. Our statements about them trying to kidnap you for a ransom fit that narrative."

"True." Tristan leans in and presses her lips against Liv's. "I'm cautiously relieved. Soon, we'll have to contact Iris's stepdaughter and let her know what's happened. Once the trial is over, we'll be able to contact her and her father more openly."

"Of course." Liv hopes Tristan won't insist on doing everything at once. Even though she was discharged from the hospital in Boston two days ago, she is still frail, which is concerning.

Most of Tristan's mail ends up on the coffee table unread, and then she stops. "Oh, my."

"What?" Liv has slumped against the backrest but now sits up straight. "What's wrong?"

"It's from the Netherlands." Tristan turns the envelope over. "No return address." She keeps turning it over in her hands.

"Want me to read it?" Liv waits while Tristan keeps staring at the letter.

"Yes. If you don't mind?"

"Not at all." Still dreading what the letter might say, Liv takes it from Tristan's unsteady hands and opens it. The letter is written by hand on regular printer paper. Clearing her throat, she reads out loud.

Dear Tristan,

I hope my letter finds you at all, and indeed finds you well, dear friend. Two of the stalkers who are after us paid me a visit a few weeks ago. I hope you have been able to stay ahead of them and their violent ways.

My contacts tell me that some of them have been dealt with, but the details are sketchy. Apparently, they ran into superior opposition, and I couldn't be gladder.

I'm healing rapidly and am now, to my physicians' astonishment, already at a 90% recovery, perhaps more. They don't know what those men did to me, but truth be told, I don't care about recovery percentages—I'm simply happy to be alive. Who thought I would say that and mean it after all these years?

I'm sending this to your address at the firm. Enclosed is a PO box address in Rotterdam. My friends here will collect the mail for me, and when I'm convinced that the men are truly made harmless, I look forward to speaking with you again.

If your young lady is still with you, give her my best.
Here's to surviving, Tristan. I hope the same is true for
you.
    Much love,
    Rosalee

Liv lowers the letter and looks at Tristan with tear-filled eyes. "She survived. And at the rate she's healing…she'll be all right."

Tristan's eyes are dry, but her hand that covers her mouth trembles. She nods, clearly unable to speak. "She might be the last one of the nine girls."

"What do you mean?" Liv runs her fingertips along Tristan's cheek.

"I'm not healing at the same rate as she is. I'm getting better, yes, but at a normal pace," Tristan says. "I'm not responding like I used to. I'm incredibly sore. You must've realized that I'm healing slowly. Normally, even. My best theory is that the blood transfusion using normal blood caused this, sort of like a reset or something. You said so yourself at the hospital. I practically bled out."

"As if they rinsed out whatever the illness caused?" Liv grips Tristan's shoulder's gently but isn't about to let go. "Can having normal blood, as you put it, make you start to age at a normal pace?" And is this why Tristan thinks Rosalee is the last one standing of the nine girls? Oh, God. What if the blood transfusion accelerated Tristan's aging process?

"I have no idea, darling. If the healing process is anything to go by, there's a chance. And as for Rosalee—yes…I think so. Her healing is like mine used to be." Eyeing Liv with a cautious expression, Tristan swallows hard. "If that's the case…?"

"If that's the case, we'll age together. If not, then I'll age faster than you. That's what I thought would happen until a moment ago. That might still happen, for all we know." Liv caresses Tristan's cheek.

"I find myself truly hoping that I'll age right alongside you." Tristan caresses Liv's face. "Truth be told, nobody knows how my body will react in the future. My life expectancy could either be a lot longer than normal, or my metabolism might speed up, and I could age faster than expected."

"And yet, here we are, right now, together. Loving each other deeply. That's more than many people ever get." Liv doesn't want to think about any strange physical manifestations that can show up in Tristan. "There's something to be said for living in the now. Just a few weeks ago, I nearly lost you. You saw that brute nearly strangle me."

"And yes, here we are." Tristan's blue eyes soften to an almost gray. "And yes, we do love each other. I know that with every fiber of my being. Perhaps that's why I've lived such a long time—to love, and be loved by, you."

Liv's heart melts for the umpteenth time. "Why don't we just go to bed? I know you're still not well enough for me to make passionate love to you, but I can't think of anything else I'd rather do right now than hold you and be safe here in our home."

Tristan chuckles and stands, though with some effort. "You have some great ideas that we need to cultivate. I knew I chose the perfect person when I hired you."

Liv throws her head back and laughs. "And here I thought I was the clever one by applying for an internship at your firm."

Tristan holds Liv close and kisses her. Pulling back, she tilts her head. "You're right. In fact, we're both right."

As they make their way to the bedroom, Liv with a hand at the small of Tristan's back for subtle support, she's certain they're both right. Looking back at all they've been through and how they've still managed to find love during it all—it is nothing short of miraculous.

EPILOGUE

Three years later

"Ready to open the doors?" Tristan steps into the foyer of Amaranthine Inc. "Your reputation must be preceding you, as there's actually a line."

Olivia pivots, making her flowing green dress billow around her. Her chestnut hair is long again and, for the evening, piled into a stylish messy updo. Her eyes are dark and widening as she peers out through the narrow window next to the door. "There is. A line, I mean."

"Well, they're coming to see your exhibition, and you're one of the most talked-about new artists in New York. Hell, the East Coast, if you ask me."

"God. I'm going to be sick." Olivia presses a hand to her stomach.

"Don't you dare. Now, how's my hair?" Tristan drags a hand through her hair, now with a lot of silver streaks among the icy blond tresses. "I'm not sure that new girl, what's-her-name, understood how I want it done."

Olivia stops rubbing her belly and steps closer. "Hey, you look fantastic. The white is amazing on you. You know that. And the new girl, whose name is Ylva, by the way, did your hair just right." Winking at Tristan, Olivia nudges a few locks. "There. And yes, I know you did this on purpose. My stomach calmed down."

"Then go open the doors and let people in to see your paintings." Tristan steps back to join Graham, Dana, and Marlena. She watches how Olivia opens the doors and greets the first guest with the grace and natural charisma that's only grown since they returned to New York.

"She's amazing," Graham says. "And you, my friend, are happier than I've ever seen you."

"Olivia is everything to me." Tristan nudges Graham's arm. "And thank you—I'm very happy." She is. The last three years have confirmed that she's aging the way any middle-aged woman would. Crow's feet, more white strands of hair, sometimes more tired, and, oh God, premenopause. Not so romantic, but *real*. She's not aging faster than anyone else, but in a way that she surmises goes for normal.

"There's the New York art critic she fears so much," Marlena says in a low whisper. "He better be fair to her."

Tristan hopes so too, as the art critic has misogynous tendencies. "Olivia will be fine. If that man treasures anything, it's his reputation for being able to judge art."

Tristan follows Olivia's movements with her gaze as more and more of her art pieces receive a sticker that shows they're sold. Eventually, she joins her wife next to the only painting in the workshop-turned-gallery that's not for sale. It's a painting of Tristan as she holds the infant Olivia gave birth to four months ago. Their little girl, Corinne, gazes up at Tristan with such a stern glance, it makes her smile every time she looks at the brilliant piece of art. Right now, Corinne is sleeping upstairs under the watchful eyes of Marlena's parents.

"You're a hit, darling. I told you that," Tristan murmurs in Olivia's ear.

Olivia beams at Tristan. "You did say something to that effect. But you're also biased."

Tristan chuckles. "Perhaps, when it comes to you. But your art speaks for itself. Congratulations. You've worked hard for this."

Merely leaning into Tristan, Olivia smiles as they stand among friends and strangers. "I could stand here and look at all of them forever."

Tristan tugs Olivia closer, thinking that she's grateful that *forever* is a more manageable concept for them these days—and she wouldn't want it any other way.

About the Author

Gun Brooke (http://www.gbrooke-fiction.com), author of almost thirty novels, writes her stories, surrounded by a loving family and two affectionate dogs. When she isn't writing on her novels, she works on her art, and crafts, whenever possible—certain that practice pays off. She loves being creative, whether using conventional materials or digital art software.

Books Available From Bold Strokes Books

Almost Perfect by Tagan Shepard. A shared love of queer TV brings Olivia and Riley together, but can they keep their real-life love as picture perfect as their on-screen counterparts? (978-1-63679-322-1)

The Amaranthine Law by Gun Brooke. Tristan Kelly is being hunted for who she is and her incomprehensible past, and despite her overwhelming feelings for Olivia Bryce, she has to reject her to keep her safe. (978-1-63679-235-4)

Craving Cassie by Skye Rowan. Siobhan Carney and Cassie Townsend share an instant attraction, but are they brave enough to give up everything they have ever known to be together? (978-1-63679-062-6)

Drifting by Lyn Hemphill. When Tess jumps into the ocean after Jet, she thinks she's saving her life. Of course, she can't possibly know Jet is actually a mermaid desperate to fix her mistake before she causes her clan's demise. (978-1-63679-242-2)

Enigma by Suzie Clarke. Polly has taken an oath to protect and serve her country, but when the spy she's tasked with hunting becomes the love of her life, will she be the one to betray her country? (978-1-63555-999-6)

Finding Fault by Annie McDonald. Can environmental activist Dr. Evie O'Halloran and government investigator Merritt Shepherd set aside their conflicting ideas about saving the planet and risk their hearts enough to save their love? (978-1-63679-257-6)

The Forever Factor by Melissa Brayden. When Bethany and Reid confront their past, they give new meaning to letting go, forgiveness, and a future worth fighting for. (978-1-63679-357-3)

The Frenemy Zone by Yolanda Wallace. Ollie Smith-Nakamura thinks relocating from San Francisco to her dad's rural hometown is the worst idea in the world, but after she meets her new classmate Ariel Hall, she might have a change of heart. (978-1-63679-249-1)

Hot Keys by R.E. Ward. In 1920s New York City, Betty May Dewitt and her best friend, Jack Norval, are determined to make their Tin Pan Alley dreams come true and discover they will have to fight—not only for their hearts and dreams, but for their lives. (978-1-63679-259-0)

Securing Ava by Anne Shade. Private investigator Paige Richards takes a case to locate and bring back runaway heiress Ava Prescott. But ignoring her attraction may prove impossible when their hearts and lives are at stake. (978-1-63679-297-2)

A Cutting Deceit by Cathy Dunnell. Undercover cop Athena takes a job at Valeria's hair salon to gather evidence to prove her husband's connections to organized crime. What starts as a tentative friendship quickly turns into a dangerous affair. (978-1-63679-208-8)

As Seen on TV! by CF Frizzell. Despite their objections, TV hosts Ronnie Sharp, a laid-back chef, and paranormal investigator Peyton Stanford have to work together. The public is watching. But joining forces is risky, contemptuous, unnerving, provocative—and ridiculously perfect. (978-1-63679-272-9)

Blood Memory by Sandra Barret. Can vampire Jade Murphy protect her friend from a human stalker and keep her dates with the gorgeous Beth Jenssen without revealing her secrets? (978-1-63679-307-8)

Foolproof by Leigh Hays. For Martine Roberts and Elliot Tillman, friends with benefits isn't a foolproof way to hide from the truth at the heart of an affair. (978-1-63679-184-5)

Hard Pressed by Aurora Rey. When rivals Mira Lavigne and Dylan Miller are tapped to co-chair Finger Lakes Cider Week, competition gives way to compromise. But will their sexual chemistry lead to love? (978-1-63679-210-1)

The Laws of Magic by M. Ullrich. Nothing is ever what it seems, especially not in the small town of Bender, Massachusetts, where a witch lives to save lives and avoid love. (978-1-63679-222-4)

The Lonely Hearts Rescue by Morgan Lee Miller, Nell Stark & Missouri Vaun. In this novella collection, a hurricane hits the Gulf Coast, and the animals at the Lonely Hearts Rescue Shelter need love—and so do the humans who adopt them. (978-1-63679-231-6)